BEWITCHED

ELIZABETH ROSE

OLIVER HEBER BOOKS

 Created with Vellum

The Sage
Isle of Denwop
Glint
Whispering Dale
Pyramids of the Gods
Quamm Caves
...sked Sea
Picajord Mountains
Macada
Kasculbough
MURA
Lake of Souls
Fae Cottage
Goeften Forest
Evandorm
Blackseed Cottage

Being conceived from both light and dark magic was an imprisonment from which there was no escape.

It was also the bane of Medea de Bar's existence.

Even with the darkness that often filled her heart, Medea decided she wouldn't wish this life on anyone. No one, no matter how evil they were, deserved what she had been living through. It felt like being trapped in her own body. Hatred, jealousy, and extreme rage often reared up, seeded in her from her late mother. It consumed her to the point that there was nothing she could do to stop it. The darkness that filled her was sometimes so strong that she even frightened herself.

However, along with this great grief, also came a gift. A light at the end of the tunnel. Darkness made up only half of Medea. In her was also imbedded the spark of goodness from her father. That light sometimes shone so brightly that it somehow managed to push the darkness aside. There was a constant battle taking place inside Medea, one side winning over the other, and then back the other way again. Medea felt like naught but a bystander, as she was not in control at all.

At twenty years of age now, Medea realized she was no longer a child, but a woman, like her sisters, Rapunzel and Cinderella. She was a lot like all of her seven half-siblings, she supposed. The only difference being that she didn't grow up with them around, and because of this, it made her feel empty and lonely. Loneliness was something that frightened Medea more than anything else.

Sitting back on her throne in Tanglewood Castle, she threw her feet over the arm of the chair, even though she wore a gown and it wasn't proper or ladylike to act this way. Nay, she didn't care what others thought of her, even if she was a queen now, since her mother was dead and she'd inherited the title. She actually didn't care about anything anymore. All she wanted was to be happy, and needed to find a way to do just that.

Yanking the crown off her head, Medea studied it, running her finger over the jewels embedded into the golden circlet. Gemstones, coins, gold, wealth—these things seemed to make most people happy. Then again, Medea wasn't like most people. Nay, she didn't want these riches or even cared about them at all.

This crown had once belonged to the rulers of Tanglewood, before her mother seized the castle, making it her own. Hecuba's victory was accomplished at the price of others' lives. It hadn't been a fair fight—it never was. The poor departed souls never had a chance against Hecuba's use of dark magic.

Medea had inherited that same dark magic from her mother, but hers wasn't yet as developed as it could be. With no one there to teach her or guide her, she didn't know what to expect.

That made her wonder. What would it be like not to have this magic at all? What if she were just human, and felt like everyone else? It was an absurd thought, but still it made her wonder, since she had a curious nature. Lately, Medea found herself not able to stop wondering about it day and night. Thoughts like these filled her head constantly, ever since she inherited the title and position two years ago.

Drumming her fingers atop the arm of her throne, Medea struggled with feeling not only alone and unwanted, but also extremely bored. She needed to get out of here and go places. She wanted to do things! This sitting here thinking, but taking no action, was only going to drive her mad.

"My Queen," came the voice of her head guard, Orson, walking up and stooping low as he bowed before her. Part of Medea liked seeing others groveling at her feet. Another part of her found it repulsive. Tension built up inside her, causing her to shake and creating sweat on her brow. Her skin crawled. It made her feel confused and as if she were going to burst.

"Stop calling me Queen! I don't like it," she snapped, knowing that stolen titles didn't necessarily make a person worthy of them at all. "I'm not a queen. How many times do I have to remind you?"

"Nay, that's not true, Your Highness. You are our Queen now, my lady, and our ruler," said another guard, Riggs, entering the great hall and stopping to bow to her as well. "We answer to you now since Hecuba is dead."

And before Hecuba, they'd answered to the true King and Queen of Tanglewood, she reminded herself. These men were naught more than puppets on strings. Why didn't anyone have a mind of their own? The struggle inside her made her feel as if she wanted to scream or run. Sometimes she had admired her mother, and other times she despised her. But no matter how evil Hecuba had been, she was still Medea's mother.

Hecuba had been the only one who had truly cared for her and looked after her. She was also the one whom Medea severely let down in the end.

"You don't need to remind me that my mother is dead!" she shouted. Anger filled her, growing stronger with each breath she took. She didn't want to think about how her mother died. It hurt too much, and the guilt she harbored ate away at her blackened soul. If Medea had the ability to do it, she would erase the memories from her mind completely about that day and never be haunted by it again.

Medea threw the crown at the guards, almost hitting them. They both ducked as the metal circlet smashed into the wall behind them and then fell, rolling across the stone floor beneath their feet. If she didn't leave here anon, she was going to wind up killing someone, of that she was sure. Mayhap her mother never had a qualm about killing or cursing people, but Medea didn't want to follow in those footsteps right now.

"So sorry, my Queen," said Riggs. "We didn't mean to upset you."

"That's right. Our wish is your command," said Orson nervously. He most likely only said this since he'd seen the extent of her powers and was frightened by them. They all were. After all, with just a flick of her hand, they could all be dead, or possibly turned into toads, or cursed for life. As far as Medea knew, there weren't any limits to her magic.

Medea had no friends, or at least not real ones anyway. Anyone who pretended to like her, was only doing it out of fear or duty. No one wanted to feel the results of her wrath.

She let out a deep sigh of frustration, glaring at her guards. Taking a deep breath, she held it until the light within her overcame the darkness, smoothing out her emotions once again. Over the last few years she had been experimenting with being able to control her magic. Sometimes she was able to stop the darkness inside with the light, but at other times it worked in just the opposite way.

There was no one to turn to in order to find out the answers. Her mother had been pure evil, and her father and half-siblings were all good. No one understood what she was going through.

This time, she was lucky, and her breathing managed to summon the light within her. Slowly, she stood up, feeling relaxed and as if all the tension had been swept away. She had been trying hard to change her ways, wanting to be more like her sister Rapunzel and the others. Sometimes, she was able to stop the darkness before it consumed her completely; however, it didn't happen often enough.

Bored beyond belief, she yawned, stretching her arms high over her head. It had been her mother's idea to seize Tanglewood by means of magic, just to gain an army to go up against Lucio de Bar. Medea didn't know anything about the previous king and queen of Tanglewood, and neither did she want to know. To even think about how the innocent rulers were killed by her mother would only make the guilt inside her grow stronger. That was something she didn't need at all.

Medea supposed it should make her happy that she was a queen, but it didn't. Not in the least. Making decisions, punishing thieves, and going to battle, was nothing she enjoyed. Medea wanted excitement in life! However, that excitement was something that she was going to have to create for herself, if she wanted it at all.

She also wanted a man in her life. Medea was curious about love. She'd been there when her sisters Rapunzel and Cinderella fell in love with their husbands

Marco Drago del Rossi the third, and Sir William Fremont. She'd also been present when one of her brothers, MacKay, fell in love with the Snow Queen. Why were they all able to find a mate and fall in love, but she wasn't? She was just as pretty as her sisters, and even more powerful than her Dragon Lord brother-by-marriage.

In the past, Medea had fallen hard for both Marco and William, but realized now it had been more infatuation than true love. All her magic couldn't stop the men from staying true to her sisters. It was unbelievable that even MacKay and Queen Eira Koldottir ended up together. After all, her mother's curse on MacKay made him infatuated with the wretched Snow Queen, who had naught but a heart of ice. The meaner Eira acted toward him, the more MacKay liked her. It was amusing, but still, it was all wrong. Or, at least Medea thought so. Right now, she was no longer sure. Her head became clouded and she seemed unable to make decisions on her own.

"Fine then," she told her guards. "If you insist on pleasing me, I have a chore for you both." A corner of her mouth lifted up into a half-smile as she thought of an adventure that would truly prove to be exciting.

"Anything at all, my lady," said Riggs, keeping his head bowed.

"What can we do for you?" asked Orson, being so fast to want to please her. It disgusted her, and made her want to strike them both down dead just so she wouldn't have to watch them grovel at her feet again.

"Riggs, I want you to saddle a horse for me. Orson, fetch my travel bag from my chamber with my things. Then, you'll both escort me on a little trip."

"A trip?" asked Orson, looking up and scratching

his nearly bald head. "We didn't know you planned on traveling today, my Queen. This is such short notice."

"I just decided to go. Besides, I don't need to report my doings to anyone."

Riggs and Orson exchanged glances.

"Of course not, my lady. But where, if I may ask, are you planning to go?" asked Riggs.

"It's really none of your concern." Medea grabbed her cloak from the back of the chair and fastened it around her shoulders. "However, I'll tell you, just because I don't care who knows it. I am going to Tavistock Castle."

"Tavistock." Orson nodded. "Then you are going to visit your sister, Rapunzel, and her Dragon Lord husband, my lady?"

"Nay. I'm not going to exchange pleasantries with anyone. That is not my purpose at all." Medea reached up and fixed her hair. "I'm going for an exciting adventure."

"An adventure?" asked Riggs. "We don't understand."

"I'm taking a ride on a dragon, since I never got the one Marco promised me."

"Oh," said Orson, seeming very uneasy. After all, Hecuba had shapeshifted into a dragon to secure this castle as her own. Dragons were not something that anyone at Tanglewood welcomed. "So, the Dragon Lord will be accompanying you then, on your ride?"

"Of course not, you fool! I'm going by myself."

"Yourself?" Riggs shook his head. "I am surprised the Dragon Lord agreed to let anyone else take his dragon."

"He doesn't know yet," she admitted with a cocky smile. "You see, I'm going to steal the dragon and take it for a ride."

"Y-you can command a dragon?" asked Orson with wide eyes. It was an unusual skill, and could only be obtained by those who were born into it. If one wasn't a Dragon Lord, the dragon could turn on them.

"Of course I can command a dragon," she answered, then made a face. Her magic might be powerful, but would it be enough to control a fierce, fire-breathing beast? "I mean, I think I can. After all, how hard can it really be?"

* * *

Medea froze as the dragon turned its head and its beady orange eyes stared a hole through her. The majestic beast filled the entire stable, its head rubbing against the ceiling as it snorted and pawed at the floor. Marco's dragon was bright red with long, transparent wings folded back. Spikes stuck out from the ends of the wings, looking just as sharp as any blade.

"My, you look a lot bigger than I remember, seeing Marco ride you through the sky," she mumbled. Once again, the dragon eyed her up, probably wondering if it should scorch her with fire to cook her before it ate her. The thing had the eeriest orange eyes with vertical black slits, reminding her of the eyes of a cat.

Her gaze roamed over its tough, scaly hide all the way from its head down to its long tail covered with sharp spikes. It had large, curved claws, or talons on its feet. She also saw a double row of long, sharp teeth emerging from its mouth. It truly was a terrifying sight. Mayhap she should have thought about this more before she decided to get this close.

On the other side of the enclosure was a second dragon that she knew to be that of Marco's father. It was blue with red stripes down its wings. It too, snorted and pawed the ground. Anxiety thickened the air. Smoke streamed out of its nostrils. The dragons could feel her presence, her fear, and most likely her intent. By their actions it was obvious they didn't like her being there.

Medea had briefly encountered the dragons before, but that day was naught but a blur in her mind right now. So much had happened so fast that it made her head spin.

"They looked a lot less threatening up in the sky," she commented, swallowing hard.

"W-we'll wait outside, m-my Queen," said Orson backing away. He dropped her travel bag at her feet. Then, he and Riggs high-tailed it out of the stables.

"Run then, you cowards, I don't need you!" she shouted. When she turned back to look at the dragon again, she jumped in surprise. The beast threw back its head and opened its mouth, enabling her to see clearly now its double row of sharp teeth. Flames shot out of its nostrils in a steady stream. The stables were constructed from metal instead of wood, and now she realized why. The dragon could burn anything... or anyone to ashes just by breathing on them. "It's all right," she spoke to the dragon in a soft voice. "I only want to ride you, not harm you."

Dragons were very finicky creatures and could pick up emotions and bad intents from people easily. She wondered if they were spooked by the darkness inside her, or just upset to see a stranger here.

Picking up her travel bag, she slipped it over her shoulder and slowly unlatched the gate to the stall, trying not to frighten the beast. The dragon pulled anxiously at the chain around its neck. The chain was fastened to a metal spike in the ground to keep it stationary. It was also forged in magic, so the dragon could not break it and escape.

"You want to fly, I know. I can tell. I want to do that, too," she spoke to the dragon, her eyes never leaving its piercing stare. "No dragon should be chained up like this. I agree."

The dragon's back was high, and there was no way to climb atop it unless the beast bowed down to her the way it did to its Dragon Lord master. That was something she was sure it would never do. So, with a wave of her arm she used her magic to transport herself, ending up sitting atop the back of the dragon before the beast even knew what happened.

The dragon lurched and pulled hard at its chained tether, snorting and trying to shake her off.

"Now, now, just calm down. You'll feel better once you're out in the open sky." Medea gripped on to its leathery mane, hoping she wouldn't be thrown to the ground. She quickly eyed the chain holding the dragon prisoner. She needed to release it, but couldn't reach it from her position. With no other way to do it, she used her magic once again. The chain dropped from the dragon's neck, hitting the ground with a loud thud. The second dragon roared from the other end of the stables.

The dragon beneath her was now free, and it knew it. The beast made an awful sound and reared up, almost throwing her from its back. She gripped on tighter, feeling her body slipping down over the hard scales. Then the dragon turned around and darted out of the barn with her atop it. She had succeeded in freeing the beast, but she wasn't sure what to do next.

"Wait!" she cried, having no idea how to control a dragon. "Calm down," she shouted as its wings started flapping wildly around her sounding so loud that it reminded her of a tornado. Orson and Riggs saw what was happening and ran in fear to hide.

"Medea? Is that you?" came the voice of her sister from the direction of the castle. Medea turned her head to see Rapunzel running toward the stable. "Nay! What are you doing?" The look of shock and also frustration washed over her sister's face.

"Stay back, Rap," Medea yelled, using the shortened name for her sister that her siblings sometimes used. "I am finally going to get that ride on the dragon that Marco promised."

"Medea, wait. I'll call for Marco, and he'll take you. He's the only one besides his father who can command the dragons. Marco!" She shouted for her husband, but her eyes remained on Medea.

"Nay! I don't want Marco to take me anymore. I'm tired of waiting for anyone to give me what I want. I'm getting it for myself."

"Nay, don't. It's too dangerous," warned Rapunzel, picking up her skirts and following as the dragon moved across the courtyard with Medea atop it. Rapunzel's once extremely long hair was now cut shorter and only hung down to her waist. Her blond tresses were interwoven neatly with colorful ribbons into one long braid that trailed down her back. "Marco, come quickly," Rapunzel shouted once again at the top of lungs.

"Goodbye, Sister," said Medea, kicking her heels into the sides of the dragon the way she would do atop a horse. The beast snorted and groaned, flapping its wings furiously now. Before Medea realized what was happening, the dragon lifted into the air and flew off over the top of the castle, into the vast sky.

"Come back!" shouted Rapunzel from below, shading her eyes and looking upward.

"Sorry," Medea leaned over and called out with a shrug. The dragon flew in a circle over Tavistock Castle, the wind biting against Medea's face. She looked down to see soldiers and servants running in chaos, looking up at the sky. Then she saw Marco exit the keep and look up at her and raise his fist in the air. She could feel him calling to the dragon, and of course the dragon had to obey. "Nay!" she cried, not wanting the dragon to return to its master. Her ride had just started, and there was no way she was going to allow it to be over so soon.

Using her powers to block out the sounds of Marco's command, she hummed loudly, filling the dragon's head with her voice instead. Medea kept the dragon from hearing Marco or even his thoughts. The dragon swooped down and then back up to the sky, causing a flitting sensation in her stomach. As terrifying as it was, it made her feel alive and happy, which is something she had never felt before. Medea reached up and yanked the ribbon from her head, letting the wind blow her long, black hair freely up around her. It felt so good. This was exhilarating and more than exciting than anything she had ever done before. It was exactly what she needed to bring her out of the slump she was in.

"Wheeee!" she cried, throwing back her head and closing her eyes, feeling so free as she flew through the sky. Holding on with only her legs, she daringly threw her hands in the air. It was good to finally get her ride on the dragon, and she hadn't had to depend on anyone else for her happiness this time.

The dragon swooped down one last time, not even hearing the Dragon Lord who shouted and waved his arms over his head now. This was working out perfectly and she didn't even feel guilty for using her magic to steal the beast.

"Goodbye, Sister," Medea called out to Rapunzel once more. But when they got higher above the castle, she felt someone's presence behind her. She jerked around to look, almost losing her balance. "Rapunzel!" she screamed. "How did you get up here?"

Her sister sat behind her on the dragon, reaching out and wrapping her arms around Medea's waist to hold on.

"You forget, little Sister, that you are not the only one with magic. I have newfound powers now as well. I used them to get up here."

"Oh, that's right," she said with a sigh, knowing this was only going to cause trouble.

"We need to take the dragon down now, Medea," scolded her sister. "You are being reckless. Someone is going to get hurt. You don't know the first thing about dragons nor how to command the beast. You don't know what you are doing."

Medea supposed her sister was right, although she didn't want to admit it. Even with Marco's anticipated reprimanding her when she got back, the ride would still have been worth it.

"Fine," she snapped. "Down, Dragon," Medea commanded, but the dragon didn't heed her words. She was figuring out quickly that only a Dragon Lord was able to control the beast after all, and that her magic might not be able to remedy this problem after all. Mayhap in her eagerness to take a ride, she hadn't thought things through. "It won't listen, Rap," she cried, starting to feel anxious. She supposed she could just use magic to transport herself to the ground, but she didn't want to leave the dragon or her sister.

"Medea? What is that?" Rapunzel gasped and pointed at a swirling mass of colors where the land and sky met at the lake.

"I don't know," said Medea. Her eyes grew wide as the dragon headed for the anomaly that looked like nothing she had ever seen before. Colors of blue and red swirled around and it almost seemed as if an opening was being created in the middle of the mass.

"Something is happening," shouted Rapunzel.

"The dragon is headed right for it and I can't stop him," yelled Medea.

"It looks like some kind of portal." Rapunzel gripped tighter to Medea.

"A portal?" Medea didn't know anything about portals, but could sense that it wasn't somewhere that they purposely wanted to go. "Turn around, Dragon," she said, pulling at the beast's leathery mane. It only seemed to anger the dragon even more. "Go down, I say," she commanded. Of course, it didn't listen to anyone but a Dragon Lord. "Rap, it's not working!" She felt scared now. This wasn't what was supposed to happen. "The dragon is heading right for that—that portal. This isn't good."

"Nay! Don't let it go through," begged Rapunzel. "Try to use your magic again to stop it, Medea."

"I did but it didn't work. I don't know what to do. This has never happened to me before. You try, Rap!"

"I can't," protested Rapunzel. "My magic isn't strong enough to work on a dragon or a portal. You need to do something. This is up to you. You got us into this mess, now fix it and do it fast!"

The dragon veered upward so quickly that Medea lost her travel bag as well as her cloak, and nearly fell from its back. The items fell to the ground as Rapunzel held on to her even tighter. Then, the dragon swooped around and headed right for the swirling mass of colors. Medea froze in fear. "I–I'm scared, Sister," said Medea, not yet able to fully control her powers, and feeling too reluctant right now to even try. She was at a loss for knowing what to do, since her mother had never told her how to handle a situation such as this.

"Hold on!" cried Rapunzel, laying her head against Medea's back. "We're going through!"

"Naaaay," cried Medea, knowing now that not only her siblings, but also her father was going to be angrier with her than ever before. Aye, when she returned—if she returned—there was going to be hell to pay.

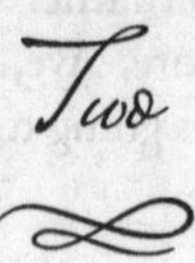

Two

Rhys Blackseed rode his oversized silver snowflake warhorse away from Kasculbough Castle in Mura, on an errand from the King. Being King Rand Osric's head knight, Rhys had been given the best steed of the land. It took a strong man to control such a large horse, but then again, Rhys was stronger than anyone.

Being the youngest son of the late Sin Eater, Ambrose Blackseed, Rhys had inherited the family trait of super strength from his great-grandfather. He also had the power to heal himself, although he rarely ever needed to use it. The Blackseed brothers had a strong presence in the land of Mura. Zann, the middle brother, was the huntsman for King Drustan Grinwald of Evandorm. Their eldest brother, Darium, was a Sin Eater who made a great sacrifice to ensure the souls of dead loved ones made it to The Haven, instead of ending up in The Great Abyss.

Rhys rode next to Zann, but could tell by the silence that his brother was still upset. With his quiver of arrows on his back and his bow thrown over one shoulder, a scowl plastered on his brother's face.

"Zann, are you still sulking about the fact our

brother has newfound fae powers?" Rhys asked, looking at him from the corners of his eyes. Zann hadn't spoken much to anyone lately, not even at their brother Darium's wedding yesterday.

"I am not sulking. I'm just not sure how to accept everything that has transpired lately," Zann answered.

Their brother Darium married the fae Talia-Glenn, who was also an Elemental of the Earth. They'd almost lost Darium when he was sucked into the portal of the Land of the Dead, but thankfully things worked out. The Kings were grateful for the closure of the portal, because this saved them from the dark spirits coming through from the other side. Two of the Kings even decided to drop the ban prohibiting magic of any kind, since it was magic that closed the portal in the end.

The land of Mura was ruled by three kings who never seemed to agree on much. Each of them was greedy and wanted to rule Mura as their own. Rhys was headed now to King Leofric Sethor's castle to try to convince the man to join the other two kings in no longer prohibiting magic.

"We should be happy for our brother. Also, thankful that we now have Mother with us again, when we thought she was dead," Rhys pointed out.

"That's something else that is going to take some getting used to," complained Zann, not wanting to forgive the woman for deserting them when they were children.

"Which part do you mean?" asked Rhys. "That we were lied to about her death, or that she is an Elemental of the Air and we nerver knew it?"

"All of the above," Zann snorted.

"Our late father is the one you should be angry with, not Mother."

"Um... Rhys?" Zann looked up over the lake and his eyes opened wide. "Do you see what I see?"

"What?" asked Rhys, turning to look, just as his horse reared up in fear. "Whoa, Sampson." He tried to still the animal, gripping tightly to the reins. Then he saw what his brother was speaking of. There was a swirling, colorful portal opening at the edge of the water. The Lake of Souls was the largest and deepest lake of Mura. "Darium has been insisting he's seen another portal opening, and I guess we should have listened to him."

"What is it exactly?" Zann stopped his horse and so did Rhys. "I mean... it doesn't look dark and murky like the portal that led to the Land of the Dead."

"Nay, it doesn't," agreed Rhys, his horse turning in a full circle since it was frightened and wanted to run. Rhys held it still. "It oddly seems... colorful and almost... comforting."

"I suppose we'd better get a closer look and figure out exactly what it is." Zann dismounted his horse and tied the reins to a tree. Rhys did the same. Together, they slowly walked toward the dreaded lake that only seemed to bring strife and trouble to the land of Mura.

"It looks like something is coming through the portal, but I can't tell what." Zann stretched his neck, trying to see clearly the center of the swirling mass that was right in front of him now. Then he reached behind him and yanked an arrow from the quiver on his back, quickly nocking the arrow in case he needed to use it.

"If it's something bad that comes through, we've got to stop it." Rhys unsheathed his sword, getting ready to fight. "I'm getting tired of this."

"Me too," agreed Zann as they stood in front of a large boulder, just waiting and watching, not knowing what to expect.

What came through the portal was something that neither of them could have ever imagined.

"Watch out!" shouted Rhys, pulling his brother out of the way as a large, red dragon swooped through the portal, its sharp talons almost scraping against Zann's back as it passed overhead.

Zann let loose the arrow, but it only bounced off the hard scales of the dragon, making the beast turn and shoot fire from its mouth.

"Dammit." Zann dove behind the boulder, but Rhys wasn't fast enough. His tunic caught fire, flames shooting up past his face. Rhys dropped to the ground and rolled to put out the flames.

"There is someone atop the dragon," shouted Zann, getting back to his feet.

Rhys looked up to see two women riding the fire-breathing beast. When the dragon rose up in fury, the girls lost their balance and fell to the ground. One loud roar from the dragon and it lifted back up into the sky, creating a whirlwind around them. Dirt, debris, and sand swirled around them in the vortex of air created by the beast's flapping wings. Rhys watched in awe as it flew up over the lake, seeming lost. The portal had already closed and disappeared from sight. The dragon couldn't find its way back through it, and flew in circles seeming to decide where to go.

"Come back here!" shouted one of the girls from the ground, as the dragon rose up higher into the sky and finally took off toward the Picajord Mountains.

"What in the name of Belcoum was that?" asked Zann, cursing, using the name of Mura's demon lord of the underworld.

"I have no idea." Rhys jumped to his feet, patting out the last of the flames on his shoulder. His tunic was burned through, causing his skin to blister. "However, I know someone who can tell us." Picking his sword back up, he gripped it tightly, clenching his jaw as he made his way toward the two women sprawled out on the ground.

"Wait for me!" shouted Zann, running after him.

"Who are you?" Rhys asked, pointing his sword at the women, demanding answers. He didn't think they were demons like his last encounter with a portal, but then again, he couldn't be sure.

One of the women had a long, blond braid hanging down her back. Her eyes were bright blue. The younger of the two had dark brown eyes and long, black hair that was loose and tousled, and sticking out in every direction.

The dark-haired one looked up and her expression changed. Her eyes became darker, almost black now. Then she lifted up her hand. "Leave us alone!" Some sort of beam of light or possibly fire shot out, hitting Rhys directly in the chest. His breath left his lungs as he sailed through the air, ending up landing on his back upon the hard earth, looking up at the sky.

"Ooomph," he groaned, feeling like he was getting beat up without even being touched today. The damned wench obviously used magic. And as if it wasn't bad enough that he'd already been set on fire by a dragon today, now he'd been knocked on his ass by a mere girl. He shot to his feet and lunged at the wench who was now standing up and brushing the dirt off her gown. His body knocked into hers and they both landed in a prone position with Rhys on top, pinning her down. He held on to her tightly.

"Nay, stop it!" shouted the other woman. "Let her go."

"Rhys, what are you doing?" asked Zann.

"The wench is not going to best me," he growled,

watching the girl make faces beneath him as she squirmed, trying to escape his hold.

"You're heavy. Get off of me, you fool," she spat.

Just as he was about to give her a piece of his mind, she disappeared into thin air. Rhys fell forward, ending up hugging dirt. He looked up to see her standing in front of him now, tamping down her hair with her hand. Quickly getting to his feet, he rushed her, but his fingers only closed around air once again. Rhys felt a push from behind, and found himself on the ground once more.

Zann laughed heartily.

"It's not funny, Brother," grunted Rhys through gritted teeth.

"Medea, stop it," begged the blond woman. "I'm sorry for my sister's behavior," she told Rhys, offering her outstretched hand to help him.

Rhys shook his head and got to his feet on his own. "Who are you, and where do you come from?"

"My name is Rapunzel, and this is my sister, Medea de Bar," the blonde told him. "Once again, I apologize for her rude behavior."

"I wasn't the rude one," sniffed Medea. "Sister, you saw the man holding me down. I could barely breathe."

"I must apologize for my brother's behavior," said Zann, stepping forward. "Hello, I am Zann Blackseed and this is my brother, Rhys." Zann kissed the back of Rapunzel's hand. When he reached out for Medea, she raised her hands and Zann went flying through the air. He landed hard and let out a groan.

Rhys chuckled now. "See what I mean, Brother?"

"Oh, you're hurt!" said Rapunzel. Her jaw dropped and her eyes opened wide in surprise when she noticed Rhys' burned tunic and blistered skin.

"Aye. Your dragon did that to my brother," said Zann, getting back to his feet.

"Mayhap I can help. I'm not sure where I am, but does this land have herbs that grow freely? If so, I know how to use them to heal." Rapunzel, looked around at her feet.

"Never mind. I can do it myself." Rhys held his open palm over his burned and blistered flesh. In a matter of seconds, his skin was healed and back to normal. All that remained was the charred tunic, now in shreds.

"Oh. I see, you have magic, too," said the one called Medea. All of a sudden she was much more interested in him than she was a moment ago. She craned her neck and walked over to inspect his wound that was no longer there. She reached out and boldly ran the tip of her finger over his skin, causing Rhys to feel as hot as when the dragon's flame hit him. "How did you do that? Are you some sort of warlock?" she asked, seeming very curious to know the answer.

"Nay, of course not. Don't be ridiculous," he scoffed.

Her brows dipped as she pulled her hand away. Her sour expression told him that she wasn't happy with his answer. "Then, tell me. What exactly are you?" She cocked her head and stared up at him, demanding an answer. Her black eyes cleared, turning back to dark brown again. It was the oddest thing Rhys had ever seen.

"Never mind what I am," he told her. "You tell me something. Where did you get a dragon?"

"I've never seen a dragon before," said Zann. "Although we've heard a lot about them, I thought they were extinct."

"Obviously not, or we wouldn't have one." Medea's answer sounded sarcastic.

"It's my husband's dragon," Rapunzel explained. "Marco is a Dragon Lord."

"A Dragon Lord? Really?" Zann smiled and nodded, seeming more than impressed by this than anything else right now.

"Why are you here and where did you come from?" Rhys continued with his questions, needing answers.

"The sky opened and we came through some sort of portal," said Medea with a shrug. Rhys wasn't sure, but he thought he saw her roll her eyes, as if his question sounded stupid to her.

"I can see that," said Rhys. "But how did you cause the portal to appear and disappear?"

"If we had the power to do that, do you think we'd still be standing here talking with you two fools?" snapped Medea, crossing her arms over her chest.

Rhys didn't like the girl's attitude in the least and was eager to send her back through the portal. However, before he could say anything about it, his brother spoke.

"So, are you two from Mura?" asked Zann, eyeing them up.

"Where?" Medea made a face and squinted her eyes.

"Mura," Zann repeated. "The land you're on right now." He held out his arms and looked around. "I am guessing mayhap you live on the other side of the Picajord Mountains? Are you perhaps one of the fae from the Whispering Dale by any chance?"

"Fae?" asked Medea. "Don't be silly. Of course we're not."

"The Picajord Mountains?" questioned Rapunzel. "We've never heard of them or the land of Mura." Her eyes darted back and forth as she took in her surroundings.

"It doesn't look much different from England," said Medea, eyeing the landscape as well.

"England? Where is that?" asked Rhys.

Both girls exchanged glances.

"We can't answer that, since we have no reference as to where we really are right now," answered Rapunzel. "Is there somewhere we can go to freshen up and talk?"

"I guess so," said Rhys. "But what about your dragon?"

"Oh, it'll be back when it's hungry," said Medea.

"Hungry?" Zann looked up at the sky nervously. "What do dragons eat?"

"Well they eat... what do they eat, Sister?" asked Medea. "I'm not really sure."

"That doesn't matter right now." Rapunzel glanced up at the sky as well. "We need a plan to get the dragon back as quickly as possible. My husband is going to be very angry about this. Not to mention, there is no telling what might happen with a dragon on the loose in a strange land."

"Rhys, let's take them home," suggested Zann.

"Home?" Rhys looked up and shook his head. "I can't take them to Kasculbough, and you'd better not take them to Evandorm. Our kings might have lifted the ban on magic, but let's not throw it in their faces. After all, once they see the dragon, they're most likely going to change their minds again."

"Magic isn't allowed on Mura?" asked Rapunzel in shock.

"Well, aye and nay," said Zann. "We're sort of in the middle of negotiations at the moment, I guess you could say."

The sound of thundering hoofbeats took their attention. Rhys looked up to see some of King Sethor's men headed their way.

"Damn. They're soldiers from Macada Castle," said Rhys in a low voice.

"Macada Castle? Where is that?" asked Medea.

"Never mind. You two need to hide, quickly." Rhys directed them behind a tall standing stone. "Stay quiet, and whatever you do, do not—I repeat—do *not* use magic."

"But I thought it was allowed now," said Medea.

"Not by all the Kings," answered Rhys, mounting his horse and riding out to meet the soldiers.

"Have you seen or heard anything odd?" asked one of the guards.

"Odd? How so?" asked Rhys, not wanting to give away information until he found out what they knew first.

"King Sethor swears he saw a flying beast over the castle."

"A flying beast?" Rhys chuckled. "Perhaps King Sethor is well in his cups again. What has he been drinking that would cause him to see such things?"

"That is none of your concern. Now answer my question." The guard's brows arched. "Did you see a flying beast? Perhaps a dragon?"

"A dragon?" Rhys tried to feign surprise. "Is that what the King thought he saw?"

"Answer me!" growled the guard. "You are standing out here in the open so you must have seen it." His hand gripped the hilt of his sword. "Do not lie, Blackseed," he warned.

Damn, Rhys now wished that he and Zann would have hidden as well. The last thing he wanted to do was to answer King Sethor's men when he was supposed to be trying to convince the King to allow magic. This wasn't going to be an easy feat after what he just saw. "I think I might have seen something large pass overhead, but I wasn't really paying attention," he told them.

"The King thinks another portal might have opened

and something came through," reported the second soldier.

"Really," said Zann, coming to join them atop his horse now.

"King Sethor wants that flying... dragon, for his own," said the man.

"Whatever for?" asked Rhys, knowing the King's greed and also that this meant trouble. "Has King Sethor accepted magic now, like the other two kings of Mura?"

"Nay," answered the first guard. "However, if he has a powerful creature like that in his possession, he might change his tune."

"Well, we'll keep our eyes opened," said Rhys, nodding to the man. The soldier grunted and directed his men to leave. They rode off quickly to the east kicking up a puff of dust.

"What was that all about?" Medea emerged from her hiding place and ran over to join them.

"They're looking for your dragon," announced Zann.

"Well, so are we," stated Medea. "Perhaps we can do it together with them."

"Nay. If King Sethor finds it first, he'll want to keep it," Rhys told them.

"Nay, he can't have it. It belongs to my husband," protested Rapunzel. "Besides, only a Dragon Lord can command it."

"Really? Then why were you two on it?" Rhys asked suspiciously, eyeing up the women.

"My sister stole it, wanting to go for a ride." Rapunzel shook her head in disgust, glaring at Medea.

"You did what?" Zann sounded as in disbelief as Rhys was right now. After all, who would do a daft thing like stealing a dragon just to go for a ride? It was preposterous. Especially when they couldn't control the beast.

"I was bored," said Medea, nonchalantly brushing dirt off her skirt.

"Bored?" asked Zann with a chuckle. "You were bored and so you decided to steal a dragon? Did I just hear that correctly?"

"You did," said Rapunzel, scowling at her sister. "My sister didn't think through the consequences before doing such a reckless thing. Now, we really need to find our dragon and head back home. Will you two please help us?"

"Help you? Hunt down a dragon? Hah! I think not," spat Zann. "Even if you two do find the damned thing, what makes you think you're going anywhere?"

"That's right," agreed Rhys. "Until that portal reopens, you are stuck here. And unfortunately, we have no way of knowing where and when it'll open again, or even if it will at all."

"Stuck here?" asked Medea. "Well, for how long?"

"No one can answer that. Until that portal reappears and opens, you're pretty much stranded on Mura," Rhys told them.

"Well, that is unacceptable," said Medea. "I need to get back to Tanglewood or my guards will be looking for me."

"Your guards?" This took Rhys' interest.

"My sister is Queen of Tanglewood Castle," explained Rapunzel.

"A queen? Her?" Rhys chuckled lowly. "You could have fooled me." He noticed the girl's eyes going dark again when he said it, but it was too late. Once more, to his dismay, he found himself on his ass on the ground, even though she hadn't even touched him. "I command you to stop doing that," he said through gritted teeth.

"No one commands me," she retorted. "I'm a queen. Didn't you hear my sister?"

"Medea," said Rapunzel under her breath, seeming as if she was trying to calm the woman down or keep her quiet.

The woman named Medea was a brash wench who seemed to fear no one and nothing. Well, Rhys was a knight who feared no one and nothing as well, and he was going to make sure she knew it.

"You might be queen of some castle from some far-away land we've never heard of, but here, you are nothing more than a simple wench." Rhys climbed back atop his horse. "Well, mayhap not simple, but of no significance or importance, that's for sure," he mumbled, thinking this girl was complicated in more ways than one.

"He's right," agreed Zann. "Even though you have powers, there are a lot of others here on Mura with powers just as strong as yours, Medea."

"I doubt it," sniffed Medea, sounding as if they'd insulted her self-worth.

"I suggest we get out of here before those soldiers come back. Give us your hand and we'll help you up. We'll give you a ride to our brother Darium's cottage." Rhys held out his hand from atop his horse toward Rapunzel, but Zann rode forward, offering his hand instead.

"That might be good, so we can all figure this out." Rapunzel let Zann help her atop his horse, and that left Rhys with Medea. Not what he wanted at all. Still, he had no choice and held out his hand, but Medea was a stubborn woman and would not take it. "Come on, Queenie, it's a far climb up to the top of this huge horse. Let me help you," he told her.

"Don't call me Queenie," she snapped. "My name is

Medea and I don't need your help." She disappeared into thin air, and materialized in front of him on his horse, making Rhys jerk backward in surprise, almost losing his balance. He hadn't expected her to do that at all.

"You are the one who had better hold on to the reins of this big horse," she told him. "After all, it seems to me you fall a lot."

"Only when I'm being pushed," Rhys told her. "I'm not sure how you behave back in the land of Tangle-wood, but it won't be tolerated here on Mura, I assure you."

Medea giggled. "Tanglewood is the castle. Our land is called England," she informed him.

"Whatever you say." Rhys headed through the woods to his brother Darium's house, feeling it in his gut that this woman and her dragon were going to bring nothing but trouble to Mura. And trouble was the last thing they needed right now.

Three

"Rap, I don't like it here," said Medea, after the girls had dismounted. As they waited for the men to tend to their horses, they looked around. It was a beautiful land from what she could see. On the way over here, besides the lake, she noticed little cottages and a lush forest of evergreens.

"Well, you should have thought of that before you stole Marco's dragon," scolded Rapunzel. "Medea, what were you thinking?"

"I was bored, Sister. Besides, Marco promised me a ride on the dragon and he never gave it to me."

"If you had shown up for even one of our family events or the births of any of our children over the past few years, mayhap he would have. Medea, since your mother died, you have been hiding at Tanglewood, refusing to come see any of us, and not allowing any of your siblings or even Father inside your castle. You have made it impossible for any of us to reach you."

"I wasn't hiding. Not really. Besides, I have my reasons," Medea answered, feeling that pang of loneliness inside her heart. Seeing her father and siblings only made the guilt she was harboring over the death of her mother even worse. When one wasn't happy, it only hurt to see others happy or in love. She didn't bother to try to explain this to Rapunzel since she was sure she wouldn't understand it. None of her family would understand her, because they all hated Hecuba for the curses she bestowed upon them. No matter how awful the woman was, she had still been Medea's mother. The only person who could have possibly understood Medea was now gone, and she was to blame.

"Father was very hurt when you all but ignored him when he discovered he had another daughter."

"What does it matter?" Medea thought her sister was making too much of a fuss over this. "I know all of you hate me for what my mother did to you."

"Nay, don't say that."

"It's true and you know it. After all, you know better than the rest that I did Mother's bidding, and wasn't very nice, either."

"Mayhap so, but it wasn't your fault that we were all cursed, or even that Hecuba tricked Father into lying with her and having... you."

Medea threw her hands in the air. "Well, if that is supposed to make me feel better, it doesn't. You might as well stop right there and don't even say another word."

"Ladies?" Rhys stood there, nodding toward the house. "Sorry to interrupt your little family quarrel, but why don't we go inside?"

"I'll wait out here," said Zann, sounding reluctant to enter the cottage.

"Nay, Brother, you won't."

"I have no desire to go inside, Rhys." Zann purposely looked in the other direction, away from the house.

"You have to face her sometime, you know," said Rhys.

"Don't tell me what to do."

"It sounds like we're not the only ones with a family quarrel." Medea pushed past the men and boldly let herself into the house without waiting for Rhys to go first. She opened the door and stopped short. A man and woman were embraced in each other's arms, kissing. This was the last thing she wanted to see right now. She cleared her throat and slowly they looked up.

"Huh? Who are you?" asked the man with the long black hair.

"Darium, sorry about this," said Rhys, brushing past Medea. Rapunzel was right behind him. Zann hovered in the doorway without actually stepping inside. "We need to talk."

"Again?" asked Darium. "Brothers, your timing is always off. I told you that I didn't want to be interrupted on my honeymoon."

"Sorry, but this can't wait," said Rhys.

"You just got married?" asked Medea, feeling as if anywhere she went, people were getting married, or at least falling in love. Everyone but her.

"Yes, we did just get married," said the man named Darium. "Now, tell me. Who in Zoroct's name are you?"

"Who is Zoroct?" asked Medea.

The man looked at her as if he thought she was addled. "One of the gods of The Haven, of course. Why do you even need to ask? How do you not know that?"

"Where exactly is this Haven?" she continued with her questions.

"Rhys? What's going on here?" asked Darium under his breath.

"Honey, you're being rude," said the woman in his arms. She walked over to Medea. "I am Darium's wife, Talia-Glenn. Are you Rhys' new girlfriend?"

"What?" Medea gasped, feeling disgusted by the suggestion.

"Nay, she's not," Rhys interrupted. "Her name is Medea de Bar and she came through a portal with her sister, Rapunzel."

"On a dragon," added Zann from the door.

"Wait. What? Seriously?" Darium looked from one brother to the next.

"It seems you were right about seeing another portal," Rhys told him.

"Damn." Darium ran a hand through his long hair, and when he did, Medea noticed a bright white streak going down the middle of his hair. She almost laughed aloud since it looked so silly. "I had hoped I was wrong. This isn't good at all."

"Excuse me. What is the white streak in your hair?" asked Medea, her curious nature getting the best of her.

"He's a Sin Eater," explained his wife. "That's just what happens to one of his kind."

"He's a what?" asked Medea, blinking twice in succession. She had never heard of such a thing before. It intrigued her.

"Sit down," said Rhys, pulling out a chair and nodding to it.

"I'd rather stand," she answered, only to purposely aggravate the man even more. She didn't like the way he acted toward her.

"We're from England," said Rapunzel, taking a seat. "My sister stole my husband's dragon. Since she's not a dragon master and can't control it, we ended up going through the portal by mistake."

"And to make matters worse, they lost the dragon," added Zann, still standing by the door. "It's flying around loose in Mura."

"Belcoum's eyes, Zann, will you come inside already?" asked Darium.

"Who is Belcoum?" Medea finally took a seat. "Another brother of yours, Rhys?"

"I should hope not," answered Talia with a giggle. Medea sneered at the woman. She didn't like anyone laughing at her. "Belcoum is the god of The Dark Abyss... the underworld," the girl explained.

"Medea, it is obviously their religion," Rapunzel told her. "Like ours with God and the Devil, and Heaven and Hell."

"Who? What?" asked Zann, finally walking in to join them.

"Never mind," said Darium, pacing back and forth. "We have more important things to discuss right now. Like, how in the world did this portal open?"

"We don't know," said Medea with a shrug. "It just happened."

"And the girl's magic can't make it reopen again," Rhys explained to his brother.

"You have magic?" This took Darium's interest.

"Are you a fae, too?" asked Talia, her green eyes dancing with light and excitement.

"Too? Oh, you must be a fae. That is why you giggle," said Media. "Nay, I'm not a fae. I'm a witch."

"Are you a witch, as well?" Talia looked over at Rapunzel.

"Yes. I suppose you could say that," she answered. "Although I just recently found out I had magic at all."

"I know the feeling," mumbled Darium.

"Darium, I think your mother should be here when we talk. She might be able to help us," came Talia's suggestion.

"Aye, we should call her," agreed Darium.

"Nay, don't call Mother or I'm leaving." Zann

sounded angry. Medea wondered if his mother was evil, the way hers used to be.

"No one has to call me, because I'm already here." A woman stood in the doorway wearing a white wispy gown that flowed in the breeze. Her hair was pulled up atop her head and intertwined with flowers. Her features were pretty, yet mature at the same time. She also had a pleasant smile on her face. Nay, she didn't look anything like Hecuba, Medea decided. This woman was not dark in any way at all.

"Mother." Zann acknowledged the woman before quickly looking the opposite way.

"The wind told me a portal had opened and that a dragon and two women came through." The woman walked into the small house. It was a cottage with several rooms, but nothing special, as far as Medea could tell. She was used to the castle, or even the tower where Rapunzel was once imprisoned and where Medea grew up. This place seemed cozy, but rather small.

"The wind told you all that?" Medea tried her best to figure out this intriguing woman.

"My mother is an Elemental of the Air," explained Rhys.

"You are? Oh, that's wonderful." Rapunzel beamed with hope. "Then, can you help us find our dragon and also assist us in getting home?"

"It's not that easy," explained Rhys. "Portals opening and closing are beyond anyone's control."

"So what you're saying, then, is that we're stuck here." Medea mentioned this for the second time since they'd arrived.

"I suppose you are," said the woman walking in and eyeing Medea up and down. "My name is Alaina. What kind of a witch are you, Medea?"

Medea's heart jumped and her head snapped up. "How do you know my name?"

"My mother just knows things," said Rhys, making Medea feel confused. Perhaps the woman had been standing there and listening longer than they realized.

"So, what kind of a witch are you?" Alaina was persistent with her question.

Medea decided the elemental must be able to sense the darkness within her, and she didn't want the others to know about it. "W-what do you mean by that?"

"I mean, are you a witch of white or black magic?"

Damn. This one was too perceptive. Medea's eyes snapped over to Rapunzel next, silently begging for her help. If these people knew some of the evil things she'd done or was capable of doing, they would shun her quickly, just like everyone else in her life. Medea had started to like the fact that no one here knew her or anything about her or her mother. She wanted to keep it that way. Mayhap she wasn't in such a hurry to go home after all, she decided.

It might be fun and also beneficial to stay here and explore this new land with their customs and beliefs. It took her curiosity. Aye, this place was already exciting, and not boring like her life back home. Mayhap, if things worked out, she'd never have to go back to Tanglewood to deal with her shadows of her past.

"We need to find the dragon," said Rapunzel, thankfully changing the subject so Medea didn't have to answer the elemental's question. "It is dangerous, and we wouldn't want anyone to get hurt."

"Or anyone to hurt it, either," added Medea. "Marco would never forgive me if anything happened to his dragon."

"I'll scout the area and see what I can find out," said Rhys. "Darium, is it all right if the women stay here for now?"

"What?" Darium's mouth fell open. "Nay, they can't. What part of '*leave me alone, I'm on my honeymoon*' don't you two understand?"

"I'm going back to Evandorm Castle. I'll see what they've heard there." Zann hurried past his mother, but she grabbed his arm to stop him.

"Son, you can't keep ignoring me," she said. "Please, forgive me."

"I've got to go," he said, shaking her hand off of him and hurrying out the door.

"I'll be back in the morning," announced Rhys, heading to the door as well.

"I'll come with you." Medea jumped up, but Rhys refused to take her.

"Nay. You'll only slow me down or cause trouble. Stay here."

"Rhys, you're not really leaving them here, are you?" whined Darium, but Rhys didn't listen to his brother's complaint. He hurried out the door, closing it behind him.

"It'll be dark soon," said Talia. "Rapunzel and Medea, you are more than welcome to spend the night here with us."

"Talia," said Darium, with angst in his voice.

"It'll be fine, honey. They are in a strange land and know no one. Plus, they are probably hungry. I'll fix something for both of you to eat," she told the women.

"I'll help you," said Rapunzel, hurrying after her to the kitchen.

Medea was left alone with Darium glaring at her, and his mother perusing her so hard that Medea was sure she would burn a hole right through her.

"I think I'll just step outside for a breath of fresh air." Medea couldn't wait to get away. She hurried out the door, and closed it behind her. Once outside, she felt dizzy and as if her heart was beating too fast. She waved her hand and materialized an apple, thinking mayhap she just needed something to eat. Taking a bite, she chewed slowly, taking in her surroundings.

Looking over the treetops, she could see tall spires and flags in several directions from what looked like three different castles. Just through the forest from the cottage was the lake where they'd come through the portal. She couldn't see anything else through the dense foliage. It was a pretty land, this place called Mura. She listened to the singing of the birds and the croaks of frogs as she finished off her apple.

Her thoughts shot back to the big man named Rhys with all the muscles. He was handsome. Even if he had been crushing her with his weight atop her, part of her liked the fact that his body had been pressed up against hers. If she hadn't been so aggravated with him, mayhap she would have kissed him, just to see how it felt. She had never kissed a man before. Her cheeks felt hot just thinking about it. A smile came to her face and her tongue shot out to touch her top lip.

"Is something wrong?" came a voice from behind her.

She spun around to see Alaina watching her from the doorway.

"Nay. Of course not. What could be wrong?" She felt uncomfortable around this woman. It was almost as if she could see into Medea's mind.

"You tell me. Your cheeks seem awfully flushed for some reason. Why is that?" asked Alaina.

"I'm not ill if that is what you mean."

"Nay. I didn't think you were. But tell me, Medea, were you just thinking about my son Rhys, by any chance?"

Medea suddenly felt extremely invaded. She wasn't

sure what kind of powers this faerie held, but she guessed it had something to do with reading minds. She didn't like that at all. Her thoughts were private and she didn't share them with anyone.

Disgust filled Medea, and she felt anger rearing its ugly head. She could do nothing to stop her darkness from surfacing. "You disgust me!" she spat, feeling a bitterness on her tongue. She also had the urge to push the woman to the ground, or perhaps send her flying through the air like she did to Rhys. It took all her restraint not to do so.

"I disgust you?" The woman looked surprised to hear this. "How so?" she asked, innocently, as if she were not guilty at all.

"You can read minds, just admit it."

"What if I can?"

Medea walked up to the fae and stuck her face up close to hers. "Stay out of my mind, I warn you. I don't like you putting your nose where it doesn't belong. You do it again, and I promise you that you'll be sorry."

They stared at each other for a minute, neither of them moving or blinking at all. Their faces were very close to each other.

"Your eyes have turned black, Medea. Why is that?" asked Alaina.

"Why don't you tell me? You're the one who invades people's minds," she challenged her.

"Medea, are you out there?" Rapunzel stuck her head out the door. "Please come inside. Talia was kind enough to fix us some food. We are going to have a bite to eat now."

"Of course," said Medea, glaring at Alaina, throwing the apple core over her shoulder. When she walked past the fae woman, she could feel the mistrust leaking out from the woman's pores. She stopped and turned, looking directly at her once again. "Is something wrong, Alaina?" she asked, not afraid to meet the fae in challenge.

"I warn you, witch," Alaina said in a low voice. "Don't you dare hurt my son, or you'll have to deal with me." She turned and walked into the house, leaving Medea standing there wondering what in the world that meant. Medea didn't even know Rhys. She'd been thinking about kissing him, not hurting him. Or was that what the man's mother was talking about after all?

Four

Rhys made his way over the drawbridge of Kasculbough Castle, realizing that everyone was running around in a frenzy, shouting in alarm.

"What's wrong?" he called out, dismounting, and throwing the reins to a stable boy.

"There was a beast that breathes fire," the stable boy told him. "It flew right over the castle."

"Was it a red dragon?" he asked.

"I believe so," said the boy, looking up at the sky. "It was terrifying, I tell you."

"Aye," said Rhys, looking up at the sky. He knew exactly how terrifying the dragon was. He also knew the extent of the beast's fiery breath. He might be able to heal himself from the breath of the dragon, but the people of Kasculbough wouldn't be so lucky. Thankfully, it didn't look as if the dragon had attacked, but the fact that it might was not a reassuring thought. If the dragon attacked, people would die. Fires could burn everything, and crops and livestock could be lost. The occupants of Kasculbough counted on this to survive. He had to do something to stop this from possibly happening.

"Sir Rhys, the King has been calling for you," said

one of the guards. "He is in the great hall now, instructing the men to don their weapons to kill the beast."

"Kill it?" he asked. "Nay, he can't do that." If the dragon was killed, Medea and Rapunzel would never leave. With the way he felt about Medea right now, the sooner they found the dragon and a way to open the portal, the better.

Rhys hurried up the stairs and into the great hall to find King Osric with a group of knights and foot soldiers gathered around him. They all seemed to be in the middle of an important conversation. Concern showed on the brows of all of them.

"Blackseed, there you are," said King Osric. "Where have you been? Get over here, anon. Your presence is required." The King was a stout man with a double chin, black hair, and squinty eyes. He wore a long, ermine-lined cloak and a tall crown on his head with lots of etchings in the gold and embedded jewels upon it.

"My King, I am sorry for my absence." Rhys hurried over to the rest of the group. "Is there a problem?"

"There's a beast in the sky that I've never seen before," the King told him.

"Aye, I know," said Rhys, figuring he needed to tell his ruler at least a little of what he knew. The King trusted him completely and this made Rhys the man's favored knight. Rhys was loyal and couldn't lie to his king. "It is a dragon, Your Majesty. It came through a portal just this day." While he didn't want to lie, he purposely didn't mention Rapunzel or Medea, just to protect them, even if he didn't know them well. He felt it was his duty since they possessed magic.

"I want you to find that dragon and catch it for me, Sir Rhys," came the King's order.

"Catch it?" Rhys looked from one man to the next.

No one was laughing. This was a serious situation. "My King, no one but a Dragon Lord can control such a beast."

"Aye, but you're my best knight, and also my strongest," said Osric, sounding as if he had total confidence that Rhys could accomplish this impossible feat. "I know you can do it, if anyone can."

This only made things worse for Rhys. How could he do his king's bidding, and at the same time help the magical women, too? "Why do you want me to capture it?" he asked. "What do you plan to do with it? Dragons are magical creatures, you realize."

"Of course I do!" snapped the King. "But that beast is dangerous. If Sethor gets to it first, he'll use it against me, as well as against Evandorm. He'll use it to seize our lands and castles. I can't have that."

"Nay, of course not, my lord."

"You'll find that dragon, and bring it to me as quickly as possible," he commanded.

"I'll do my best, Sire." Rhys felt conflicted, but he couldn't ignore a command from his king. He nodded and turned around, only to be stopped by Osric.

"Oh, and Sir Rhys? Some of my men reported that they saw a woman or two atop the dragon when it came through the portal."

"They did?" Rhys turned back toward the King, holding his breath.

"Aye. These women are probably dangerous, and can't be trusted. If they were on a dragon, they must have magic."

"What are you saying, My King?" Rhys was afraid of where this conversation was heading.

"I'm saying, you need to find these women and bring them to me, anon."

"What will you do to them once I deliver them?" he asked, afraid he already knew the answer.

"If they can fly a dragon, they've got to be very powerful and will need to be stopped."

"Mayhap so, my lord. However, you and King Grinwald stated you no longer have a ban on magic."

"Well, I've changed my mind. If they came through the portal, they are dangerous and also our enemies. I cannot take a chance."

"What does that mean?" asked Rhys, surprised that the King could say such a thing when he'd never even met the women.

"What do you think it means?" he growled. "I want you to bring me those women, because I have no choice but to take drastic measures. They will be executed at once."

* * *

Medea was just about ready to go out and look for Rhys when the door to the cottage swung open and he and Zann entered once again. She had been doing her best to stay occupied, and also to avoid looking into the eyes of the fae woman, since she thought that might be how she was reading her mind. Of course, there were two faeries here, and that made her extremely nervous. She didn't like being around even one.

"Rhys. Zann." Darium, the one they called a Sin Eater, got up from his chair. "What did you find out?"

"It seems King Grinwald has seen the dragon and is bothered by it," reported Zann.

"As well as King Osric," added Rhys. "He wants me to hunt it down and bring it back to him."

"He does?" asked Medea. "Whatever for?"

"He's afraid it will be used against him."

"So, what is he planning on doing with the dragon once he has it?" asked Rapunzel.

"He didn't say."

Medea could tell that Rhys was holding something back.

"All the Kings are going to want it," Darium pointed out. "Either to use it against each other, or perhaps to kill it."

"Kill it?" Rapunzel's head snapped upward. "Nay! That is Marco's dragon. We need to protect it."

"I agree," said Rhys. "That is why I suggest we go out and find it before they do."

"And do what, when we find it?" asked Zann. "It's not like we're skilled in the art of capturing flying beasts that can singe us with their breath alone."

"I'll go out and look for it," offered Medea. "After all, it was my fault it flew through the portal in the first place."

"I won't argue with that," said Rapunzel. "However, I can't let you go alone, Sister. I am coming with you."

"Wait, please don't leave," said Rhys, holding up his hand. "I will go with Zann and Darium to find the dragon. It will be better that way. The women will all stay here where they are safe."

"Me? Hunt down a dragon?" Darium's brows dipped. "I never agreed to such nonsense. I'm on my honeymoon, in case anyone has forgotten."

"Mayhap this is just a waste of time," stated Zann. "After all, we don't even know where to look for it."

"I know someone who can help," said Alaina.

"Who, Mother?" asked Darium. "Can you just ask the wind where the dragon is?"

"I can try, but it'll do no good if we still can't open the portal. I know someone who will be more beneficial in this matter." She looked over at the door. "Elric, please come inside the cottage."

"Elric? Oh, nay. Please, anyone but that irritating elf," groaned Darium, with his hand covering his face.

Medea jumped when a blur whizzed past her. Then she realized it was a little man, moving so fast that she couldn't even see him until he stopped.

"Are you Elric?" she asked, looking at the man who was so small he was more the size of a child even though he seemed old enough to be her father.

"Mayhap I am, and mayhap I'm not," came his reply. The little man crossed his arms over his chest. "Who's asking?"

"Elric is a sage, Medea," explained Alaina.

"And an elf," mumbled Darium. "A pesky one, at that."

"Hush, Sin Eater," snapped the elf. "If you want me to tell you how to open the portal, you'll be nice to me."

"Can you do that?" asked Rhys. "Do you really know how to find and open the portal?"

"I'm a sage, aren't I?" The elf seemed so insulted by Rhys' questions.

"Can you help us find the dragon first?" asked Medea. "My sister Rapunzel and I cannot go back through the portal without it."

"I don't know. Mayhap." The elf looked Medea up and down, wrinkling his nose.

"What's the matter, Elric?" asked Rhys.

"There's something about this one." He nodded at Medea with his head. "Something I don't like at all."

Medea's eyes went from the elf to the elemental and then over to Rhys. She tried her hardest to keep her emotions at bay, but she didn't like that they saw something in her that they didn't trust. She didn't know exactly what fueled her dark side, but she noticed it happened more so when she got angry or when she was truly bored. Therefore, she took a deep breath and tried to relax. She faked a smile and tried to think of happy things. Things that had no place where dark magic existed. It didn't work.

"Please," said Rapunzel, stepping in front of Elric. "Where can we find the dragon?"

"What have you got to trade me for my information?"

The stupid elf truly was stubborn. Media didn't like him in the least. She felt her anger growing again, and she could no longer hold it back.

"Tell us!" she shouted, using her powers to flip the man over without even touching him. He caught himself in midair, and zipped behind Alaina, peeking out from behind her.

"Well, after that, I'm not telling you anything, Witch," said the little man.

"Medea, stop it," said Rapunzel. She pulled off her wedding ring and held it out in her open palm. "Here. I'll trade you my ring if you'll give us the information of where to find the dragon and how to get back home."

"Sister, no," said Medea. "That is your wedding ring."

"I know, but we need to get back home." Rapunzel looked so sad as she held the ring out to Elric.

"Paaaalease," said the elf, sounding extremely insulted. "I don't want your jewelry. It means nothing to me."

"Then how about a punch in the nose?" asked Medea, feeling feisty.

"Medea," warned Rapunzel, reaching out and grabbing her arm to keep her from making trouble. "Elric, what is it you want in trade for this information?"

"I want some locks of your hair. You, and the mean one, too," he said, still hiding behind Alaina.

"My hair?" Rapunzel slipped the ring back onto her finger, and smoothed down her hair with her hand. Medea knew how much Rapunzel's hair had meant to her at one time. Of course, since Hecuba's curse that made her hair grow and grow and grow, Rapunzel didn't seem as if she thought it was so valuable anymore. "Done," said her sister. "Medea?" She looked over to Medea.

"What could you possibly want with our hair?" Medea asked the elf.

"I still can't figure it out either," mumbled Darium.

"That's my business," said the wiry man in a crackly voice. "Now, will you agree to it or not?"

"Do it, Medea. Please," begged Rapunzel.

Medea didn't want to give this pesky little elf anything of hers, and certainly not her hair. But when she saw the pleading and desperation in her sister's eyes, she realized she had no choice. Rapunzel had been willing to give away her wedding ring to get them back home. This was all Medea's fault, so she had no choice but to agree.

"Fine," she said, blowing air from her mouth.

"Good! Hee hee," laughed the man. "Talia, get the scissors."

Medea clenched her jaw as Talia first took a snip of Rapunzel's hair, and then one from Medea as well. Talia put down the scissors, and handed the locks to Elric. The elf's fingers moved in a blur as he braided the hair together, making a colorful twist of the light and dark hair. Ironic, thought Medea. It was not unlike her magic, having both dark and light twisted together inside her. The elf quickly tucked the braid into his pocket.

"All right. You have our hair, now spill the information," commanded Medea, having no more time for this nonsense.

The elf still seemed scared of her, clinging to Alaina's skirts, peeking out from behind her.

"Go ahead, Elric," said Alaina. "You need to keep your end of the deal."

"Oh, all right," whined the elf. "You'll find the dragon hiding in the Quamm Caves."

"Great. Where is that?" asked Medea anxiously. All she wanted to do was to get Marco's dragon and head back home.

"They're the caves of the gnomes," Talia explained. "They are on the other side of the mountain where the magical beings live."

"Magical beings?" This perked up Medea's interest. Mayhap somewhere in this odd land, could there be someone else like her? It made her want to find out more.

"What about the portal?" asked Rhys. "How do we open it?"

"You'll need a crystal key from the Pyramids of the Gods to do that," said Elric.

"Pyramids of the Gods? Is that on the other side of the mountains too?" asked Medea.

"They are," said Alaina. "However, the pyramids are sacred temples of the gods and goddesses of Mura. Not many have ever entered, and strangers from another land will not be allowed inside. They are off-limits to anyone not from Mura."

"I highly doubt that we're going to be able to walk in and steal a crystal key, even if we are allowed to enter," said Rhys.

"I'll do it," offered Medea, eagerly. This sounded like just the kind of excitement she'd been longing for in her life. "I'm not from Mura, so your gods hold no power over me. I'm not afraid of them. I'll go inside and retrieve the crystal key."

"Medea, I don't like this idea. It sounds dangerous," Rapunzel tried to discourage her. "I don't think you should do it. Let someone from Mura go inside the pyramids instead."

"I like to try new things, Sister, you know that," Medea answered with a smile. "I'll go myself. I don't need any of you to help me."

"You can't. You don't even know how to get there," said Rhys.

"I'll figure it out." Medea felt as if she'd rather go alone, rather than to have all these people tag along. She was used to being alone and doing things by herself. Being around a lot of people made her feel insecure. This would be no different.

"Don't even think about it," said Rhys in a stern voice. "It is a treacherous journey over the mountains and I will not allow it."

"I don't remember asking for your permission," she told him, not used to taking orders from anyone besides her mother. "Besides, I won't need to hike the mountains. I can transport there in the snap of my fingers," she explained. "Rap can do it, too."

"You can?" asked Darium. "That's impressive."

"Medea, the rest of them might not be able to do what we can," Rapunzel told her. "We have no idea how to catch the dragon and we'll need them to be with us. We're in a strange land. We need their help."

"Fine," she said, crossing her arms over her chest and letting out a frustrated sigh. "I just thought it would be faster if I did this alone."

"Darium, are you joining us?" asked Rhys.

"I'd rather stay here with my new wife. Go on

without me," said Darium, putting his arm around Talia.

"Darium, I'm a fae," Talia reminded him. "They might need me. The pyramids and caves are just outside the Whispering Dale. You know that no one but the fae can stay there. This trip is going to take several days, so mayhap I can talk them into taking in a few guests."

"I'll go and do that," offered Alaina. "My powers of the air might be needed. Darium, you and Talia stay here and enjoy the rest of your honeymoon. Alone."

"Fine, then. We'll head out first thing in the morning," said Rhys, sitting down on Darium's bed, stretching and yawning.

"Wait a minute," said Darium. "You're not all staying here. Not tonight."

"If we're going to get an early start, we'll have to," said Zann. "I can sleep on any chair." He sat down on a padded chair that had a tall back, putting his feet up on a stool, placing his hands behind his head.

"Girls, you can share one bedroom, and I'll stay in the other with Talia," said Rhys' mother. "The men and Elric can stay out here."

"Me?" Elric's eyes opened wide. "I'm not staying here with the Sin Eater."

"I still don't understand what a Sin Eater is," remarked Medea.

"Don't worry about it." Darium plopped down on the other side of the large bed, falling to his back. He turned away from his brother and buried his face in the pillow. "This has got to be the worst honeymoon ever," he muttered.

"I'll be leaving then," said Elric, getting ready to run out the door.

"Mage, you'll be back here in the morning, or you'll deal with me," warned Darium. "And don't think that

I'm not capable of taking back every lock of hair we've ever given you."

"You've given him hair before?" asked Medea, thinking how odd this was. Perhaps this whole land was full of strange customs.

"I'm a sage, I told you, not a mage," Elric told Darium, his hand patting his pocket with the braids of hair. "I'll sleep outside. I'm headed back to my home in Glint in the morning, so I'll let you all travel with me." Once again, in a blur, he was out the door.

"Rap," said Medea, pulling her sister over to the side, speaking softly.

"What is it?" asked Rapunzel with a yawn. It was getting late and they were all tired.

"I don't want the elemental and the elf coming with us."

"Why not?" she whispered back. "They seem nice enough, and they have powers. They might be able to help us."

"I don't feel as if they like me." Medea never knew when her darkness would overtake her. Having others around only seemed to trigger it more often. Having people around her who didn't like her was only going to make it worse. She would be defensive and lash out at anything they said about her that wasn't kind.

"You're just imagining things. After a good night's rest, things will look better in the morning. Now, let's get some sleep."

"Mayhap you're right," said Medea, following her sister to the bedroom, feeling very tired. She looked back at Rhys lying on the bed. Her eyes roamed down his opened tunic that was still shredded from his bout with the dragon, as well as with herself. His chest was visible. It looked strong and sturdy, and she wondered what it would feel like if she touched it.

"The room is this way." Alaina stepped in front of her to block her view of her son.

"Thank you," said Medea, trying to shake the thoughts of Rhys from her head before the man's mother read her mind again. After all, from the way the woman was acting, Medea was sure that is what she was doing.

Medea headed to the bedroom, knowing this trip was going to be nothing but trouble. She could feel it deep in her bones. Back home, the only magical people she really knew were the members of her own family. She didn't feel threatened by it there. Here in Mura, almost everyone so far seemed to have magic. She wasn't sure how she felt about that. To make matters worse, tomorrow they were traveling to the other side of the mountains where all the magical beings lived. Why, she wondered, did that make her feel so uneasy? She had her powers, so it shouldn't be a problem. Still, she had a feeling that something bad was about to happen.

Five

R hys was up early the next morning, anxious to leave on the journey. He stood outside, down at the Lake of Souls, waiting for the others to awaken. The sun was just rising, lighting up the Picajord Mountains, making them glow with tones of purple and orange. The birds chirped happily, and the scent of spring filled the air.

"It's rather pretty here in Mura, I must admit."

He heard a voice and turned to find Medea sitting atop a tall boulder, tossing rocks into the lake. The morning breeze lifted her loose, long hair, and then set it down again gently over her shoulders. She was a pretty girl with quaint features. Her skin was smooth and pale. She wore a purple velvet gown that made her ebony hair seem to glow in the early morning sun.

"What are you doing here?" he asked her. "And how did you get way up there?" It was a tall standing stone with smooth sides. Several of these stones could be found along the shore of the lake. They were high, steep, and slippery. There was no way anyone could actually climb them.

"I followed you," she admitted. "And I didn't climb

all the way up here, if that's what you're asking. I just… transported."

"Oh, that's right. You can do that disappearing and reappearing thing," he mumbled, turning back to look up at the sky. The rays of sunlight filtered through the air above the lake. The change in the morning temperature had caused a fog to slowly rise up from the water. "How do you do it? And what else can you do?"

It wasn't two seconds later that the witch was standing right next to him. He jumped, startled by her sudden appearance.

"Did I scare you?" she asked with a giggle.

"I'm just not used to the way you do that."

"It's a much faster way to travel."

"I can see that." He glanced over at her, his eyes focusing on hers. In the sun rays breaking through the fog, her eyes looked to be even a lighter shade of brown this morning. Quite different from the darkness in them he had seen when she became angry. Up close like this, he could really see that she was still a very young woman. She had the innocence of youth about her, yet at the same time she held a dark, dangerous edge to her that he couldn't explain.

Everything about her was mysterious, calling out to him, tempting him to find out more. He had never really known anyone quite like her.

Medea's face was heart-shaped, and her eyes were deep set and shaped like almonds. Her cheeks were rosy and she had the cutest little button nose. However, the most enticing thing about her had to be her smile. It was pretty and inviting. That is, when she wasn't trying to knock him on his ass. Her teeth were white and straight, and her full lips looked like they'd be just right for kissing.

"What are you staring at?" she asked, sounding suddenly uncomfortable by his perusal.

"You," he answered directly, not even trying to hide the fact her was checking her out. Her cheeks blushed and her gaze dropped to her feet.

"So... are you saying I'm... pretty?" she asked, hope resounding in her words. She had a sing-song, captivating voice this morning, much like that of a fae.

"I didn't say that."

"Oh." Her smile turned into a frown and she seemed sorely disappointed.

"Of course, I might have been *thinking* it," he added with a grin. Her smile was back again as quickly as it had disappeared, and he had managed to do it.

"Were you? Thinking it, I mean." There was no doubt that his playful, flirting nature was making her happy. Her lips turned up into a charming smile. He meant every word, but was somehow surprised by how well she responded to compliments. He hadn't expected it at all from a woman who seemed to have such a hard edge.

"Tell me about yourself, Medea." Rhys was intrigued and truly wanted to learn more about this woman from another land.

"Me?" Her eyelids flickered, and she seemed so surprised that he had asked. It was almost as if she were at a loss for words. That made him wonder if anyone had ever asked her this before. "Why do you ask? What do you want to know?" Her words started sounding suddenly defensive and Rhys almost felt as if he had done something wrong.

"Calm down," he said, turning to face her. "I didn't mean to make you so upset."

"I'm not upset. Why would you think I am?"

"Oh, I don't know. You are just acting like you've got something to hide."

There was silence between them for a few minutes as they both stared up at the sky and said nothing at all to each other.

"What did you mean?" she finally asked, breaking the silence.

"Huh?"

"I mean, what did you want to know about me?"

"I don't know," he said with a shrug. "Just normal stuff, I guess." He peeked out from the corners of his eyes to notice her slowly dropping the walls she'd put up around her. Being a knight, he'd seen this before from those who had been interrogated before being sentenced or thrown in the dungeon. Aye, she was hiding something, he was sure of it. But perhaps this wasn't the right time to ask about it.

"Oh," she said, releasing a breath. "Sure, then. Go on. Ask me whatever you want."

"Well, how about, how old are you?" was his first question. Unfortunately, that seemed to upset her again. He thought it was a safe thing to mention, and couldn't for the life of him understand why she reacted the way she did.

"How old do I look?" she asked, not answering the question but throwing one back to him. He knew this maneuver, and it was a sly way of dancing around an answer.

"I don't know," he said, drinking in her beauty once again. "Maybe, eighteen or twenty at the most."

"I'm twenty," she said quickly. "How old are you?"

"I'm the youngest of the brothers, at twenty-three. Zann and Darium are twenty-four and twenty-five."

"No sisters?" she asked.

"Nay. The Blackseed line has had only boys for generations." He skipped a stone into the lake, watching the ripples move outward as it hopped across the water.

"Only boys? I wonder why."

"It's just the way it is, I suppose. Do you have more siblings besides Rapunzel?"

"I do. Well, they are all half-siblings, and I'm the youngest. There are eight of us in all."

He whistled lowly when he heard the number. "That's a lot of children in one family."

"Aye. I suppose it is," she agreed.

"Are you all witches, then?"

Her head snapped up. She looked quickly in one direction and then the next before answering, as if she wanted to make certain no one else was listening. "Not really. Although some of my siblings have proven to have... powers."

"I thought you were about to say magic."

"They all had magic within them, since each of them was cursed. My brother Hugh still is."

"Really?" That took his interest now. "Who cursed them?"

"It doesn't matter." She looked down and played with her fingers.

"Well, what kind of curses did they have?"

"I think we'd better get back to the others. They'll wonder where we are. Plus, we really should start on our journey, since we'll be hiking up a mountain and that will take some time. I still think it would be faster if I just transported."

"All right, we'll go. But first, at least tell me what curse your brother Hugh still has. You've made me curious, so at least allow me the answer to that."

"I'd rather not talk about it right now."

"Sorry," he apologized, seeing this was upsetting her and he was getting nowhere. "I've got my horse. Get on, and we'll ride back together."

He expected her to just transport up there like she

did before. Instead, she stopped at the side of his horse and looked up to him with longing in her eyes.

"Will you help me up?" she asked, flashing a killer smile.

Rhys knew damned well that she didn't need help to get on the horse, but still, he didn't mind playing the little game with her since it was a form of flirting. He hadn't had a girl in his arms in some time now. This was starting to sound inviting to him. When the girl wasn't trying to knock him down or take off his head, she was very alluring indeed.

"Of course," he answered, putting his hands around her waist and lifting her up to sit atop Sampson. He quickly pulled himself up after her, wrapping his arm around her to keep her from falling.

"You're very strong," she said, looking down and placing her hand on his arm. He felt the warmth of her gentle touch.

"You have no idea. Being strong is a trait I was born with."

"If your mother is a fae, does that mean that you and your brothers are, too?"

"I suppose it does, in a way."

"What do you mean?"

"We are only half fae. Our father was a Sin Eater."

"Can you please explain that to me? I have never heard of a Sin Eater before, and I'm afraid I just don't understand it." She looked back over her shoulder at him as they rode. The scent of wildflowers drifted on the breeze from her soft hair.

"A Sin Eater helps the dead by absorbing their sins."

"Absorb? How? Why?"

"A Sin Eater eats bread and drinks ale or wine off of the chest of a corpse. My brother, Darium is a Sin Eater, just like our late father."

"Oh my. That sounds horrible! Why would anyone purposely do that?"

"It is done at the request of the family of the dead one, or the King. The dead are all people who passed away suddenly and did not have a chance to confess their sins. Sin eating gives the dead a chance to go to The Haven in the afterlife."

"Oh, I understand now. And The Haven is what we would call Heaven. Still, it all sounds so silly to me." She turned around, no longer looking at him.

"Not any sillier than the rest of us in the family and what we do."

"Really?" She looked back once again. "I know you have super strength and also the ability to heal yourself. Is that all?"

"It is, as far as I know."

"What is it that your brother, Zann can do?"

"He... I'd rather let him tell you that."

"Why?"

"Because I'm not sure you'd understand."

"If you tell me, I promise to tell you what curse it is that my brother Hugh has." She wasn't going to stop talking, so Rhys just decided to go along with it. At least he could find out more about her family this way.

"Well, all right. Zann is a shapeshifter," he told her.

"Really?" She got so excited, that she almost fell off the horse.

"Whoa, careful there." He put both arms around her now.

"What can he shift into?" Her eyes were wide with excitement.

"Just a wolf." He shrugged.

She started laughing.

"I don't think it's funny. I'm not sure why you do," he said, not liking her reaction at all.

"I only laugh because my brother, Hugh's curse is that he shapeshifts into a wolf. Actually, back home, everyone even calls him Wolf."

Now it was Rhys' turn to laugh. "I suppose I shouldn't have been so hesitant to tell you. After all, you're a witch. You can probably shapeshift, too."

"Nay, I can't. Or at least, I never have. However, my mother was a seasoned shapeshifter. She could turn into any animal, person, or even just objects, like a chair."

"That's amazing. She sounds intriguing. I'd like to know more about her."

"She's dead now," she answered. Then she stopped talking altogether.

Rhys felt as if he'd said something wrong, but had no idea what. He was about to question her about it when they heard a roaring noise in the sky, coming from behind them. His horse became spooked and rose up on its back legs, pawing the air.

"I've got you," said Rhys, holding her tightly, all the while trying to calm Sampson. "It's the dragon. I can see it over Kasculbough Castle."

Rhys turned the horse, shocked to see fire and smoke coming from the direction of the castle now. Something was burning, and he had the feeling it was damage brought on from the dragon.

"Bloody Abyss and damnation, I think the dragon attacked the castle. Zann! Darium!" he shouted for his brothers.

"What is it? What's the matter?" Zann opened the door to the cottage, wiping the sleep out of one eye.

"It's Kasculbough. I think the dragon just attacked it," he told him. "I can see smoke and fire coming from that direction."

"Nay!" shouted Zann as Darium appeared at the door as well.

"What is all the shouting about? I was trying to sleep," complained Darium. "You two don't make it easy."

"It's Kasculbough," said Rhys. "The dragon attacked. We've got to get there, quickly."

"I can transport there and find out for sure." Medea started to move off the horse, but Rhys held her back.

"Nay, Medea. This is not your land, and you don't know it. There are many dangers here that you are unaware of. You'll stay with me. Let's go!" he called out to the others.

"I'm coming after all," said Darium, quickly pulling a tunic over his head. "If there are dead, they'll need me to sin eat."

"We're all coming with you." Talia appeared at the door with Alaina and Rapunzel.

"We've got to get there quickly," said Rhys, turning his horse. "I need to stop that dragon before it destroys the Kingdom."

"Just don't hurt it, please," called out Rapunzel, running for Zann's horse.

"Hurting a dragon is the least of my concerns," grumbled Rhys. "If King Osric was killed, we're going to have a war on our hands, as the other two kings try to claim his castle and lands for themselves."

Six

Rhys wasn't sure what to expect when they rode up to Kasculbough, but the devastation was worse than he thought. Small fires burned inside the castle's courtyard. There were broken items and rubble scattered across the ground. Black, billowing smoke curled up into the sky from the thatched roofs of the outbuildings as they smoldered. It almost reminded him of some of the evil faces from the demons they'd experienced with the portal of the Land of the Dead.

Acrid smoke filled his nostrils, making him want to retch. When Rhys directed his horse over the drawbridge, he saw scorched wood beneath his horse's feet. The castle's crops outside the castle were scorched and broken. Debris floated in the moat, looking as if something had exploded.

Chaos reigned all around him. Soldiers, nobles, and peasants cried out and yelled to one another. They all moved with urgency as they ran to long troughs filled with water, and even headed to the moat to fill their buckets to help put out the fires.

"It looks like the dragon did some damage," remarked Medea.

"Aye. The thatched roofs of the outbuildings have

been burned. I wonder how many people were wounded or even killed."

"Blackseed, get over here!"

Rhys looked up to see King Osric emerging from the keep. He let out a deep sigh of relief that the man hadn't been harmed.

"I'll be right back, Medea. Stay here," he told her, dismounting and making his way over the rubble and through the puddles of spilled water to speak with his king. "My King, how do you fare?" he asked with a slight bow.

"I'm angrier than a wet vabesta-bee in the middle of a downpour." The vabesta-bee was a cross between a bee and a bird. It was a very large flying insect that had a long, sharp stinger and hated to get wet.

"Are there any deaths?" asked Rhys with concern.

"Nay, thank the gods, not from the dragon. However, there are quite a few injuries. Some are severe."

"King Osric." Darium rode into the courtyard with Talia, stopping his horse and helping his wife dismount before rushing over. Zann and the others were right behind him. "I thought perhaps my services might be needed."

"Sin Eater," said the King with a slight nod. "There were no deaths from the dragon, but since you are here, my kennel groom did die unexpectedly this morning."

"Did you want me to sin eat for him, my lord?"

"I suppose it would make his mourning family happy, and would take any weight off my shoulders too. I'm always the one blamed somehow when there is a sudden death without the chance of a confession. His body is being kept in the mews until the undertaker can get here. Hopefully, there isn't too much damage there from the dragon."

"I'll go right away, my lord." Darium started away, but Talia reached out to stop him.

"Darium, I see quite a few wounded. Perhaps my healing skills are needed."

"My king?" Darium looked over to King Osric.

"I don't know," he said, hesitantly, looking her up and down. "She's a fae, is she not?"

"Sire, my magic has naught to do with my healing abilities," said Talia. "I was recently employed as the healer of Evandorm. Please allow me to help those of your kingdom who have been hurt by the dragon."

"Well, I suppose so," he said, looking down and shaking his head. "Go! But be discreet about it. I'm still not sure how I feel about allowing a fae in here."

"Your wish will be respected," said Darium, taking Talia's hand and heading toward the mews.

"Sir Rhys," said the King. "You need to find that dragon immediately."

"Aye, my lord. My brother and a few others will be accompanying me. We know where it is, and are headed across the mountains right now to capture it and bring it back to you."

"Put it in the pit until I can decide what to do with it. I suppose that might hold it."

"The pit?" asked Medea, suddenly standing behind Rhys. He groaned inwardly. This could only mean trouble.

"He's talking about the oubliette—the large pit over there." Rhys pointed to the large hole in the ground that was used to keep prisoners. Those captured were thrown inside and the lid closed. They were more or less forgotten until they died. This pit was huge and could hold more than a dozen men. Rhys wasn't sure but supposed it might be large enough for a dragon.

"Nay! You can't put the dragon in that pit," cried Medea. "I need to return it to my brother-by-marriage."

"The dragon is responsible for all this." The King held out his arms. "I'm sorry but it needs to be stopped." The King looked over to some of his guards. "We have a healer here now. Make sure she is brought to each of the injured. The Sin Eater is also here if any of them are to die."

"Aye, Your Majesty," said one of his men with a nod of his head, hurrying to do as ordered.

Mothers holding the hands of their crying children rushed past them, pulling their little ones to safety. A few dogs followed and barked at their heels. A whole line of people still worked with passing water buckets, dousing what was left of the flames.

Rhys felt terrible about what happened. This was his home. He lived with these people. Part of him felt responsible. As much as he didn't want the dragon harmed, he could see the King's concern. Next time, the dragon might do worse and people could die. He couldn't let that happen. His first duty was to his king.

Rapunzel ran up to them with Zann on her heels. Alaina watched from a distance.

"Please, don't hurt my husband's dragon," cried Rapunzel.

"Who are these wenches?" snapped the King, irritated by the disturbance.

"They came through the portal with the dragon," Zann told him before Rhys could stop him from announcing it.

"They did?" The King looked at the women and shook his head. "Then we'll keep them in the pit until the dragon is found. They are as much to blame as that fire-breathing beast. Guards, seize them!"

"Nay, Your Majesty, they aren't dangerous, I assure you." Rhys tried to convince the man, but King Osric wouldn't listen. Several guards came forward. Rhys could see this wasn't going to end well, and that there was nothing more he could do at the moment to protect them. He turned and whispered to Medea.

"You'd better get out of here any way you can. Take your sister with you. I'll meet up with you at the Quamm Caves as soon as I can."

"Come on, Rapunzel," said Medea. "We don't need anyone's help." Medea took her sister's hand in hers. Then, just as the guards were about to seize them, they disappeared into thin air.

"What?" gasped the guard, frantically looking back and forth. "What just happened? Where did they go? Where are they?"

"They were right here and now they're gone," shouted another of the guards. "They disappeared into thin air."

"They have magic!" yelled the King, becoming very angry. "Sir Rhys, why did you bring fae into my courtyard?"

"They're not fae. They are witches, Your Majesty. And I assure you they mean no harm. They only want to find a way to get back home."

"Find them!" Osric called out to his men. Then he looked back at Rhys. "You better bring not only the witches, but the dragon back here to me. If not, *you'll* be the one I'm throwing into the pit instead. Understand?"

"Aye, my lord," said Rhys with a nod, knowing it would do no good to argue with his liege lord. He had given a command, and it was Rhys' duty to carry it out.

He turned toward Zann and spoke in a low voice. "Go to the mews and warn Darium to get Talia out of here at once. It's no longer safe for her. Then meet me at the foot of the Picajord Mountains."

"Aye," said Zann, taking off at a run.

Rhys looked up to see his mother standing near the

gate. He needed to get her to safety as well. Since she was able to read minds like all fae can, he sent her a silent message. *Go, Mother. Find Medea and Rapunzel and meet me at the caves.*

His mother looked up and nodded slightly before turning and leaving the courtyard.

"Sir Rhys!" bellowed the King.

Rhys turned around, not wanting to hear more, but having no choice.

"I'm counting on you to bring back that dragon."

"Your Majesty, you realize, I don't have training in capturing dragons. No one does. We have never encountered one before, and there is no telling what will happen."

"The beast is deadly and needs to be stopped. If you can't manage to catch it... then kill it instead. As well as those witches. Catch and kill them all, do you understand? They'll only cause us trouble."

Rhys' heart picked up a beat when he heard his new orders. He could never kill women. Besides, he liked Medea and her sister, and wanted to protect them, not harm them.

"I assure you, the women will be no trouble. They only want to collect their dragon and leave Mura through the portal that brought them here."

"I'm sorry, but I don't believe that."

"You said you were willing to accept magic again."

"Well, I've changed my mind. It is apparent that magic only means trouble for everyone on Mura. I'm depending on you, Sir Rhys, to help me abolish it."

"My King, with all due respect, how can you ask me to do that? You know my mother as well as my sister-by-marriage are both fae. I would never do anything to hurt them."

"Then take the fae back across the mountains and

leave them there. That is where creatures of magic belong, not here."

"They are not creatures. They are people, the same as you and me. And you're asking me to desert my family." Rhys was torn. As a knight and right hand of the King, he had never disobeyed an order before. But this was a command that affected not only Medea and Rapunzel, but his family, too. He'd had hope that things would change when King Osric said he had finally accepted magic. Now he realized that the man's words were naught but an empty promise. It was clear to see magic would never be accepted at Kasculbough, and this made Rhys very upset indeed.

"Sir Rhys, I admire you. You are my best and favorite knight. You know that. You're like a son to me. A son I never had."

"Thank you, my lord." This meant the world to Rhys, since the King had been more of a fatherly figure in his life than his own father. He didn't want to let the man down.

"My wife is deceased, and I only have daughters left," continued the King.

"I know this, my lord. Why are you telling me?"

The King dismissed his guards with a shake of his head. Once they departed, he took a step closer. "Listen closely to me, Sir Rhys. When I am dead, I want you to be the one to take my place as King of Kasculbough."

"My lord?" Rhys couldn't believe his ears. "I don't understand. You want me as your heir?" This truly surprised him, since he had no idea that the King valued him that much.

"I do. You are the son I never had, and I trust you more than anyone. I want you to carry on in my stead when I leave this world."

"I'm flattered, My King, but it isn't normal for a knight to wear the crown. Are you sure about this?"

"Of course, I'm sure. I am so certain, Sir Rhys, that I've had my advisor write up the papers already."

"This is all so sudden," said Rhys, not sure what to say. Being king and having his own castle was everything that Rhys ever wanted. He had a hard time believing what the King was saying, and it made him wonder why he decided on him as his heir. "May I ask why you've decided this so suddenly?"

"My second advisor was the one who convinced me it is the right thing to do. I trust the man completely."

"Second advisor?" asked Rhys, not knowing the King even had any advisor except for his man, Raudfer, who Rhys was sure didn't even like him.

"Aye, I've had Cirle undercover at Macada Castle for some time now. He gave me valuable information about King Sethor's defense plans. He goes back and forth from Macada to here, and he's also been keeping an eye on you and your family for me."

"What?" asked Rhys in surprise.

"Don't be alarmed. His report was a good one. He's told me wonderful things about you, Sir Rhys. Things that made me confident I was making the right decision."

"With all due respect, I'm not sure I like the idea of being spied on, Your Majesty."

"It's a good thing, I assure you, Sir Rhys. You should be thanking my spy, since it was on his word that I've based my decision to make you my heir."

"Well then, if I ever meet the man, I will be sure to thank him. But what about your three daughters, Sire? Surely, you'd put them in line in front of me to sit on your throne?" Rhys had a hard time believing this was true.

"Bah!" The King swiped his hand through the air in

a dismissing manner. "They are just women, and cannot be my heirs. You know that."

"I am sure that someday they'll marry, Your Majesty. Wouldn't you prefer one of them and their husband to rule in your stead, rather than me?" As much as Rhys wanted this position, he needed to know it was truly the King's wishes, and not just an impulsive decision that the King would soon regret.

"Nay! I don't trust anyone but you. I've left a signed and sealed missive with Raudfer. It is to be opened upon my death. In it, I name you, Sir Rhys, as heir to all I own." This shocked Rhys so much that it left him tongue-tied, and not able to speak. Even if he had been able to talk, he wasn't sure he knew how to respond. This was a stroke of luck. He would someday get every-thing he ever wanted. This was an amazing dream come true.

"I am honored, my lord," he finally managed to squeak out. "That is, if you are sure you want me." This was a tough position to be in. As the proclaimed king's heir now, how could he possibly deny any command the man gave him? He couldn't. And the King just gave a command that Rhys wasn't sure he could possibly carry out.

"Are you saying you don't want this opportunity, Blackseed? What is the matter with you? You would turn down a kingdom and title of king?"

"Nay, of course not. It is an opportunity that only a fool would pass up," he answered, feeling excited, hesi-tant, and confused all at the same time.

"Just follow my orders exactly, or I'll make someone else my heir instead," he warned Rhys. "Unless you are trying to tell me you're turning down my offer?" The King looked at him suspiciously, almost as if he had started to doubt his decision. Mayhap Rhys' hesitancy had caused this. He needed to be more careful. The last thing Rhys wanted right now was for the King not to trust him.

"Nay, of course I wouldn't turn down your offer," he answered, shaking his head, feeling very confused right now. "I didn't mean that at all, Sire. After all, doesn't every knight want to someday own his own castle and be a ruler? Of course, I do. I am just surprised, as well as honored, that you should choose me, that's all. I really didn't expect it."

"Through the years, you have served me well, Sir Rhys. You have always done what I've asked, and have been more loyal to me than even any of my hounds. You have never questioned my word, nor have you given me doubt that you would ever betray me."

"Thank you, Sire. I assure you, that you can trust me completely."

"You are the best man for the position, once I am gone. The last thing I want is for Kasculbough to fall into the hands of my enemies."

"Of course not. I understand."

"Good. Then, prove to me that I haven't made an error in judgement. Bring back that dragon and the witches as I've commanded. Dead or alive. But either way, you will be required to kill them all. I know you can do it, Sir Rhys."

"I will do my best, Your Majesty." He bowed his head. "But concerning the witches..." He tried again to change the King's mind.

"You know what you have to do! Don't make me question my choice of naming you heir."

"Of course not, my lord."

"Now, go! And in the name of all the gods in The Haven, do not even think of letting me down."

Seven

Rhys mounted his warhorse and rode out over the drawbridge of Kasculbough Castle, feeling as if someone had just punched him in the gut. What the King was offering was everything that he had ever dreamed of. It was almost too good to be true. Of course, it didn't go into effect until the man was dead, but the way things were going on Mura lately, that could happen sooner than later.

He took the path around the east of the castle and rode along the shore of the sea. He had never disobeyed an order from the King before, but this time was different. How could he carry out the order to kill Medea and her sister? And in regards to the dragon, he had no idea how to even capture it, let alone kill it. He was more than sure that he might be the one to get killed just trying to carry out the order.

"Rhys!" called out his brothers from behind him. He turned to see Zann and Darium riding their horses fast, trying to catch up with him. He stopped and turned around.

"Did the women get to safety?" asked Rhys, hoping they did.

"Aye," said Darium as they both stopped their steeds

in front of him. "I thought it best if Talia and her family stay in hiding for now. I instructed her to stay in their cottage until I return."

"Will they be safe there?" asked Rhys.

"I believe so," said Darium with a nod. He tied back his long black hair, which only made the white streak down the center more noticeable. He had been ridiculed a lot from people calling him a skunet because of it. No one wanted to be compared to the hairy black and white animal of Mura that had a stench worse than the garderobes on a hot day. "They will be hidden by their fae magic. No one will find them, so we don't need to worry. What happened to Mother?" asked Darium "I didn't see her anywhere, and she was with us when we crossed into Kasculbough."

"I gave her a silent command to meet us at the caves along with Medea and Rapunzel," Rhys explained. "Thank goodness, Medea and her sister have the power to transport. They are in grave danger and were lucky to get out of there alive."

"What do you mean?" asked Darium.

"King Osric has commanded me to... to kill them."

"What?" Zann's eyes opened wide. "You're not really going to do it, are you?"

"I have never disobeyed an order from my king."

"Well, mayhap now is the time to start," said Darium. "Rhys, are you really planning on killing the women?"

Rhys had never killed a woman in his life, and didn't want to start now. But the situation he was in would determine his future. He'd worked so hard to please the King, and now was so close to getting what he always wanted. The King trusted him enough to name him as heir. How could he let the man down?

"I'm in a terrible predicament, Brothers." Rhys

shook his head in despair. "The King also wants me to bring back the dragon. He wants the dragon killed, too."

"So, it sounds as if he's changed his mind about magic again," said Darium.

"He has. He says it needs to be stopped, and he is counting on me to do it."

"Well, he's got another guess coming then," said Zann with a chuckle. "After all, we know you'd never carry out those crazy orders."

Rhys remained silent. This only caused concern from his brothers.

"Rhys?" asked Darium. "Please tell me you are not truly considering doing what King Osric wants you to do."

"You know that the last thing I want to do is to hurt or kill a woman. That's not who I am," said Rhys.

"Then why the long face, Brother?" asked Zann.

"Aye. Tell us exactly who you are," said Darium.

"Rhys, why do you look like you're not sure of your decision?" asked Zann.

"I'm not," admitted Rhys, blowing air from his mouth. "You see, King Osric told me that he has named me as his heir when he dies."

"What?" both his brothers said together.

"That's great!" said Zann.

"Congratulations," added Darium.

"Nay. You don't understand." Rhys closed his eyes and shook his head.

"Rhys? What's going on?" asked Darium, glancing over at Zann and then back to him again.

"King Osric warned me not to let him down," explained Rhys.

"So you mean, if you don't carry out his orders you

will no longer be his heir?" Zann was starting to understand the situation.

"That's exactly what I mean." Rhys felt like he was going to be sick.

"Brother, this is a tough one, and I don't envy your position," said Darium.

"It is a dream come true to be a king's heir," Zann told him. "Rhys, you might be a fool to turn it down."

"At the expense of two innocent lives?" Darium scowled at his brother. "How can you even say that?"

"Aye. You're right." Zann shrugged and looked the other way. "So, Rhys, you're damned if you do and damned if you don't."

"And I thought I was the one who was damned when I almost ended up trapped in the Land of the Dead forever," mumbled Darium.

"Let's go." Rhys turned his horse and continued riding for the mountains.

"Wait. Are you going through with this or not?" asked Zann from behind him.

"I have a job to do," Rhys told them without even looking over his shoulder. "The first thing I need to concern myself with is catching that dragon before it destroys all of Mura."

"What's the second thing?" asked Zann.

"Aye. What about the girls? Are you going to kill them as ordered?" Darium wanted an answer.

"I don't know what to do," said Rhys, feeling like screaming out loud. "I guess I'll deal with that when the time comes."

"I think I'd better come along on this little journey of chasing a dragon after all," said Darium.

"What about your honeymoon and spending time alone with Talia?" asked Zann.

"How in the name of Zoroct can I relax and enjoy

myself when I know my little brother might make a choice that he'll regret for the rest of his life?"

Rhys wondered if Darium meant the choice to listen to the King, or the choice to ignore him. Either way, it didn't matter. He already regretted any decision he was about to make.

* * *

Medea materialized with her sister, right in front of a grouping of caves that were layered one on top of each other and spread out across the coastline. The waves of the sea washed into the bottom caves, then receded and slipped back out again.

"Well, I'm not sure this is where we're supposed to be, but at least I see caves," said Medea with a satisfied nod.

"I wonder how long it will take the men to join us?" Rapunzel looked around and then sat down on a large, flat rock in the sun.

"I'm sure it'll be a while. After all, they're on horses and need to cross the mountains," Medea told her. "Oh well. Mayhap I'll cool off my feet in the water while I wait." She sat down on a rock and removed her shoes.

"Medea, you have been very bad by stealing Marco's dragon." Rapunzel lay back on the flat rock with her eyes closed, sunning herself.

Medea didn't like her sister scolding her the way she always seemed to do. It only stoked the fires of her anger. "Well, if Marco would have kept his promise and given me a ride on the dragon, I wouldn't have had to steal the damned thing!" She got up and sloshed through the water.

"It seems as if your darkness is taking over again,

Medea. You need to control it, or you'll end up just like Hecuba."

"Nay! I won't!" Medea's anger grew so fast that any thought other than revenge was masked in her mind. She spun around, using her dark magic to blast Rapunzel, sending her flying through the air.

Rapunzel was used to this, and prepared to defend herself. When she hit the air, she was able to levitate, using her own powers to send a wave crashing over Medea, knocking her to the ground.

"Stop it!" cried Medea. "You are always so rude with the way you speak and treat me."

"Mayhap you're forgetting all the horrible things you have done to me in the past, Sister," answered Rapunzel. "I could never be as mean or as rude as you have been to me."

"That was before. I've changed since then." Medea made a limb of a tree shake, and the branch came crashing down, nearly landing atop her sister. Rapunzel was able to stop it, and send it sailing right back at Medea. Medea blasted it with her powers causing the thing to splinter and shatter into a million pieces, raining down around them.

"Have you really? I don't see it," said Rapunzel. "You're just as mean as you used to be when Hecuba was alive."

"I am not, and stop saying that or you will be sorry." Medea could feel her eyes turning black. It was as if a dark shadow snaked up through her body taking control and she didn't know how to stop it.

"Your darkness is going to destroy you someday, Medea," warned Rapunzel, climbing atop a large boulder. With the way her gown blew in the breeze and with the sun shining down upon her, Rapunzel looked like a queen ruling from her rock. That only made Medea angrier, since Rapunzel was the spoiled one in the family, and always got everything she wanted. Medea wanted what Rapunzel had.

"If you'd stop goading me, mayhap I wouldn't have to use my dark magic." Medea waved her arm in the air using her powers again, feeling something odd happening this time. It was a feeling that she'd never had before. Her body tingled at first, and then it became heavy. She felt so heavy that it was as if she could barely move or even breathe. It was a feeling she didn't like in the least. She found herself crouching down behind Rapunzel, and she didn't feel like herself at all.

"Medea? Where did you go?" Rapunzel turned and looked right over Medea's head, but her sister didn't even seem to see her. "Come out, Sister. We need to talk."

Medea tried to talk, but couldn't seem to do it. It was almost as if she had forgotten how. Then Rapunzel took a step and stood right on Medea's head, causing her anger to grow stronger.

"Medea? Where are you?" called out Rapunzel. "Come on. I'm sorry for fighting with you."

It was then that Medea realized that her sister didn't see her, because she was no longer in her human form. She struggled to stand, pushing out her arms, trying her hardest to get to her feet. Rapunzel teetered with the movement and cried out.

"Oh!" shouted Rapunzel, falling to the ground as Medea shifted back into her human form. "Medea?" Rapunzel pushed a stray lock of blonde hair from her face, looking up from the ground. Her eyes were wide and her mouth dropped open. "Y-you just... shapeshifted."

"I did?" It took a minute, but then Medea felt like

herself again. She looked over to Rapunzel in question. "W-what was I?"

"You were a rock! Are you saying you don't remember? Didn't you mean to do that?"

"Nay! I guess I was thinking about you standing on the rock, but... did I really just shapeshift the way my mother used to do?"

"Yes, you did. I guess your powers are growing. Shapeshifting is only something that older witches, or those with very powerful magic can do."

"I suppose you're right," she said, looking at her arms and feeling them to make sure she was still in one piece. It had been such an odd experience and she couldn't say that she liked it. "Interesting," she mumbled. She wasn't sure how she shapeshifted or even if she could do it again. Mayhap in time she would learn how to control it. Being a rock didn't feel great, but this made her wonder what else she was capable of doing.

"Hello, girls."

Medea turned to see Rhys' mother Alaina heading their way, walking along the shore. Medea groaned.

"Hello, Alaina," called out Rapunzel, waving to the woman. Then, she turned and spoke lowly to Medea. "I can tell you don't like her. Why not?"

"The fae is the one who doesn't like me," Medea said in her own defense. "I think she can read minds, Rap. Be careful what you think. And don't tell her about my new power of shapeshifting."

"Why not?" asked Rapunzel. "You should be proud of it. Besides, it might come in handy to help us catch Marco's dragon."

"Just the same, I would rather she didn't know."

Alaina walked up to them with Medea's shoes in her hand. "I found these shoes in the water." She held them out. "Why are you all wet?" she asked Medea.

Medea's eyes shot over to Rapunzel and she shook her head slightly. She didn't want the fae to know about their fight. And especially not about her newfound power to shapeshift. The woman didn't like her, and Medea wasn't sure she wouldn't cause her trouble. Therefore, Medea purposely blocked her thoughts, hoping Rapunzel was doing the same.

"My sister went for a walk in the water to cool her feet," stated Rapunzel. "I suppose the waves caught her off guard." She turned and winked at Medea.

"Yes, I suppose they did. Thank you," said Medea, snatching her shoes away from the woman, and sitting down to don them.

"I see you ladies found the Quamm Caves with no trouble." Alaina smiled and looked over at the caves.

"Oh, so this is the right place to meet the men, after all?" asked Rapunzel. "Good."

"Aye, it is. I probably should have offered to get the boys here faster using my powers to control the wind, but I didn't think Zann would agree to it," Alaina told them.

"Why not?" asked Rapunzel.

"He doesn't seem to like you much," Medea said bluntly, standing up and smiling. She wanted to point out to Alaina that there were others besides herself who didn't like her.

"I suppose Zann doesn't like me much right now, that is true."

"What happened?" asked Rapunzel.

"It's a long story," Alaina answered, her smile disappearing. "I think Zann is just harboring ill feelings toward me from the past. I'm sure he'll get over it eventually."

"Hrmph," said Medea, reaching up and squeezing the water out of her hair.

"You're an interesting one," said Alaina, her eyes boring into Medea again.

"Shall we proceed to the caves and see if we can find the dragon before the men arrive?" asked Rapunzel, thankfully changing the conversation before Medea did something nasty to Alaina.

"Nay." Alaina shook her head. "I wouldn't suggest going into the caves without the men."

"Why not?" asked Medea defiantly. "I'm not afraid of the dragon. Are you?"

Alaina didn't react. Instead, she slowly turned her head and looked out over the sea. "There are magical creatures here that you've yet to encounter. Those caves are filled with gnomes who don't like to be around people like us."

"Gnomes?" asked Medea, laughing. "Do you mean those little people with the tall pointy hats?"

"You know of them?" asked Alaina. "Do you have them where you come from?"

"We've heard of them, sure," said Rapunzel. "I don't believe we've ever encountered them, though." She looked over at Medea when she said it. "Perhaps it would be best to wait for the men after all."

Medea thought it was ridiculous, but didn't want to object. She knew it would only bring about trouble. "What other kinds of creatures live on Mura?" asked Medea.

"Most of the magical beings are only on this side of the Picajord Mountains, not down south near the humans," explained Alaina.

"So, where are they all now? I don't see any." Medea looked around but saw no one other than themselves.

"The Whispering Dale is where the fae folk live," Alaina explained. "Next to it is Glint, the home of the elves."

"Elves? Like that sage, you mean?" asked Medea. "Where is he, anyway? I thought he was coming along on the journey."

"Elric lives in his own home atop a rock," she explained. "He'll be here, don't worry. He travels so fast, that I'm sure he's been waiting for us for quite some time now."

"I am intrigued by these magical beings and can't wait to meet some," said Rapunzel with a smile.

"Don't be too anxious. They're not all friendly," Alaina warned them, looking back at the caves.

"You can't possibly be talking about those little gnomes," said Medea.

"Them, and the giants who live on the Isle of Denwop." Alaina pointed to an island just beyond the caves, isolated from anything else.

"Giants, huh?" Medea squinted her eyes to see the island better. "I hope they won't eat us."

"Anything is possible," Alaina told them. "However, the giants' favorite food is elves. Then again, they are huge and eat a lot. They have been known to eat anything when they're hungry."

"I don't want to go there," said Rapunzel, looking very nervous now. "We'll just find the dragon, get the crystal key, and use it to open the portal to get back home."

"Where are those pyramids that were mentioned?" asked Medea, looking around. "Mayhap we can collect the key while we're waiting for the men to arrive."

"Those are the Pyramids of the Gods," said Alaina. "We'll have to make some sort of offering when we go there, so we don't anger them. They don't allow many inside, even if someone has come to worship them."

"Seriously?" Medea laughed. "You would think they'd want a large following. What kind of offering are you talking about? Are they going to want a snip of hair like that crazy elf, or mayhap they are even more addled and want something like... shoes?" She held up her foot and water dripped from the shoe.

"I wouldn't speak that way about the gods if I were you." Alaina's eyes scanned the sky. "If you anger them, it can be very dangerous indeed."

"This is silly." Medea sighed and plopped down atop the rock. "I'm not afraid of any magical being or any of your so-called gods either."

"Really?" The woman raised her chin and stared at Medea, causing a shiver to go up her spine. "Well, my dear, mayhap you should be."

Eight

"Zann, mayhap you'd better shift and run ahead of us to make sure the women are all right. Tell them we'll be there soon." Rhys started regretting telling the women to go ahead of them.

"Really?" Zann's tone told Rhys that he wasn't looking forward to doing this. "I'm sure they're fine. They're witches. Besides, Mother is there, too."

"Oh, and that's why you don't want to go," said Darium in a knowing manner. "Zann, you need to get over your issues of the past."

"It has nothing to do with it."

"Doesn't it?" asked Rhys, knowing it most likely had to do with not wanting to be by their mother.

"Fine, I'll go," said Zann, most likely just trying to prove his brothers wrong. Zann stopped his horse and hopped off, tying the reins to Darium's steed. "Don't say I never help you two, because that is all I ever seem to do." He undressed as he spoke. Once naked, he stuffed his clothes into the travel bag tied to the horse. "You two enjoy the fact I am going to have to parade around in front of the women stark naked, don't you?"

"Zann, stop your complaining," said Rhys. "We are doing this for the sake of everyone in Mura. Besides, it'll be good if you are there with them in case they run into any trouble with the dragon before we arrive."

"And tell me what should I do if that happens, Brother? After all, I'm sure dragons love the taste of wolf."

"Mayhap so," said Rhys. "But I wouldn't worry about it if I were you."

"He's right," said Darium with a chuckle. "You're too bitter for anyone's taste, even a wild beast."

"You both owe me for this, big time. The only reason why I'm agreeing to it at all, is because I have the need to run and clear my head. If I didn't, you'd be out of luck." Zann hunkered down on the ground, taking a deep breath and releasing it. He shook his head back and forth and started shifting into a large white wolf. Then he threw back his head and howled loudly. After snapping at the air in what looked like an act of aggravation, he took off at a run up and over the mountain.

"So, what do you think of the witch?" Darium asked Rhys as they traveled up the mountain on horseback.

"Which one?" asked Rhys.

"You know damned well which one. The one that isn't married."

"Oh. You mean, Medea."

"Yep, that's the one."

"What about her?" Rhys didn't really want to think about the girl that the King ordered him to kill. He had started to become fond of her, and that only made the confusion in his head worse.

"I can tell by the way she looks at you that she likes you."

"Really?" Rhys raised his brows, feeling excitement course through him. "Do you think so?"

"Mmm hmm," said Darium with a chuckle. "And I

see by the way you just perked up that you must have feelings for her, too."

"Nay. You're wrong, Brother. Medea means nothing to me. And I haven't noticed her taking any liking to me at all."

"I'm sure you did, but you just won't admit it."

"Darium, what are you getting at? Just spit it out already because you're starting to irritate me with this little game." All Rhys wanted was silence. He'd had enough of his brother's nonsensical jabbering. Right now the confusion in his head was loud enough and he didn't need more chaos.

"I'm just saying, wouldn't you rather kiss the girl than kill her?"

"Of course I would!" he spat. "You have no idea how hard this is for me. Do you think I really want to kill women? I don't."

"Then what's the problem?"

"The problem is that I've never purposely disobeyed one of the King's commands before."

"You're not seriously thinking about carrying out King Osric's orders, are you?" asked Darium. "Murdering innocent young wenches isn't something I pegged you for even considering doing."

"Brother, King Osric has named me as his heir once he dies. It's in writing."

"I heard you the first time you told us."

"Well, this is huge! It is everything I've worked so hard for, and all that I've ever wanted. Don't you understand? I'm going to be King of Kasculbough someday. I'll have my own castle, not to mention my own army. Soldiers will answer to me alone, and I will make all the decisions. I'll even make sure magic is allowed within the castle walls. I'll have so much power, wealth, and everything that goes along with the title, if I don't manage to anger the King. If I do, he will change his mind, and I can't let that happen. I will be set for life, Darium, and that means you and Zann will be too. I'll have money and lots of food so we'll never have to go hungry again. I'll make sure my family never wants for anything. This affects all of us. Do you understand exactly what this means?"

"Yes, I think I do," said Darium, not looking at all pleased with the conversation. "It means my brother is going to sell his soul for greed."

"Greed?" Rhys' head snapped around and he scowled at his brother. He didn't like to be called greedy. It was just his way of self-preservation. "Now, wait a minute. That's not fair."

"It's accurate, Rhys, and you know it. What is not fair is what you're considering doing to Medea and Rapunzel, or even the dragon. They are not here of their own will and all they want to do is to get home. How can you not let it bother you that you're considering taking the life of a woman who likes you and whom you care for as well?"

Rhys didn't answer. He didn't appreciate his brother speaking this way to him, calling him greedy and a murderer. He especially didn't like him talking about matters concerning the heart. Rhys barely knew Medea. She was naught but a witch and a stranger to him. He didn't have feelings for her in the least. Sure, the wench was pretty and also powerful, but he didn't feel as if he owed her a thing.

Except mayhap her life, he sadly realized.

He released a deep sigh, knowing what his brother was trying to do. No one deserved to die just because they had magic. Especially, not because a greedy king ordered it. These women were innocent. How could he ever take their lives? He couldn't. Not for all the wealth in the world. If he did so, he would never be happy or able to live without guilt.

"Damn it, I was so close," he grumbled. "But you're right. I can't do it, Darium. I won't kill the women, no matter what the King says."

"That's more like the brother I know and love," Darium answered with a smile.

"I guess I'll have to get used to eating snails and seaweed the rest of my life, since I won't have a job or a home once the King finds out I am not going to follow his orders."

"I'll teach you to fish, Brother. And Zann is a hunter, so we'll make sure you don't go hungry, don't worry."

"Let's find a way to get the witches and their dragon through that portal before I have to report back to the King," said Rhys, feeling as if he'd made the right decision, but at the same time hating himself for letting such a great opportunity slip through his hands. Kicking his heels into the sides of his horse, he sped up the mountain path. Right now, he wanted nothing more than to send the wenches and their pet dragon back through the portal, because looking at them would only remind him of the life he almost had and lost. Aye, he was sure he never wanted to have to see any of them again.

* * *

Medea waited with the women all day, wishing the men would hurry up and arrive. Bored out of her mind and wanting something to do, Medea finally took off into the caves to explore on her own. She'd been warned not to do it, but she really didn't care what her sister or Rhys' mother said. Medea wasn't used to taking orders from anyone. She was a queen and would do what she pleased.

Looking over her shoulder, she saw both Rapunzel and Alaina lying back in the sun with their eyes closed. For all she knew, they were sleeping. Good. This was the perfect opportunity to get away on her own.

Medea had excused herself hours ago, walking by herself along the coastline. She was used to being alone. This wasn't out of the ordinary for her, although she couldn't say she really liked solitude. It felt so lonely. She peered across the sea to the Isle of Denwop. Alaina said this was where the giants lived. It made her wonder what a giant even looked like. Was it ugly like an ogre, or did it just look like a tall man? She really had no idea since she'd never seen one before. Medea also was curious about the other magical beings such as the elves, and fae, and these cave gnomes that were supposed to be so mean.

"Impossible," she said, throwing a rock into the water as far as she could. It landed with a splash. To her surprise, something reared up out of the water that looked like a giant pink sea serpent. It caught the rock in its mouth and then sank back down under the water. It disappeared from sight just as fast as it came. "Did you see that?" she said, turning to look back at her sister and Alaina, but neither of them heard her. Both the women still lay there with their eyes closed and their faces turned up to the sun. "This place is amazing," she mumbled, finding the land of Mura much more fascinating than back home in England. She was sure she'd never be bored for a minute if she lived here.

A low rumbling sound caught her attention, and she swore it sounded like Marco's dragon. The noise was coming from the cave closest to her. If the dragon was in there, she needed to go and find it before it flew off again. She was told to wait for the men, but Medea decided she was tired of waiting. After all, she had powers, so she wasn't really in any kind of danger. She'd just use her magic to try to control the dragon, even if she couldn't seem to fly it straight. Having to always fend for herself, this shouldn't be that difficult. Why wait for the men to help when she could have the dragon captured and bound before they even showed up?

Tiptoeing to the mouth of the cave, she tried to see inside but it was too dark to make out anything clearly. Moving further into the entrance, she stopped and listened. Yes, she was sure she heard the snort of the dragon. What luck to find the exact cave where the dragon was hiding, and so quickly, too. This would save a lot of time searching for it.

It was dank and damp and smelled musty, like old wet stockings inside the cave. The rocks inside were wet and slimy. She lost her footing and slipped, landing on her butt. When she looked up, she was surprised to see a dozen tiny odd-looking men and women surrounding her.

"Gnomes," she muttered, knowing this is what they must be. They were small, but looked fierce, and the furthest thing from friendly.

"Hello?" she said, releasing a nervous giggle. "Are you gnomes?"

They didn't answer. Instead, they moved closer to her, closing in all around her. When they did, she realized they were holding weapons of some kind. Well, not actually weapons. In their hands were rakes, shovels, and some type of long pointed spears. A few of the gnomes even held wooden poles with axes or large stone hammers attached to the tops. She supposed these farming tools could be used as weapons, after all.

The gnomes were not much more than knee-high to

her, but still they were plenty threatening. The men were clad in earth-colored tunics and breeches. They had white hair and long, white beards down to their bellies. The women wore long dresses that touched the ground. The females were round and stout and big busted. Each had long, loose hair down to their elbows. Both the men and women wore pointy hats in a multitude of colors.

As they moved in closer and closer to her, they aimed their array of weapons, all pointing directly at her!

"Now, wait a minute you little gnomes. I mean you no harm. Just leave me alone," said Medea, feeling fear at first. When they started making some sort of grunting noises that grew louder and louder, she became defensive. One of them poked the sharp end of their spear at her, pricking her on the behind. "Stop it!" she shouted, anger filling her quickly. Like her late mother, it didn't take much to awaken her dark side.

She jumped up and held out her hands, no longer caring if she hurt them or even killed them. They were irritating her and they had to go. A black wisp of smoke shot out of her palms, knocking down the gnomes as easy as rolling a ball at glass bottles. They didn't like that. All of a sudden, she found herself being attacked. They rushed at her and jumped atop her, hitting her and poking her with their weapons. All the while their grunts of communication between them became louder and louder, hurting her ears.

Medea tried to transport to get out of there, but her powers didn't seem to be working well now, with all these magical beings piled atop her. "I'll kill you. I swear I will," she cried, trying to get up, feeling their boots pounding into her back as they jumped up and down, continuing to hit her. Medea was ready to explode. She felt the flow of dark magic through her body, and would use it to stop them, not caring what happened to them in the end. But before she could use the dark magic to do her bidding, something else took her attention.

She heard a low growl coming from the mouth of the cave. Instantly, the gnomes scattered, hiding behind rocks and in the shadows. When she finally managed to sit up, a large white wolf faced her, snarling, and showing its elongated teeth. Its eyes were orange and seemed to almost be glowing. This was the last thing she needed right now.

Medea was about to do away with the wolf, when she realized it was snapping at the gnomes, not her. It seemed to be keeping the gnomes away from her, oddly protecting her for some reason. The wolf made some sort of half-bark, half growling noise, its eyes blazing with a possessed look. She was about to hit it with a beam of her own magic when Alaina and Rapunzel ran into the cave.

"Nay, stop, Medea!" Alaina called out to her. "Do not hurt the wolf."

"Why not?" she asked. "It's going to eat me if I don't."

"Nay, it won't, I promise," said Alaina. "That wolf is my son, Zann."

That's when she remembered Rhys telling her that his brother was a shapeshifter and could turn into a wolf. She supposed this could be Zann Blackseed after all.

"Quick, Medea, get out of the cave." Rapunzel grabbed her and pulled her outside into the sunlight. Alaina followed with the wolf right behind her.

"We need to protect ourselves from those gnomes," Medea told the others.

"They won't come out into the direct sunlight,"

Alaina explained. "They prefer cloudy days, or to stay inside their caves."

"They're mean. Just like you said. They attacked me!"

"They did?" Alaina looked over to her in question, as if she didn't believe her. "Are you sure?"

"Of course, I am. I have a prick on my backside as well as bruises from their feet on my back to prove it."

"The gnomes only attack if they feel threatened," the fae explained. "They have children in those caves. You must have done something to them first, or they wouldn't have been so defensive."

"I did not! And I was the one having to defend myself, not them."

"Medea? Did you do something to rile them?" asked Rapunzel, narrowing her eyes and folding her arms over her chest.

"You think I purposely attacked the gnomes for no reason?" asked Medea.

"It wouldn't be the first time you did something like this," said Rapunzel. "Or have you forgotten all the trouble you gave me while growing up?"

"That's when I was naught but a child, Sister."

"Perhaps Medea was innocent, like she says," commented Alaina. "It is best not to bring up incidents from the far past that happened between siblings."

"Oh, it's not so far in the past as you think," said Rapunzel.

"Rap! Let it go." Medea's eyes flitted over to the fae. The less the woman knew about her and their siblings, the better. For some reason, Medea felt as if Alaina would take information about her and use it against her. She also decided she'd better confess before the damned fae read her mind and called her a liar. "All right, I did blast the gnomes with my power, but only because they pricked me with their spear first."

"Pricking another is their way of investigating you and saying hello," explained Alaina. "They weren't trying to hurt you, but rather trying to figure out just who you are, since they haven't seen you before."

"Now is a great time to mention that," she mumbled, brushing the dirt off her clothes.

"Well, that was just so much fun, I can't even stand it," came a male voice from the mouth of the cave.

The women looked over to see Zann getting up off the ground, having shifted from his wolf form back into his human form again. Medea gasped when she realized he was naked.

"Son, please," said Alaina, hiding her eyes. "Put on some clothes."

"Well, it's not like I can carry clothes while I'm in my wolf form, Mother," Zann told her with an edge to his voice. "I can't wear what I do not have." He picked a large leaf off a nearby plant and held it in front of his groin. Then he did a sidestep, hiding behind a boulder that was up past his waist, trying to seek cover. "Darium and Rhys sent me ahead to tell you they'd be here soon. Also, to protect you."

"Good thing they did," said Rapunzel. "It seems my sister has a knack for getting into trouble."

"It's not my fault," said Medea in her defense. "I was bored just waiting around for the men to show up. And curious, too. Besides, how was I to know that gnomes were so finicky?"

* * *

It was already starting to get dark before Darium and Rhys showed up.

"We're here," called out Rhys, getting off his horse, seeing Zann standing behind a rock. The women were all sitting around, but no one was talking. "I'm sorry it took so long, but the horses have a difficult time traveling over the steep mountains."

"Brother, I've got your clothes." Darium took clothes from a travel bag and brought them over to Zann.

"So, what's been happening?" asked Rhys, feeling the tension in the air. Each of the women stared out in a different direction rather than to look at each other. That told him something happened before he arrived.

"Oh, not much is going on," said Zann, pulling his tunic over his head. "Just little things like Medea being attacked by gnomes, and me saving her neck, that's all. I'm still waiting for a thank-you."

"What?" Rhys looked up with a jerk. Just the thought of Medea possibly being hurt bothered him for some reason. He supposed it shouldn't have, since just this morning he had been considering killing her. The thought of what he might have done bothered him even more, now that he laid eyes on her again. "Are you all right, Medea?" He hurried over to her, putting his hand on her shoulder.

"I'm fine," she said, looking up at him and smiling. "I know where the dragon is hiding, Rhys."

"Aye, in the caves. The elf already told us."

"Yes, but there are many caves, and I know the exact one. Shall we go capture it now?"

"Not yet," said Rhys, holding up his hand. "First, I think we need to go to the pyramids and find the crystal key."

"Can't we do that after we get the dragon?" asked Medea, sounding eager to prove to everyone that she was right.

"Nay. This way, you'll have a means to open the portal when we do find the dragon," Rhys explained. "You see, there is no telling how the dragon will react when we approach it. Medea, if you and your sister can manage to get atop it, then you'll already have the key, and also your means to get home quickly."

"I agree," said Alaina. "We should go after the crystal key first."

"Where are these pyramids?" asked Rapunzel.

"I'll show you. Follow me. They are right over that hill." Alaina started to walk and the rest followed. Rhys held the reins of his horse, catching up to Medea.

"I'm glad you weren't hurt, Medea," he told her, feeling like a traitor even though the girl had no idea of what he'd been ordered to do.

"I'm glad you're here, Rhys," she said, surprising him, since he didn't think she even liked him.

"Y-you are?" he asked.

"Aye," she said. "You're not as boring as everyone else around here."

"Uh, thank you. I think." Rhys looked at the girl in confusion. He wasn't quite sure what she meant. Darium told him Medea liked him. If she did, he wasn't sure he was seeing it. He decided it must be her odd way of complimenting him.

Medea stopped, letting the others go ahead of them. He waited with her, feeling as if she wanted to speak with him in private.

"Rhys, I think I like it here on Mura," she told him.

"Good," he said with a nod of his head, wondering why this even mattered since she'd be leaving soon.

"It's much more exciting and intriguing than back in England."

"Uh huh," he said, feeling as if she were leading up

to something. He wasn't sure where she was going with this conversation.

"I like to explore and discover new things."

"That's nice." What did she want him to say?

"Therefore, I've decided I'm going to stay right here in Mura and not go back to England at all."

"Wait. What?" That shocked him, as it was surely nothing he thought she'd say. It was also the last thing he wanted to hear right now. He planned on getting the women and the dragon out of Mura before the King sent his men to kill them. Having her hanging around was only going to be an invitation to getting herself killed.

"Does that make you happy?" she asked, sounding hopeful that it would.

He wasn't sure how to answer. "Medea, how can you decide such a thing so quickly? You don't even know anything about my land."

"That's right. And that is why I want to stay. To find out more."

"Nay, you can't do that. You need to go back through the portal as soon as possible." He started worrying. If she stayed, King Osric would demand that he killed her, and he just couldn't do it. The only way to ensure her safety was to make damned sure she went back through that portal and that she did it soon.

"Why do I have to return?" she asked. "I don't see a need. I'm perfectly happy here."

"You don't belong here, sweetheart. Your being here is by accident. We need to fix that."

She looked at him and smiled, her eyes twinkling with happiness. "Did you just call me *sweetheart*?"

Too late, Rhys realized his mistake. He never should have used the endearment, because she seemed to like it a little too much. She also focused on that and didn't seem to hear a word he said about her leaving here. "You have a home. Back in England, not here," he continued. "You have a family and people who will miss you if you don't return."

She looked up directly into his eyes and he watched her smile quickly fade. Sadness, as well as pain filled her big brown eyes. It made him curious as to why this was happening or what was making the girl look so sad. He wanted to ask about her and her life, and figure out exactly who she really was, but if he did, it might just lead her on. Rhys liked an independent woman like her. He also liked a woman who was powerful, and that was something that surely described her. He had never met anyone like Medea before. Even though she had a way of irritating him with her stubbornness, he was starting to enjoy being in her presence. Medea wasn't just a beautiful wench, she was also someone who seemed to know what she wanted, and someone who wouldn't let anyone stand in her way once she made a decision. If only he could feel as confident with his own choices right now.

"I don't belong back in England, either, believe me," she said in a soft voice. "I promise you, no one will ever miss me if I don't return."

"How can you say that? I'm sure it's not true."

"It is true."

"It can't be."

"It is, I tell you!" she said, with a stomp of her foot upon the ground. Her hands went to her hips. He seemed to be making her angry, and he hadn't meant to do that. "You don't know the first thing about me and my family, Rhys, so don't pretend that you do. You know absolutely nothing about me at all. Nothing, I say!"

"Medea?" He was almost afraid to speak since his

words were making her filled with emotion, and not in a good way. Her eyes seemed to turn from brown to black, unless it was his imagination. Something deep inside warned him to stay quiet. Unfortunately, another part of him needed to know what was upsetting her so much. For such a young woman, she seemed to hold the weight of the world upon her shoulders, and he wondered why. "What do you mean by that?"

"Never mind." She almost looked as if she were going to cry. She turned away from him, but he grabbed her arm and gently pulled her back toward him.

Medea looked up to him with tears in her eyes. He didn't want to see her so sad, plus he certainly didn't understand it. She seemed so innocent that his heart went out to her, and he found himself wanting to protect her. She'd made it sound as if her family didn't want her, but how could this possibly be true? A tear dripped down her cheek, so he reached up and softly brushed it away with his thumb.

All he wanted to do was to make her happy and keep her safe. Disgusted by his greed, he now wondered how he could have been tempted to carry out the King's plans. Guilt ate away at him, and he hoped she would never find out what he had almost agreed to do.

Rhys knew now that he could never purposely harm her. If he had carried out the King's commands just to get what he wanted, he'd be no better than the greedy, ruthless, black-hearted kings of Mura. Rhys could never be that way. Although he'd had a weak moment, he hadn't been thinking clearly at the time. It just wasn't worth the steep price he'd have to pay just to attain wealth and someday claim the throne of a king.

Darium was right, although Rhys hated to admit it. Rhys could never hurt a woman, and certainly not someone like Medea.

"I don't like seeing you so sad," he said, noticing a stray tear making a trail down her cheek. Gently, he reached out, cupping her chin in his palm, and using his thumb to brush away the tear. Her eyes closed and she leaned in to his touch. Slowly, he rubbed the back of his fingers over the swell of her soft cheek.

"Thank you for putting up with me and for being so kind," she said, her eyes flickering open. Once again, the color was brown, the black disappearing completely. "No one has ever treated me this way before."

He saw her gaze drop from his eyes to his mouth. His gaze dropped to her mouth as well. She wasn't leaving or pulling away, and neither did he want her to. Lost in his thoughts, he couldn't stop wondering how her lips would feel against his.

Boldly, he bent down and pressed his mouth against hers. She didn't fight him, nor did she pull away. Instead, her arms went around his neck and she deepened the kiss on her own. In the kiss he felt power, passion, and even a little pain. But at the same time, if he wasn't mistaken, he felt a sense of gratitude, mixed with a tinge of desperation. Nay, he didn't know Medea, she was right. But now, he wanted to find out everything about this mysterious lady before he sent her back through the portal and never saw her again.

Slowly their lips parted, and he found himself lost in the depths of her beautiful, mesmerizing eyes.

"Brother? Are you coming?" Darium walked back to find them still standing there. Rhys quickly pulled away from Medea, and stood up straight, clearing his throat. Why did he feel like a youth being caught doing something he wasn't supposed to?

"Aye, we were just... resting for a bit." Rhys cleared his throat again.

"I see," said Darium, raising a brow.

Medea smiled sweetly at Rhys, and then turned and ran to catch up with the rest of the group.

"Bad timing, Brother," Rhys grunted once she'd left.

Darium chuckled. "Glad I can repay the favor, after all the times you interrupted me."

"I'm going to hate to see her go, but it's imperative that she returns to England through that portal." Rhys watched Medea as he spoke. She seemed so full of life and energy as she talked with her sister. If he didn't know she was a witch, he'd swear she had qualities of the fae. As if she knew he was watching her, she shyly glanced over at him, smiling once again.

"So... does this mean you're no longer going to be in line to inherit the Kingdom of Kasculbough?" asked Darium, pulling Rhys' attention away from Medea.

Rhys looked at his brother, shaking his head. "I never said that."

"Then you're going to actually carry out the King's orders?"

"I never said that either," Rhys told him, not wanting to discuss this with his brothers any further.

"Well, which is it?" asked Darium. "You can't have it both ways. I saw you kissing the girl just now. So, are you going to save her and lose your royal inheritance because of it, or are you going to kill her and someday become king?"

Rhys looked up in the air in thought, biting at his bottom lip. "Neither, and a little of both," he answered.

"What?" Darium chuckled. "That makes no sense."

"It makes perfect sense, Brother. All I have to do is help Medea leave here with her sister and the dragon. Then I'll tell the King I did my best to carry out his orders, but unfortunately, they escaped."

"I see." Darium nodded. "So, you'll still inherit the

title of king and everything that goes with it someday, but won't have to kill the women to do it."

"I suppose, you could look at it that way."

"What if it doesn't work?"

"Why wouldn't it work?"

"If you're sure."

"Aye, I think so," said Rhys, rubbing the back of his neck. "Then again, Medea did just say she wants to stay in Mura, so that might create a little problem. If she does that, it would ruin everything."

"I'll say," answered Darium. "So what are you going to do?"

"I guess I'll just have to make sure she leaves, and does it fast, that's all. Yes, that's what I'll do." He started to walk away from Darium, but stopped in his tracks when he heard his brother mutter from behind.

"That might not be so easy to do, Brother."

Rhys turned back to Darium. "What do you mean by that?"

"Oh, nothing, I suppose." Darium shrugged his shoulders. "It's just that mayhap you should have thought about that plan before you decided to kiss her." He motioned with his head to Medea.

Rhys' eyes followed, to see Medea grab on to her sister's arm, giggling and whispering in her ear. She was so excited that she couldn't stand still. *Giddy* would be the right word for how she was acting. *Crap* would be the word for how he felt. He had no doubt she was telling Rapunzel about what just happened. He'd seen the dreamy look in her eyes when he'd kissed her. She had mentioned she didn't want to leave, and now all he did was give her more reason to stay.

"Damn it," he growled, wondering how he could have been so careless. For one brief moment he had let down his guard. One little kiss that was meant only to ease his own guilt, now brought him even more problems than he had before, because now he wasn't so sure he really wanted her to leave. "It looks like I'll be naught but a peasant by the time this is all over."

All his hard work, all his loyalty for fighting for the King, and his one wonderful chance for someday being the heir to the throne of Kasculbough, had all fallen by the wayside so quickly. The worst part was, his plan might have worked if he hadn't kissed her. But now, it was going to be next to impossible trying to convince her to leave, without telling her why he needed her to go.

Nine

Medea hummed a happy tune as she traveled with the others to the Pyramids of the Gods. Rhys had kissed her, and she liked it. It made her feel special and wanted. A feeling she wasn't used to. She'd been waiting her entire life for a kiss from a man, and now that she'd had it, she realized she didn't want it to stop.

"Rapunzel, I am starting to really like Rhys."

"It was just a kiss, Sister. It didn't really mean a thing. After all, you don't even know him."

"I know him enough to realize that he wouldn't do something he didn't believe in. He wanted to kiss me, I'm sure of it"

"How can you know?"

"Well, I was not the one who initiated it, to put it that way."

Rapunzel placed her hand on Medea's shoulder. "Please, don't get too caught up by it. After all, we will be leaving here soon."

"I'm not sure I want to go back anymore."

Rapunzel looked at her and blinked. "Are you talking about Tanglewood Castle or England in general? Because if it's just the castle you don't want to return to, you know you are always welcome to come live with Marco and me."

"Thanks, Rap, but I like it here in Mura and I'd like to explore it more. Plus, there are a lot of people who have magic so that makes me feel more comfortable."

"I hear magic is also outlawed, and that those using it will get executed," Rapunzel reminded her.

"I don't believe all the kings think that way."

"All you need is one to think that way, and your life might be over."

"I'm not worried about it. I can take care of myself. Nothing is going to happen."

"Something already did, Medea. You are infatuated with Rhys the same way you were with Marco, and Cinderella's husband, William. Just let it go. We don't belong here."

"I don't want to let it go. This is the first time I actually felt happy and that mayhap I belonged somewhere. Because of my mother, I never feel that way back home."

"I'm sorry about that, Medea, but you know we can't change the past. No one will ever forget the evil curses that Hecuba bestowed upon our family, and I'm sorry you were born into that," Rapunzel told her.

"Mayhap not. But here on Mura, I can start a new life. Mayhap possibly with Rhys."

"Oh, Medea, I'm sure you will someday find that same happiness back in England. But right now, we've got to focus on capturing the dragon and getting home where we belong. Everyone will be worried about us. Besides, you'll never see Rhys again once we leave, so do yourself a favor and don't go falling for him."

"Too late." Medea stopped in her tracks, turning to look back at Rhys. "Rap, I think I've just met the man I want to marry." Rhys was everything that Medea thought a man should be. He was handsome, big and strong, and also an honorable knight. He was gentle and caring with her, and she could tell he would risk his life to protect her if need be. He was also honest, always speaking directly to her about what he thought. She appreciated that and respected him for it as well.

"You are getting your hopes up and you're only going to be let down in the end. I'm sure Rhys already has a sweetheart here and that he doesn't want you," said Rapunzel. While Medea appreciated Rhys speaking bluntly to her, she couldn't say she felt the same way when her sister did it.

"Rhys does want me," she insisted, watching as his shoulder-length brown hair lifted a little in the breeze with every step he took. Holding on to the reins of his gigantic silver horse that looked to have white snowflakes on it, made Rhys even more enticing. He was the sexiest man she'd ever seen. "He kissed me, so that proves it."

Rapunzel kept trying to discourage her, but Medea didn't want to hear it. "A lot of men kiss girls, but that doesn't mean they want to marry them."

"Not Rhys. He's different, I can tell."

"Medea, stop it. Get these crazy ideas out of your head, because I plan on going home, and I am not going to leave you behind."

"I'm staying here in Mura, Rapunzel, I've already decided. I'm not going back with you through the portal."

This time Rapunzel stopped, looking at Medea and shaking her head. "You don't know what you're saying, Sister. Besides, you need to be around your family. You know that you can't control the darkness inside you." She looked over at Rhys and sighed. "Don't drag Rhys into this—he seems like a nice man."

"What is that supposed to mean?" asked Medea.

"You make it sound like no one should want me because I am nothing but bad news."

"I didn't say that."

"But it's what you meant, isn't it?"

"All I meant is that back home, you have seven half-siblings who understand what you've been through and care about you, even if you don't believe it. Here, you have no one who will understand or even care about the battle of light and dark magic that brews within you. At any minute, one side can overtake the other, and I know you can't help it. But if that darkness wins, you know as well as I that someone is going to wind up getting hurt, or even worse, killed."

"That's nonsense, Rap. You're just worrying because that is what you always do. If you'd just mind your own business, perhaps we wouldn't be having this conversation." Medea felt that darkness that Rapunzel spoke of growing stronger right now.

"Medea, you brought it up to begin with. Besides, I am not worrying, I am just looking out for you since you're my sister."

"Well, don't even think of trying to change my mind, because I won't let you." The emotions grew stronger and stronger inside of Medea. She knew when she felt this way it was the darkness rising to the surface. Usually, the feeling didn't last long, but it also didn't stop until it found a way to be released. That could mean hurting someone, doing something awful, or acting in a manner that she couldn't reverse.

Medea ran ahead of the rest, wanting to get away. She really didn't want to hurt anyone, but then again, neither did she want to be hurt. Could Rapunzel be right in saying she was better off back in England? She couldn't go back to that way of living. She wanted to start anew. She wanted Rhys.

Looking back at the others one last time, Medea swiped her hand through the air and transported away from them, rather than to let the darkness inside her be released, possibly hurting her friends or her sister. Mayhap Rapunzel was right in saying she didn't belong here. She thought Rhys felt something for her, but what if he didn't after all? Perhaps people on Mura were no different from back home. Mayhap her own desires were tricking her into believing that she could be happy here... or anywhere.

Either way, she needed to get away from everyone, because if she didn't, the anger taking over her emotions right now was going to make her want to kill someone.

* * *

As they approached the Pyramids of the Gods, Rhys realized that Medea was no longer with them. He tied the reins of his horse to a tree and walked over to speak with the girl's sister.

"Where is Medea?" he asked, looking around, but not seeing her anywhere. Nightfall had set in. The area was lit by occasional torches placed around the lake that held the three pyramids.

"I guess she left, for now," answered Rapunzel.

"Oh, you mean she needed to use a bush?"

"Nay. We had a little squabble and she transported off somewhere. Don't worry, I'm sure she'll return. Eventually."

"I see," said Rhys, getting the feeling that he knew what this was all about. "Would this by any chance have anything to do with the kiss?" he asked her.

When Rapunzel looked up at him but didn't answer, he could tell he was right.

"She's just being Medea," said Rapunzel. "She has

quite a temper sometimes and also a lot of crazy ideas running through her head."

"Did I do something to upset her? Because if so, I didn't mean to."

"Nay, not at all. You're fine, Rhys. Now, I can't wait to explore these pyramids. They sound so intriguing." She left Rhys standing there, wondering what was going on. His mother came up behind him.

"She's no good, Rhys. You'd better stay away from her."

"Huh?" He turned to face his mother. He could see the concern in her eyes. "Rapunzel seems harmless. Why would you say that?"

"Not her. Medea."

"What do you mean, Mother?"

"Rhys, being a fae and also an elemental, I can pick up things that others cannot."

"You mean, you've been reading minds again." Rhys shook his head. "That is so invasive, Mother. Everyone is entitled to some privacy, so please stop doing it."

"That is not what I am talking about, although I couldn't help reading the girl's mind about the way she feels about you. There is something about the girl that is dark and dangerous. Rhys, she cannot be trusted."

"You don't know what you're saying." Rhys didn't want to hear anything bad about Medea, and felt the need to protect her, even against nasty words. "Medea is a strong, beautiful, yet mysterious woman. At first, I had the wrong impression of her, but not anymore. She just comes across that way until you get to know her. Besides, sometimes, we don't even trust ourselves." He was still thinking about the deal he had almost taken concerning the King.

"Just be careful around her, Son. Don't get too close

to her. I feel that if you do, it could mean the death of you."

Rhys let out a sigh. "Mother, thank you for your concern, but I don't think my love life is any of your business."

"Love life? Please don't tell me you have feelings for the girl."

"Medea is a young, innocent girl who has some powers, that's all. I assure you, there is nothing dark about her."

"Nay, it's more than that," his mother insisted. "There's a darkness about her, Rhys, believe me. I can feel it when she is near."

"The only darkness about Medea is that she feels lonely and unloved. However, I have a feeling she might feel differently now that I kissed her."

"Nay! Please tell me you didn't." The look of horror on his mother's face was almost laughable.

"Mother, enough! I am a grown man and Medea is a woman, not a child. What happens between us is none of your concern. Now, tell me, how do we get this crystal key out of the pyramids?"

"That's what I want to know." Zann walked over with Darium at his side. "I've heard that no one has ever entered the Pyramids of the Gods to take something, and returned alive to tell about it. I, for one, am not willing to risk my life for two silly girls and a dragon."

"I'm not sure I want to go into the pyramids either," said Darium, looking over to inspect the three pyramids that were surrounded by water. "Being a Sin Eater, and with my past doings in the Land of the Dead, I don't think the gods of The Haven are going to welcome me into their abode with open arms."

"Nay, you're right. It's probably best that neither of

you try to retrieve the key," agreed their mother. "I'll do it, instead."

"Nay. I am going to be the only one to enter the pyramids," said Rhys. "Now, tell me—what does this crystal key look like, and which of the three pyramids is it in?"

"I don't know," admitted their mother.

"Then who does?" asked Rhys. "We need to know what it is we're looking for."

"Only the sage knows," said Alaina, getting a groan from Darium.

"The elf again?" asked Darium. "Why couldn't it be someone else? *Anyone* else?"

"Where is Elric?" asked Zann.

"He might have gone home. I'll go get him." Alaina raised her arms above her head and the wind started to swirl around her. It lifted her up into the sky, and she disappeared toward Glint, the elven village.

"Well, what do we do now?" asked Zann.

"We sit down and wait." Darium sat down on the grass, lying back and putting his arms behind his head.

"There's nothing else we can do, I suppose," said Zann, lying down on the ground next to him and doing the same. "A little nap right now sounds good to me."

Rhys didn't want to sleep or rest or even wait. He felt the need to find Medea and decided to go look for her himself. He made his way over to Rapunzel. "Do you have any idea where I might find Medea?" he asked. "I'd like to talk with her."

"With Medea, who really knows?" said Rapunzel, sounding disgusted. She sat down on a log, seeing a mouse nibbling around the ground next to her in the torchlight.

"Why do I get the feeling that everyone wants me to

stay away from her?" asked Rhys. "Is there something I should know?"

"Medea is... different," said Rapunzel.

"I know," said Rhys.

"You do?" Rapunzel's eye opened wide. The mouse came over and climbed up on the log next to Rapunzel.

"She's young, I understand that," said Rhys, nodding his head.

"She's younger than you think, Rhys."

"What does that mean?" He sat down on another stump nearby.

Rapunzel let out a sigh. She looked around her and then leaned in and spoke softly. "If Medea ever finds out I told you this, she'll kill me."

"Tell me what?" he asked.

"She is... born of both light and dark magic," explained Rapunzel. "Her mother was an evil witch, and her father, my father, is a good warlock."

"Are you saying Medea is bad?" The mouse started to squeak. Rapunzel tried to swish it away.

"I'm sure everyone has good and bad in them; it is just that sometimes it takes years of experience to control it at all." Rapunzel seemed to choose her words carefully.

"The girl has had twenty years to do it. How much more time does she need?" asked Rhys.

"You don't understand. She's been forced to grow up quickly. Very quickly," said Rapunzel, moving away from the mouse that was now down by her feet.

"I and my brothers had to grow up quickly, too, and without the guidance of a mother." Rhys said this to prove a point. He felt that everyone was overreacting concerning Medea.

"Believe me, my sister would have been better off without her mother around to guide her."

The mouse bit Rapunzel on the foot. She cried out and jumped up.

"Damned mouse," said Rhys. "I'll take care of it. We'll have it for supper." He stood up and drew his sword. The mouse squeaked and then started growing before his very eyes. He jumped back in shock, seeing it shift into Medea.

"Medea! You bit me," complained Rapunzel, rubbing her foot.

"Well, you deserved it, Sister. You spoke ill of my mother," Medea answered.

"Y-you shapeshifted," said Rhys, trying to wrap his head around what he just saw. "I didn't know you could do that."

"I couldn't before now. I accidentally learned how to do it, today," said Medea, looking quite proud of herself. "I must have inherited the skill from my late mother."

"Let's hope that's all you inherit," muttered Rapunzel, limping away to join Zann and Darium.

"Medea, I wanted to talk to you," said Rhys.

"Go ahead," she said, fixing her sleeve.

"I just realized, you shapeshifted and have clothes on. When Zann does it, he has to be naked."

"My powers are far more advanced than your brother's, I'm sure. As a matter of fact, I don't want to wear this gown anymore. I'm tired of it." She waved her arm and instantly was clothed in a different dress entirely. This one was green with brown ribbons lacing the bodice. "That's better." She let out a deep breath and smiled at him. "Now, what did you want to talk about?"

Rhys stared at Medea in disbelief not saying a thing. She was proving to be a very powerful witch indeed. He had never known anyone who could shapeshift into so many different creatures or be clothed in a different outfit just with the wave of her hand. This girl's power intrigued him, yet almost at the same time frightened him a little. He started wondering if he should listen to all the warnings he was getting from Rapunzel and his mother. Was Medea someone to fear? Was there really a darkness in her that she couldn't control? What was she able to do, and would she be angered and use her powers against him?

"Oh, for heaven's sake, I know what you want," she said, acting as if nothing was wrong.

"You do?" he asked, not sure what it was he even wanted to say anymore. So many thoughts were crowding his mind right now, and they all had to do with Medea.

"You want to kiss me again, just admit it."

"I do?" he asked, sounding like a dolt, but not being able to even formulate a sentence right now after what he just witnessed.

"Let me help you decide." She reached up and grabbed the front of his tunic, pulling him to her. Standing on her tiptoes, she plastered a big kiss on his mouth, making him forget about anything else, since it was so passionate and inviting.

"Mmmm," he moaned, liking the way it felt. His arms went around her waist and he pulled her closer, returning the kiss. She tasted sweet, like honeyed mead. And she smelled like a field of wildflowers on a breezy summer's day. His hands roamed lower. Without thinking, he cupped her bottom, giving it a squeeze.

"Stop that, you fool!" came the voice of the stupid little elf, accompanied by a slap to Rhys' wrist. "You're a bigger oaf than even your sin-eating brother, and I didn't think anyone could top that."

"You," said Rhys with a groan, releasing Medea and

stepping back. A swirl of air came down from the sky, and his mother appeared right behind the elf.

"We've got work to do, and you need to keep your mind on the game. Both of you," said Elric, sneering at Medea now.

"Elric." Rapunzel ran over, followed by Zann and Darium.

"Tell us what we need to know, elf," commanded Darium.

"What did you call me?" Elric's hands went to his waist and his eyes closed to slits.

"Darium, please don't goad him," begged his mother.

"Sorry, mage," said Darium.

"It's *sage*, Sin Eater," spat the little man.

"Are you still King Sethor's fool?" asked Rhys, only managing to upset the elf even more.

"Rhys," warned his mother.

"I meant *jester*. In my defense, he was the King's jester." Rhys held his palms up in the air.

"Well, not anymore, I'm not," said Elric. "And I had a purpose for being there."

"What purpose could anyone ever have for pretending to be Sethor's fool?" asked Zann. "I mean, jester," he corrected himself.

"My business is my concern," said Elric. "If I wanted any of you to know, I'd tell you. But since I don't, it's none of your damned business."

"Is a sage supposed to curse?" Zann asked Darium under his breath.

"Elric, can you tell us how to get the crystal key from the Pyramids of the Gods so we can open the portal and get home?" asked Rapunzel.

"Aye, and nay," he answered, playing his silly games as always.

"Look, Elric, these ladies need to get home, and we have to also collect a dragon," spat Rhys. "Now, tell us what we need to know."

"I'll tell you that the gods will expect an offering before anyone will be allowed inside the pyramids. And even if you do happen to find the right crystal key, there is no guarantee they'll allow you to take it, or even that you'll be able to use it."

"Can you explain?" asked Alaina.

"Sure, but it'll cost you," said the elf, holding out his palm, wanting some kind of payment.

"This is ridiculous," said Medea. "I've got enough magic that I'm sure I can get inside the pyramids, find the key, and return before this greedy elf is done playing his stupid games."

Rhys watched in awe as Medea raised her hands above her head and disappeared. "Where did she go?"

"I'm not sure, but my guess is that she's in the pyramids," said Rapunzel.

"She should have listened to me," said the elf, picking at a hangnail. "She's only going to anger the gods and that is not going to be a pretty sight, I promise you."

"I'd better go after my sister," said Rapunzel. "I can transport there as well."

"I'll go with you," offered Alaina.

"Stop!" said Rhys, holding up a halting hand. "No one is going anywhere. No one, that is, except me. I am going after her, and I don't want any of you to follow. I am the knight, and I am going to protect you all. I will handle this myself, since I have the most experience with battles."

"And you all call me the fool?" asked the elf. "I'm out of here. Good luck, oafs." In a blur, the elf disappeared.

"Rhys, don't go in there," said Darium. "None of us knows what to expect."

"He's right," agreed Zann. "It could be dangerous."

"I'm not letting Medea do this by herself," Rhys told his brothers. "She might need my protection."

"The girl has magic! Why would she need you?" Zann started to pace back and forth.

"I don't know," said Rhys, heading toward the pyramids. "But something tells me she's about to get into trouble. I swear, I'm not going to let her do this alone."

Ten

Medea transported over to the edge of the water, looking out at all three pyramids situated in the center of a small lake. Entirely surrounded by water, they were not very approachable at all. Lily pads and pink flowers floated on the surface. Each pyramid, or temple, had a long, wooden hanging bridge leading from the shore to a doorway in the middle of the structure. At each doorway were tall burning torches. Lit torches around the entire lake lit up the pyramids and parts of the water as well.

The first pyramid on the left had yellow fire burning from a torch by its entrance. The next had green flames on the torches, and the last had red. On the shore in front of each pyramid and at the end of the foot bridge, was a stone statue depicting one of the three gods worshipped here. Burning torches surrounded the statues as well. She figured that the god carved in stone was the certain one worshipped for the temple behind it.

It all seemed so mysterious and magical.

"This is interesting, but it doesn't look like anything to fear," she scoffed, not seeing anything dangerous at all about it. "Now, which of the pyramids holds the crystal key?" She put her hand to her chin in thought, trying to decide which one it might be.

Finally, she chose the middle pyramid. There was no real reason, other than it had green fire in the torches and she liked the color green. As she approached the bridge, she saw a statue of a man carved out of stone. She wondered just who he was supposed to be, since she was not familiar with Mura's gods. He looked old, and wore long robes with a hood. The statue also had a very long beard. Its face seemed to have wrinkles. There was some writing at the base by the statue's feet, but she couldn't read it because it was in a language that she had never seen before.

Just as she was about to start over the bridge, Rhys ran up and stopped her.

"Nay, Medea, wait."

"I think the crystal key is in this one," she told him, pointing to the pyramid in the water at the end of the bridge. "I'm going to go inside and take a look around. If not, I'll try one of the other pyramids. I'll keep looking until I find it."

"Look, Medea, this is the temple of Zoroct, the god of power." Rhys pointed at the stone statue of the old man and the writing by its feet.

"It says that?" she asked, looking down at the symbols or possibly letters carved into the stone. She wasn't really sure what it was.

"It is written in Murian, Medea. I know you are not versed in our written language—that is why I'm telling you. The other two temples are for Hapsren, the goddess of the home, and Cnoir, the goddess of love."

"Murian? But you speak like I do. I don't understand why this is different."

"Yes, we speak the same, but this is the way our written language looks."

"Oh. Interesting," she said, perusing one of the goddess statues and then the other. "Power, home, and love. These are all things I like. Hmmm. Mayhap I should try the temple of love first. Nay, I think I'll stick with power. I'm sure that is where I'll find the crystal key."

"But Medea, this is the temple of Zoroct, the most powerful of the gods."

"I know that. You already told me." She was becoming impatient, and just wanted to go inside and look around.

"You can't go in there."

"Why not?" she asked. "I'm powerful, too. I don't see a problem with it."

"True, you have powers, Medea, but this is different. Besides, you heard what the elf said. You are going to have to make an offering or sacrifice of some kind to the god in order to be granted entry."

"That's silly. No one can keep me from going inside. I'll just pop in, get the crystal, and pop back out again. It'll be easy." She waved her arms and disappeared, leaving Rhys standing there, feeling as if something horrible was about to happen.

"Zoroct's eyes, don't tell me she transported inside, Brother." Darium ran up, followed by Zann. The women were right behind them.

"She did," said Rhys, feeling as if Medea was doomed. "I tried to stop her, but she just wouldn't listen."

"The girl can't go in without first giving an offering," explained Alaina. "If she doesn't, the gods will just take something from her in return."

"Stay here. I'm going after her," said Rhys, starting across the bridge. He got to the door, and heard a sound from above. He looked up to see what looked like an old wizard. He was standing on a small balcony that pro-truded from the pyramid.

"I am the guardian of the temple of Zoroct," said the old man who looked more like a spirit than a physical being. "What offering will you give to the god of power? Tell me, and I will let you know if he grants you entry."

"I—I don't know what to offer. What does he want?" asked Rhys, hoping he did everything correctly. The last thing he needed was an angry god.

"Zoroct likes power," came the old man's crackly voice.

"Power," he said, pondering the word. "Well, I have super strength that I was born with, but I really can't give it up," he told the old man. "I need it. You see, I'm a knight. Is there something else I can offer instead?"

The old man looked over the balcony, stretching his neck. "I suppose Zoroct has all the strength he needs. What about that ring on your finger?"

"This?" Rhys held up his hand with a gold ring embedded with a ruby in the center. King Osric had given it to him last year when he had earned the title of head knight.

"Yep. That'll do. Throw it up to me," said the man, holding out his hands.

Rhys removed the ring. "Are you sure you're going to give this to Zoroct?" he asked suspiciously, having a feeling the guardian was going to keep it for himself.

"Don't you trust me?" When the man said that, Rhys figured this was all some sort of test. He didn't question it further. Instead, he tossed the ring up to the old man. The man caught it, shimmering brightly. "Wait here," he said, and then dissipated into a cloud of smoke.

Rhys waited as instructed, but after several minutes

with nothing happening, he wondered if he'd been made a fool of by some trickster or thief. He was about to enter the pyramid anyway, but after one step, he stopped in midmotion.

"You may come into my pyramid to worship," boomed the mighty voice of Zoroct from the clouds, as he gave Rhys permission to enter. The bridge shook beneath his feet as the god spoke from The Haven. Rhys let out a breath of relief, thinking that he was about to be struck down dead instead.

"Thank you, mighty and powerful god, Zoroct," he answered, looking up to the dark sky, not seeing a thing. Still, he thought he needed to be grateful and polite.

"However," the booming voice continued. "The witch will pay for not bringing me an offering."

"That girl is not from here, my god, Zoroct," said Rhys, still looking up at the sky, feeling a little foolish speaking to the air. "She doesn't understand. Please, can you forgive her?"

"She's a stranger to Mura and yet she sneaks into my temple? That is one of the worst offenses ever." The bridge shook again and this time Zoroct's voice was filled with anger.

"Uh oh," mumbled Rhys. Once again, Rhys said the wrong thing and now he was sure there was going to be trouble. Medea was in great danger.

"She's stealing the crystal key!" The god's voice boomed, shaking the land. A bright light lit up in the dark sky.

"Please, listen," said Rhys. "Medea came through a portal by accident from another land. She needs to get back there with her sister and the dragon. We were told by the elven sage that we needed the crystal key in order to do that." Rhys knelt down on one knee, not able to look up at the sky now, since it was shining so brightly.

"The elven sage?" asked the god.

"Aye, that's the one," Rhys confirmed the information.

"Hmph! Elric is not to be trusted," warned Zoroct. "Neither is the witch. And like I said, the girl will pay for what she's done."

"Nay, please," begged Rhys, hoping to change the god's mind. He lifted his hand in front of his face to keep from being blinded. "If we don't have the crystal key, then how are we going to open the portal to send them home?"

"I will grant you the key, but only because I don't like strangers in Mura, and I want them gone," boomed Zoroct's voice once again. Rhys still didn't see the god at all, just the bright light. "When the crystal glows, you will have the power to open the portal. However, it will only open one portal – the one that leads to the witch's land. No others."

Rhys wasn't aware of any other portals at this time. He wanted to ask Zoroct about it, but decided to wait. Right now, his first concern was to find and help Medea. "Thank you, god of power, oh mighty Zoroct," said Rhys, trying to sound humble.

"Heed my warning, Rhys Blackseed. The girl who takes what she wants without asking is only trouble. There is a horrible darkness inside her that she cannot control. She has set things in motion, and soon she will pay for her greedy mistake. She will pay dearly, and will wish she hadn't tried to deceive the gods."

Thunder boomed, shaking the hills. Winds whipped around Darium, and lightning flashed in the sky. Then, the radiant light above him disappeared, and all was silent once again.

"She will pay dearly?" he repeated, realizing that Medea was about to be punished by the gods. The thought horrified him. "Nay. Medea," cried Rhys, rushing into the pyramid, knowing that he had to help her somehow.

"Medea?" he called out, walking forward where oil burned in a trough, and a dozen more burning torches lit up the inside of the pyramid. Another large stone statue of Zoroct sat atop a dais with five stairs leading up to it. Rhys half expected to find the girl lying dead in a puddle of blood. Instead, Medea was standing atop the dais, looking around at items that had been placed at the statue's feet. "Medea. Come here," he called out, his voice echoing off the stone walls. He looked up to the apex of the pyramid, swearing he saw eyes staring down at him. This place was chilling. He needed to get Medea out of here as fast as he could.

"Rhys? Isn't this the ring I saw you wearing earlier?" She bent down and picked up his ring, holding it up for him to see. Somehow, the ring he'd given the guardian was now in here.

"Leave it there. Put it back," he warned her, approaching the dais with his hand on the hilt of his sword as he continuously scanned the area for trouble. "It was my offering to get inside."

"Bah! That's ridiculous." She inspected the ring, admiring it, blowing on the gemstone and shining it against her sleeve. "There was no need to give up something of such great value. After all, I entered without any silly offering. What does it matter?" She slipped his ring on to her finger.

"Put it back, Medea. Leave the ring here, and come with me. We need to go at once," he said, holding out his arm and constantly scanning the area back and forth, not sure what was about to happen. "We need to get out of here, right now."

"You really want me to leave the ring behind?"

"Yes, I do."

"Hmmm," she said, spinning the ring on her finger and kneeling down. "Just let me look at some more of these items that were left as offerings before we go."

When she did nothing to join him, Rhys knew he would have to remove her by force. He rushed up the stairs and grabbed her hand, dragging her back down the stairs behind him.

"Wait, Rhys. Stop that! What's your hurry?" she asked. "I haven't located the crystal key yet. It might not even be here. Mayhap we should check another pyramid."

"Nay. No more pyramids." That's the last thing Rhys wanted to do. If Medea transported into all three pyramids without giving an offering, she was sure to wind up dead. Mayhap even in The Dark Abyss for all eternity. He didn't know what would happen to her, but neither did he want to hang around to find out.

"We're going," he commanded, taking a step and accidentally kicking something with his foot. It made a noise and went sliding across the floor. He looked down to see a crystal shard made into a pendant, attached to a necklace of chain. "The crystal key," he said, sure it had been placed here for him to find by Zoroct.

"Oooo, it's pretty," said Medea, reaching out for it, but he got to it first.

"I'll hold on to this," he told her, snatching it up and slipping the chain over his head. The crystal rested against his chest, feeling warmer than he thought it would. When he looked down at it, he saw it glowing.

"Why is it glowing?" she asked, reaching out to touch it. When she did, it made a zapping sound, and she pulled her hand back, rubbing it. "That hurt!"

"Medea, we're leaving. Now." Rhys pulled her out the door and on to the wooden bridge. Before they could even cross it, everything around them started shaking. He heard a noise from the lake, and turned to look. Something large started to emerge from the dark water.

"Oh, look," said Medea. "It is one of those sea serpents I saw in the water over by the gnome caves."

"It most certainly is, and it is coming right for us. Run!" shouted Rhys.

Holding on to her hand, he ran over the bridge, dragging her along with him. The serpent shot through the water, rising up, getting ready to strike. Rhys released her hand and yanked his sword from his side, ready to fight. Medea stumbled and fell to her knees, not moving.

"Medea, what are you doing? Get up!" he shouted, but she didn't obey.

"I c-can't," she said. "I can't m-move."

"Then transport out of here if you have to, just do it now before we're both eaten by that creature." He held his sword up, trying to think of the best place to stab the water creature. He wasn't even sure he could kill it, since he'd never been confronted by one before and didn't quite know what to do.

The sea serpent rose higher out of the lake, almost seeming to grow in size. It was pink in color and had two curved horns atop its head. It looked even slimier than the arcines—the snakelike reptiles of Mura. When the serpent of the sea hissed and its forked tongue shot out of its mouth, its tongue was so long that it almost hit the bridge. Rhys had never seen one of these before in his life, although he had heard of the creatures. He thought they were nothing but a myth, but now he realized myths all came from something, and this sea serpent was real. He found himself wondering just what this creature ate, truly hoping it wasn't people.

Medea screamed and waved her arms frantically in circles, trying to use her magic, but nothing happened. To Rhys' horror, she did not transport out of there to safety. Instead, she was left there helpless, and about to become the sea serpent's dinner. He couldn't let that happen.

"It doesn't work. My powers are gone," she yelled. "I have no magic. Help me, Rhys."

The sea serpent rose up right above them now, being as tall as the pyramid.

"Damn it, I wasn't planning on fighting off a sea serpent today as well as a dragon." Rhys shook his head, not believing how this day just kept getting worse. "Oh well, I suppose it'll be good practice for when we see the dragon," he mumbled. With a war-like shout, he shot forward, using his power of immense strength to grab the serpent around the neck, holding on tightly.

The sea serpent hissed and pulled back its head, dragging Rhys up into the air with it. Flipping its head one way and then the other, the creature tried to free itself of Rhys' hold. Rhys' legs flapped around in the air, but he didn't let go.

"Rhys!" he heard Medea scream from her position on the bridge.

If he could manage to stab it with his sword, he might just be able to kill it. Then again, if it was a creature of magic, that might not work. Part of him feared killing off the being, since it belonged to the gods. The last thing he wanted to do was anger them, but he had to protect Medea. If this sea serpent ate her, he would never forgive himself for not being able to stop it.

When the serpent's head lowered back to the bridge, Rhys got his footing, lying atop the beast and holding it down with all his strength. "I've got it, Medea," he shouted. "Get yourself to safety. Run. Go, quickly before it gets loose."

Rhys' brothers both ran down the bridge to join him with their swords drawn, ready to help Rhys fight off the sea monster.

"We're here to help you, Brother," shouted Zann, swiping at the air, but not hitting the serpent. Steam flared from the sea serpent's nostrils and it squirmed under Rhys' hold. Its hissing turned to growls now, and Rhys realized it was getting angrier. He wasn't sure how long he could hold it there.

"Damn it, Zann, you're a bad aim. Let me do it." Darium tried the same thing, but it seemed as if their swords went right through the beast and didn't harm it at all.

"We can't kill it. It's sent by the gods," shouted Rhys. "Get Medea out of here."

Both of his brothers tried to help her, but she seemed to be stuck to the bridge.

"Something's wrong, Rhys. We can't move her," Zann told him.

"She's being punished. It's because she didn't give an offering," said Rhys, realizing now why this was happening. The sea serpent moved its head and a long, forked tongue shot out of its mouth, almost touching Rhys' face. He jerked backward, just managing to get out of the way and at the same time not lose his hold on the monster.

The crystal pendant Rhys wore on a chain around his neck glowed again. When he looked back over at Medea, her eyes were opened wide in fear. The poor girl looked so scared and also so helpless that his heart went out to her. That's when he noticed something. She still had the ring on her finger—his ring, the one she stole from the temple. She hadn't put it back like he'd told her to do after all. "Damn it, Medea, don't you ever listen?" he spat.

"What now, Brother?" yelled Zann.

"Darium. Zann," he called out. "Take the ring off her finger. Hurry."

"What? Why?" asked Darium, looking down at her hand.

"It was my offering to Zoroct and she stole it," Rhys explained, jostling the sea serpent, managing to pick it up, holding it over his head. He had once chance to rid them of it before the monster tried to bite him again. Using all his strength, he hurled it as far as he could, throwing it back into the lake. It hissed and screeched as it splashed down, creating such a wave that all four of them nearly got washed over the edge of the bridge.

"The ring is stuck on her finger," yelled Darium, struggling, trying to remove the jewelry.

"It won't come off," shouted Zann. Both of his brothers tried to pull the ring off, but it wouldn't budge for either of them.

"Damn it, do I have to do everything myself?" grumbled Rhys, hurrying over to them, taking hold of Medea's hand.

"Rhys, I'm scared," she cried, tears streaming down her cheeks. "Why can't I move or use my powers? What's happening to me?"

"You should have listened to me, Medea. Now, you are being punished by the gods." He slipped the ring off of her finger easily, scowling at his brothers.

"It wouldn't budge," said Darium.

"We swear it," said Zann, shrugging.

"Rhys, behind you!" shouted Medea.

Rhys turned to see the large mouth of the serpent with all its sharp teeth, lowering over all of them now. He jumped out of the way, swinging his sword at it, but the sea serpent managed to bite him on the shoulder. His abrupt action caused him to knock into his brothers who stumbled and fell into the water.

"Sorry about that," Rhys called out, once again grabbing the monster's neck, making sure to keep his head as far from it as possible. "Medea, can you move now?" he asked, wondering if removing the ring from her finger helped anything.

"Aye," she said, getting to her feet.

"Good. Now run to shore and don't stop until you get there. I'm not sure how much longer I can hold back this damned thing."

"I'm going!" Medea ran over the bridge and didn't look back. Rhys saw both his brothers swimming for the shore. When he was sure they were all a safe distance away, he lifted the sea serpent over his head and tossed it once more into the lake. This time, it grew in size, and came after him with twice the vengeance. Its eyes glowed orange and fire shot out of its nostrils.

"Uh oh. This can't be good," he muttered to himself. "What does it want?" Then a thought hit him that he hoped was the answer. He still clutched the ring in his hand that he had removed from Medea's finger. Mayhap they didn't like the fact that Medea had taken back his offering to the gods. Mayhap he was supposed to return it. He wasn't sure of anything anymore, but figured it was worth a try. He threw it hard up into the air. The sea serpent shot up high, opened its mouth, and caught the ring. Then it settled back into the lake, disappearing under the water. The chaos was over, the waters were calm, and everything was silent once again.

"Amazing," he said, shaking his head, surprised but thankful that it worked. Rhys turned and headed over the bridge, being met by Medea running to him, throwing herself into his arms. She wept bitterly, her tears dampening the front of his tunic. He truly felt sorry for her. While she seemed fearless and reckless when she had her powers, without them she was vulnerable and scared. Rhys scooped her up into his arms and carried her the rest of the way to the shore.

Darium and Zann were both wringing out the water from their clothes and hair when he got there. Rapunzel and his mother rushed over to meet him.

"Rhys, what happened out there?" asked his mother.

"Is everyone all right?" asked Rapunzel in concern.

"We had a little setback, but it's all taken care of now." Rhys' arm hurt like a demon. He put Medea on her feet, his hand going to his bloody shoulder.

"Rhys, you're injured!" gasped Rapunzel.

"He was bitten by the sea serpent," said Medea. "He's bleeding."

"Calm down, everyone." Rhys put his palm over his bloody wound, using his healing powers to close the gap and stop the flow of blood. "I'm just glad it was only me and not any of you who were hurt." He inspected the wound. It was already healed.

"Did you find the crystal key to open the portal?" asked Rapunzel.

"Yes. I've got it." Rhys nodded to the crystal pendant hanging from the chain around his neck.

"Oh, can I hold it?" asked Medea, reaching out for it.

"Nay." Rhys' hand covered her wrist. The god's warning about Medea echoed in his head. "I'll hold on to it for now. Zoroct doesn't seem to like strangers. He told me I will be able to use this to open the portal whenever I see the stone glowing."

"Well, at least we have a way to get home now," said Rapunzel, hugging Medea. "Sister, I'm so happy that you weren't hurt. I was terrified that something was going to happen to you."

"You were?" Medea looked up at Rapunzel, sounding stunned that her sister should even care.

"The both of us are fine as well. Thanks for asking, everyone," Zann called out motioning to himself and Darium, trying to dry off his sword on his wet breeches.

"Sorry about that, guys," said Rhys with a grin. "But think of it this way. At least now you two won't need to bathe for a while."

"It is getting cooler now that the sun has set, and you boys need some dry clothes," Alaina told her sons. "Gather your horses. We'll spend the night in the Whispering Dale."

"The Whispering Dale?" Darium looked up. "I thought only the fae were allowed to stay there."

Alaina calmly answered. "Boys, you're forgetting that you all have fae blood in you, even if you don't possess the powers of a fae or an elemental."

"Hey, that's not true about me anymore," Darium reminded her.

"Well, I'm not going to complain, because I don't want to have to go hunt down a dragon tonight," said Zann. "I'm tired and just want to sleep."

"We're also hungry," added Rhys. "Warding off sea serpents really works up a hunger."

"Damn," spat Zann. "I just remembered something. I don't suppose any of the faeries eat meat, do they?"

"Sorry, Zann," said their mother with a smile, causing Zann to groan because of his love of meat.

"What about us?" asked Rapunzel. "Will Medea and I be welcomed in the Whispering Dale too? We're not fae or elementals, but witches. I'm not sure if they'll accept us."

"You are witches and have magical powers," said

Alaina. "You will be welcomed as guests, although you won't be allowed to stay for more than a night or two at the most."

"Let's go," said Darium. "Zann and I will get the horses."

"The Whispering Dale is just up ahead. We can go on foot. It's not far," said Alaina.

"Rhys?" Medea held on to his arm.

Rhys looked down to see such a frightened look in Medea's eyes that all he wanted to do was comfort her. "What is it?" he asked, slipping his arm around her shoulders and pulling her closer.

"I'm sorry for causing so much trouble. I didn't mean to."

Everyone saw darkness in Medea, but Rhys didn't see it that way. What he saw was a form of innocence within her that was being controlled by a darker side. Medea seemed curious and wanted to learn about everything and anything, and he liked that. Her mind was like the palette of a painter, just waiting for the first brush stroke.

She didn't seem to like to stay put in one place long, and got bored easily. He could understand that, since at times he was the same way. She liked to stay active and so did he. Medea seemed to have a strong curiosity and a sharp mind. Learning new things and seeing new places is what seemed to make her tick.

Rhys was sure Medea didn't do the wrong things with a premeditated evil intent. Nay, it wasn't that way at all. The way he saw it, it was more like a struggle within her that she was still trying to control. Didn't everyone have that? She was not different than anyone else in his opinion.

"I know you didn't mean to cause trouble," he told her. "Mura is a new land to you, and you just need to learn how things work here. Don't worry about it. Everything turned out all right in the end and that is all that matters."

"You're not angry with me, then?" she asked, as they walked, his arm around her shoulders and hers around his waist.

"Nay. I'm just glad that you weren't hurt, Medea."

"I felt so helpless when my powers didn't work. I have never felt that way before. I'm not sure I liked it. It really frightened me, and being scared is a feeling that I have never really experienced until now," she admitted.

He stopped in his tracks. "Do your powers work now?" he asked, wondering if this had something to do with Zoroct's warning that Medea would be punished.

"I don't know. Let me try them and see." She held out her hand and materialized a peach. "Yes, that seemed to work. Let me try something else." She looked over at him, next. With a nod of her head, she repaired his clothes that had been torn by the sea serpent, and dried both of their clothes as well. "Hmmm. I think I'm fine. My powers are working again." She patted herself to check things out, the scared look leaving her and a sense of relief replacing it instead.

"Good," said Rhys, still feeling uncomfortable about what happened. "Medea, I can't be sure, but I believe you were being punished by Zoroct for taking back my ring that I used as an offering."

"These gods seem petty to me," she said, with a shake of her head. "I'm just glad it's over."

"I'm not sure it is."

"What do you mean?"

Rhys didn't want to be the bearer of bad news, but Medea needed to be aware of the consequences of her actions and what might still transpire. "We were told that an offering had to be given to the gods before we entered the pyramids."

"And you did," she said.

"Aye, but you didn't."

"Oh. Do you think that's going to be a problem?" she asked.

"I can only hope not, but I have a feeling that the gods won't let it go. Don't be surprised if this isn't over yet, Medea."

"Well, I've got my powers back and I'm not going to worry about it. By the way, thank you for saving me from the wrath of the gods today." She reached up and kissed him on the mouth. "Later, I plan on thanking you even more." She winked, making him realize exactly how she intended to show her gratitude. Not that he minded it in the least, but he still had a nagging feeling deep in his gut that Medea was not yet done being punished by the gods, and that whatever they had in store for her was going to be even worse than what she'd been through today.

Eleven

Medea sat next to Rhys later that day, eating a meal with the fae folk. She was so taken with the Whispering Dale and these friendly faeries that she felt as if she never wanted to leave.

Everything was so cheery here. Little cottages, some made of stone and others made of wattle and daub, were cozied up next to each other. Each had a bright roof of a different color. There were several stone arched bridges going over the river, and colorful flowers bloomed everywhere one looked.

The sweet scent of what they called lippenbur lilies intoxicated her senses. Something about the scent made her happy and brought her to life. The fae folk had been kind enough to even let her wear a lippenbur lily in her hair. It made her feel pretty and special. She had never felt this way before. She'd always wanted to be pretty like here sisters Rapunzel and Cinderella, with their golden locks and perfect figures. Instead, she had black hair that always made her think of soot on a hearth. She also never felt quaint and feminine, like her sisters. That is, not until now.

There was a strong sense of family here in the Dale. That was something that Medea never really had before.

Being the bastard child of a wicked witch didn't make her half-siblings particularly friendly toward her. And since it was her mother who cursed her half-siblings, killed their mother, and deceived Medea's father more than once, it made her sort of an enemy by association with Hecuba.

"Tomorrow, at first light, we'll head back to the Quamm Caves to find the dragon," Rhys announced, taking a bowl of fruit from one of the faeries they'd met, balancing it on his lap. They all sat on the ground around one of the many campfires that lit up the Dale.

"Yes, that will be good," agreed Rapunzel. "We're getting closer to finding and opening the portal to go home. All we need now is Marco's dragon."

"The sooner this is over with, the faster I can get back to Talia and my honeymoon," complained Darium.

"And I can get back to my family as well," said Rapunzel.

"Boys, your help is truly appreciated." Rhys' mother made a point to thank them all. Rhys figured she was trying to get Zann to accept her.

"Do we really need to leave so soon?" asked Medea. "I am not in a hurry. I like it here."

"You're forgetting, Sister, that I have a husband and baby back home, and I miss them." Rapunzel got up and started taking the empty dishes from everyone.

"A baby?" asked Alaina with interest.

"Yes, his name is Zane," Rapunzel told her. "He looks a lot like my husband, Marco."

"How nice."

Medea took a spoonful of fruit that Rhys offered her. It was pretty, in colors of royal purple and vibrant green. "Mmmm, that is really good. What is it?" she asked.

"I'm not sure what all is in it," said Rhys. "I just eat it and don't ask questions."

"The purple are pazzleberries, and the green ones are limsta fruit," Alaina told Medea. "It is one of the favorite treats of the fae. The fruit is grown right here in the Whispering Dale."

"I can see why it's their favorite," said Medea. "It is delicious. Between the food and the Whispering Dale with all the beautiful flowers, I think I want to be one of the fae folk, too."

That got giggles from all the fae there. Most of them were women, she realized.

"Where are all the male faeries?" asked Medea.

"You're looking at most of them," said Darium, swigging down some dandelion wine.

"You're talking about you and your brothers," Medea said with a nod.

"I'm not a faerie," said Zann. "Neither is Rhys. Just our big brother, Darium."

"That's not true, Zann," said their mother. "You all have the blood of the fae in your veins, even if you don't possess the magic that fae or elementals have."

"So, there aren't a lot of males then?" asked Medea, taking another mouthful of fruit that Rhys offered. Looking up into Rhys' eyes, she swallowed it down and licked the sweet aftertaste from her lips. She noticed his gaze dropping to her mouth. She was sure he wanted to kiss her again, and she wanted the same thing.

"The male fae line is weak," explained Alaina. "Since so much intermarriage with non-fae has been happening for such a long time, it has weakened our kind."

"Aye, but I'm going to change that," said Darium, sounding proud of it. "When Talia and I have children, they'll probably be boys since that is all the Blackseed family seems to have. Hopefully, they'll get more of her bloodline than mine."

"I don't understand about the Blackseed line," said Medea. "So, you all have… different powers?"

"The first son inherits being a Sin Eater, like Darium did," Rhys told her. "The second son born is always a shapeshifter—that's Zann. And the third one born has super strength. That's me."

"But you have the power to heal yourself, too," Medea reminded him. "Where did that come from?"

"Mother, did that come from the fae part of me?" asked Rhys. "I don't remember any other Blackseeds having the ability to do that."

"Yes, that is a fae quality. Partially, anyway. I think it is a combination of the two sides," said Alaina with a yawn. "If nobody minds, I am going to go to bed. The fae have been generous enough to give us two of their cottages during our stay here. One is for the girls and the other for the boys."

"Oh," said Medea, being disappointed to hear this. She had hoped to spend the night in Rhys' arms.

"Show us the way," said Zann, flirting with several of the faeries. They giggled in their normal fae way, and escorted the men as well as the women to the proper cottages.

"Are you coming, Medea?" asked Rapunzel, looking back to her.

"Go on, Sister. I'll be there soon."

"Rhys, we'll leave a spot on the floor for you," said Darium.

"Thanks," he answered, but did nothing to get up to follow them.

"Look at the moon and all the stars, Rhys." Medea leaned back, resting against his chest. His arms closed around her. "I wish the skies looked like this back home.

In England, it rains a lot, and the skies are never this clear. I've never seen so many bright stars in my life. Mura is such a magical, happy place. I have never experienced anything like it."

"Not all of Mura is that way," he told her, his low voice rumbling in his chest. "Remember, south of the Picajord Mountains is a whole different story. That is not a happy place at all."

"Still, you are lucky to be here on Mura."

"What is it like where you come from?" he asked, gently stroking her arm with his fingers. Everyone had left now, and they sat there alone at the fire.

"I don't know how to explain it," she answered. "Some things are the same as here, but nothing seems as alive and vibrant as it does on Mura. The flowers are more colorful and much bigger on Mura. The fruit is prettier and tastes more flavorful than that back home. Everyone here on Mura seems so friendly. It's not like that back home at all."

He chuckled.

"What is so funny?"

"How soon you forget about the three kings of Mura, or the gods and their sea serpents."

"Oh. I suppose you're right. Not everyone here is that friendly after all."

"I think people tend to only see what they want to see. So, sometimes it looks bad, but to others it looks very good."

"Do you really think so?" she asked, looking back at him.

"Aye, I do."

"It is such a beautiful night, that I'd like to go for a stroll. Will you come with me, Rhys?"

"Well, put it this way. I am not letting you go anywhere alone again. Especially not at night."

They both got up and walked hand in hand back to the bridge that crossed the bubbling brook.

"I hear frogs croaking," she told him, looking over the edge of the bridge.

"Well, we are standing over the water," he answered. "It is their home."

"Oh, Rhys, look at that." She pointed from atop the bridge at a moonlit field of tall flowers nearby. "It looks like a whole field of flowers lit up by the light of the moon. It seems so magical and inviting. I want to go there and explore it." Her intense curiosity drew her to it.

"That is a field of lippenbur lilies," he told her. "All right, we'll go," he said, walking too slowly for her. She broke away at the run, traipsing through the flowers that were up to her shoulders. "Medea, wait up."

"Hurry up, slowpoke," she said, spinning in circles with her arms out. "This scent is so strong and intoxicating that it is making me dizzy!" She fell to the ground, giggling.

"I think all that spinning made you dizzy. You're starting to sound like one of the fae now with all that giggling. Medea? I can't see you," said Rhys. "Where are you?"

She was lying on the ground in the shoulder-high field of flowers, staring up at the moon and stars. Playfully, she kept silent.

"Medea? I know you're here somewhere. Now, answer me." When he got closer, she reached up, surprising him, pulling him to the ground, laughing.

"Whoa!" he cried, landing next to her on his back. "That wasn't a good thing to do."

"Why not?" she asked, smiling, feeling happier than she ever had before. The scent of the flowers seemed to be doing something to her. Suddenly, she was becoming very randy.

"I could have smashed you with my weight, sweetheart. And stop all that giggling. You really do sound like a fae."

"I can't help it. I think it is the strong, sweet scent of all the flowers that is making me heady." She crawled atop him, kissing him passionately. "It's making me do things I don't usually do."

"I see," he said, not even trying to stop her. "I think I kind of like just lying here. Mayhap I'll sleep here all night."

"Nay you won't." She sat up and started pulling off her clothes, being able to think of nothing else but making love with Rhys.

"Medea? What are you doing?"

"We're going to do a little more than just sleeping tonight." She kissed him again. He reached out and finished undressing her. She didn't mind in the least. Medea hurriedly helped him to remove his clothing next, gasping when she looked down to see the moonlight bathing his nakedness. "You are beautiful!" she exclaimed.

"That's funny," he said, running his fingers slowly up her bare legs. "I was going to say the same thing about you."

"Rhys, I want to make love to you," she blurted out. "I've never done it before, but I think it's time I learn how."

"Oh. All right."

"So, you don't object?"

"Medea, where I come from, making love isn't something that is... shall I say, planned?"

"It's not? Then how do you know when it's going to happen?"

"You don't. That's the fun of it. You just enjoy being with someone special, and let things happen. Sometimes, it ends up in two people coupling."

"Oh, I see." She almost felt as if he was saying he didn't want her, and this upset her.

"On the other hand," he continued, pulling her down on top of him. "I like your way of being blunt about it, too. It sort of excites me." He kissed her passionately, his tongue entering her mouth, surprising her since she hadn't expected it.

"Oh!" She pulled away and put a hand to her mouth.

"Don't you like that way of kissing?" he asked her.

"I don't know. I've never done it before. However, I must admit it was nice."

"I can see you need to be guided in the art of making love. I hope I'm not moving too fast."

"It is not fast enough for me. Will you guide me, Rhys? I want to learn. I want you to be the one to do it."

"Well, since you put it that way, I can't refuse."

Rhys almost laughed aloud. Medea was eager to learn, and he was just as eager to teach her. He wanted to make love to her just as much as she seemed to want to do it with him. Something about being here in the Whispering Dale made all his worries fade. It was odd, but also a nice change of things. All he could seem to focus on was the passion inside him that he felt for Medea. He enjoyed being intimate with her, and she seemed to enjoy it, too.

"The first thing you need to do is to relax," he instructed. "Lie down next to me. The flowers are soft."

"Okay." She did as he told her.

"Now what?" she asked, looking up with wide eyes and blinking a few times in succession.

"You have beautiful eyes, Medea."

"I do? No one has ever said that to me before."

He reached down and gently kissed her closed lids. "Well, it is about time someone does."

She giggled. "That tickles."

"I also like your nose and your cheeks." He kissed the tip of her nose and then kissed her on the cheek.

"What about my mouth?" she asked anxiously, relaxing and seeming to enjoy this game.

"This mouth?" he asked, kissing her lips. When the kiss broke, he took her bottom lip gently in his teeth and then released it.

"I'm surprised such a big man like you can be so gentle. I didn't expect it," she admitted, reaching down and wrapping her hand around his erection, giving it a squeeze. "Oooo, it's so hard."

"Ah... yeeeees," he said, taking her hand in his. "I didn't expect such an innocent girl like you to be so bold on the first time."

"I'm curious by nature and also a fast learner." Her smile was intoxicating. Almost as intoxicating as the strong, sweet scent of the lilies. All Rhys could think about, now that she touched him in this manner, was what it would feel like to be inside her.

He slowly ran his hand down to her breast, putting his mouth to her nipple and suckling her, using his lips and tongue to stimulate her. She squirmed beneath his touch.

"Something's happening," she said in a breathy whisper.

"That's the idea," he told her, repeating his action on the other side.

"Oooooo, I like that. It makes me tingle." Her back arched and she threw back her head. He didn't need to instruct her after all it seemed. She was progressing nicely on her own.

"If you like that, then how about this?" He gently ran his hand up her leg, cupping her womanly mound with his palm. Then he worked his own manly magic on her, using his fingers to tease her as he played with her womanly folds. She moistened quickly. This only made him more excited than he already was. Daringly, he entered her, using just the tip of his finger.

"More, Rhys. I want more." She grabbed his hand and pulled it toward her, until his entire finger was inside. "Ooooh, yeeeessss," she cooed, with her eyes closed and her head thrown back. He slid another finger into her, being guided by her own liquid passion. Sliding them in and out, he used his thumb at the same time to play with her sensitive nub.

"Rhys," she said, her breathing becoming labored. "I —I feel like something else is happening now."

"You are awakening sexually, Medea. You will climb to your peak and then find your release. Don't fight it, sweetheart. It will be a pleasurable experience, I assure you."

She started to move her hips on her own, meeting the thrusts of his hand in a unified rhythm. Aye, she was ready to accept him now, and he was more than ready to make love with her.

Climbing atop her, he made sure to hold himself up so he wouldn't smash her with his weight. "If this hurts at all, just tell me and I'll stop," he whispered, getting in position, feeling so excited that he was about to burst.

"You stop, and I'll kill you, Rhys."

"If that is supposed to excite me, I'm not sure how to take it."

"It's a matter of speaking, nothing more. You know I don't really mean it."

"Good to hear it," he said, realizing she had powers that were so much stronger than his own. Still, he didn't want to think of that now. Right now, all he wanted was to get lost between this beautiful woman's thighs. Rhys wanted to make her cry out with the pleasure that he knew he could give her.

Once he entered her, their bodies worked together. It started out slowly, but she kept moving her hips faster and faster beneath him, moaning with elation, about driving him out of his mind. In the moonlit field of sweet-smelling lilies, he forgot all his troubles as they joined together doing the dance of love.

"Rhys, oh my! This is so wonderful."

"I agree," he said, feeling some sort of exchange between them that was more than the usual love-making. It felt right. It felt good. It was almost as if both of their magic were intermingling, making the experience even more pleasurable than usual, with heightened senses of all kinds.

Wanting for the freedom to let loose, he rolled to his back, pulling her atop him. She didn't object, but rather took the lead. Not bad for a girl who didn't know what she was doing. Like she said, she was a very fast learner.

Medea reached her peak quickly, but just to make sure, he looked up to see her face in the moonlight. She rode him like a stallion. Her hands gripped at his chest hair, and her nails scratched his skin, but he didn't mind the pain. Somehow, it only excited him even more. With her head thrown back and her eyes closed, the moonlight spilled over her smooth skin and made her long, loose black hair seem to glow with a halo of indigo. Her perky breasts were pushed forward as she arched her back, the hard nubs of her nipples pointing up to the moon. She was a beautiful woman, more appealing to him than any faerie could ever be. Being together with her felt right. The connection between them was real.

When he was sure she was sated first, he released his pent-up emotions. Growling, he drove into her, spilling his seed within her warmth. Her eyes popped open. When he thought mayhap he'd frightened her, she smiled wickedly. Her hips moved even faster as she found her release once again.

Finally, she collapsed atop his chest. Rhys held her tightly, feeling the rapid beating of both their hearts as if they were one.

"Thank you, Rhys," she whispered. He felt her tears against his bare chest. Reaching up, he smoothed back her hair with his hand, kissing her gently atop her head.

"Medea, you don't have to thank me. This coupling was warranted by both of us."

"Nay, I do," she said, looking up at him with wet eyes. "I want to thank you, because no one has ever made me feel the way you did tonight."

"Well, this is the first time you've made love, so that is understandable."

"That's not what I mean, Rhys. I'm saying that this is the first time in my life that I haven't felt lonely. And this is the only time in my life that I have ever felt loved."

Twelve

"**G**et up, you big oaf!"

Rhys awoke to the sound of the damned irritating elf and the feeling of the little man's foot kicking him in the side. His eyelids drifted open to see a daytime sky above him. It took a moment for Rhys to remember he was lying in the field of lippenbur lilies. The sweet scent was intoxicating and overwhelming. Yes, he realized, he'd made love with Medea last night and fallen asleep with her in his arms.

"Medea?" Rhys called out, and sat up. He looked around for her, but she wasn't there. Her clothes were gone as well.

"She's not here, you fool," grumbled the elf. "I see she lured you to the lippenbur lilies to have her way with you, didn't she?"

"What do you mean?" asked Rhys, trying to wake up.

"You coupled with the witch, didn't you?"

"You know I did, so why do you even ask?" he growled.

The elf laughed.

"What is so funny?"

"I would think that being the son of a fae, you would have realized the power of this field of lilies."

"What power? What are you talking about?" Rhys didn't know much at all about the fae folk or their ways, since he had grown up on the other side of the mountain and without a mother to tell him these things.

"I'm talking about the scent of the flowers and the effect they have on people. Don't tell me you didn't know they are an aphrodisiac, Rhys? Every fae knows it."

Rhys groaned. "Nay, I didn't know. And since I didn't even know I was part fae until recently, that is why."

"Well, I'm sure the witch knew what the scent of the flowers was doing to you."

"Quit calling Medea a witch. She didn't know either, and it doesn't matter. We both wanted to make love, so it wasn't anyone trying to fool the other."

"Whatever you say." The elf put his finger to his mouth, biting at a hangnail. "By the way, your brothers are looking everywhere for you."

"Damn," he spat, hurriedly pulling on his clothes.

"You made a big mistake hooking up with the witch," said Elric. "No matter which of you fooled the other."

"How so?" he asked. "Not that I care what you really think, or that it's any of your business what I do."

"She's rotten to the core, I tell you. She's like a mealy worm in an apple."

Rhys pulled his boots on, looking up and scowling at the magical being.

"I don't want to hear another bad word about Medea come out of your mouth. She's a wonderful woman and there is nothing bad about her."

"Hah! I've heard otherwise."

"From whom?" Rhys stood up and strapped on his weapon belt.

"Never mind where I get my information. All you need to worry about is the fact that she is going to betray you, and it's going to be baaaaaad," he said, stretching out the word, sounding like a damned goat.

"Nay! You're wrong. It's not true." Rhys didn't want to believe it.

"It is true, you fool. Her mother was an evil witch. As bad as they come. You do realize, don't you, that the apple doesn't fall far from the tree?" The elf snapped his fingers, and suddenly he was holding an apple. He chuckled, tossing it up and down.

"Stop it!" Rhys grabbed the apple from the elf, meaning to throw it, but it became rotten in his hand, caving in upon itself. His palm was suddenly covered with apple mush and also a dozen squirming worms. "Oh!" he cried, throwing it to the ground and wiping his hand off on his breeches.

"Told you so," laughed the elf.

"I ought to wring your neck, you irritating little barnacle!" Rhys reached out to grab the elf, but in a blur the man was gone. Rhys' fingers closed around naught but air. "Damn you!" he growled.

"Rhys? Is that you?" Darium stood over by one of the bridges with Zann. He stretched his neck, trying to see over the tops of the tall flowers.

"Yeah, it's me," he mumbled, making his way over to his brothers.

"Where have you been all night?" asked Zann. "Mother was starting to get worried when we told her that we hadn't seen you since dinner yesterday."

"I was with Medea," he told them, seeing them grin.

"Oooooh, I see," said Zann. "So, how was it?"

"How was what?" he asked, trying to avoid the truth.

"Rhys, we know you coupled with her, so don't bother trying to lie to us," said Darium.

"What?" Rhys shrugged. "How do you know that? Are you reading minds now like Mother, Darium? Have your fae powers turned to that now?"

"Whoa! Stop being so defensive," said Darium with a low chuckle, holding out his hands. "I can't read minds, but if I could, I'd say something is severely bothering you, Brother."

"I'd have to agree," said Zann with a nod. "We only figured you were coupling with her since we saw you in the field of lust-making flowers."

"You two knew the scent of the flowers were naught but an aphrodisiac?" asked Rhys.

"Sure," said Zann. "Doesn't everyone know that?"

"Apparently not," Rhys mumbled, shaking his head and looking at the ground, feeling foolish.

"Don't take it so hard." Darium chuckled. "Zann is only jesting about knowing. We had no idea about the effect of the flowers either, until this morning when we heard it from the fae."

"Thanks. I guess that makes me feel a little less foolish," Rhys answered.

"So what's bothering you, Brother?" asked Darium.

"Is it something to do with the witch?" Zann wanted to know.

"Her name is Medea." Rhys was getting tired of everyone referring to her as a witch. "Look, I already started out the day badly with that damned elf warning me about her. I don't need you two telling me to stay away from Medea as well." There was already a seed of doubt in the back of Rhys' mind about Medea. The last thing he wanted was for the seed to sprout.

* * *

Medea picked wildflowers along the bank of the river, humming softly to herself. She'd had such a wonderful night making love with Rhys that she'd been too excited to sleep. So, she got up early and decided to explore the land of the fae folk while she waited for Rhys to awake. Having a handful of the sweet-smelling flowers, she started weaving them into her hair. She made a long braid down her back, the same way that the fae wore their hair. She wished she was one of them. She also wished she could stay here forever in the Whispering Dale, and on Mura. This place was so much better than back home.

Medea noticed Rhys talking with his brothers by the bridge. She swore she heard him mention her name and it made her smile. It was the best night ever. Rhys made her feel so special and so loved. Curious to know how he felt about the love-making, she decided to spy on him. After all, it was probably what he was talking about with his brothers. Isn't that what men did when the women weren't around to hear? Well, she wanted to know what he would say. She just had to find out if he'd enjoyed coupling as much as she had, but didn't want to come right out and ask him.

Not wanting to be seen, she decided to use her new-found powers of shapeshifting to aid her in this task. That would be the easiest way to listen in to their conversation in secret. They would never even know she was there. She hunkered down on the ground, deciding to shapeshift into a bee this time. This would ensure she was small enough to remain unnoticed. No one would expect it to be her. She giggled as she shifted, and then flew over to the bridge to find out how much Rhys had enjoyed being with her.

* * *

"The elf told you to stay away from Medea?" asked Zann. "Why?"

"Aye, he did," answered Rhys. "Elric said Medea was evil, just like her mother. He compared her to a rotten apple, saying the apple didn't fall far from the tree." A bee whizzed past his head and he swatted it away.

"Well, I suppose she does seem rather harmless," said Darium.

"I agree," said Rhys. "However, there is more."

"More what?" asked Zann.

"Well, when I was at the Pyramids of the Gods, Zoroct gave me a warning about her as well.'"

"He did?" Darium raised a brow. "If Zoroct spoke to you, it must be important. I've never known anyone who received a message from the gods before."

"What did he say?" asked Zann.

"He told me that the girl cannot be trusted. Of course, he also said not to trust the elf, either, so that is rather confusing, I suppose." The damn bee was back, buzzing around his head now. He stepped back, swatting at it again.

"Not trusting the elf is something I can see. But why would Zoroct say that about Medea?" asked Darium. "She's a stranger to Mura, and he doesn't even know her."

"Zoroct said she was greedy, taking things she wanted without asking. He also said she'd be punished for her mistakes."

"Ah, like what happened to her on the bridge." Zann nodded.

"I suppose," said Rhys. "However, I get the feeling this isn't over with yet." The bee was back, aggravating him by buzzing right next to his ear.

"So, do you regret coupling with the witch?" asked Darium. "I mean... Medea?"

"No, not really." The bee flew away.

"Then don't worry about it," said Zann with a shrug.

"It's just that both Mother and Rapunzel warned me about Medea's darkness as well," Rhys told his brothers. "I don't want to believe it, but after hearing it from so many people, it makes me wonder." He felt something crawling on his arm and looked down to see the bee. He tried to smash it, but the bee was fast and he missed, smacking his arm with his open palm instead.

"You sound like you are having second thoughts about Medea, Rhys," said Darium. "You're not thinking about taking the King up on his offer after all, are you?"

"Why do you even feel the need to ask me that?" Rhys didn't want to think about this at the moment.

"Because," said Zann. "King Osric is going to make you his heir if you kill Medea, her sister and the dragon. It is a big decision, Brother."

"I can't take the offer. I can't kill Medea or any woman," Rhys answered.

"Nay, I suppose not," said Zann in thought. "But still... that is an offer that won't come twice. Just think. You can be one of the rulers of Mura and make sure magic is never prohibited again."

"I know," said Rhys. "I have to admit, I did consider the offer for a brief minute. Who wouldn't? Ow! Damn it," he shouted, feeling a sting on his ass. He turned around to find the damned bee buzzing furiously around him now. "I just got stung. I'll kill that damned bee." This time, he used his strength to swat at the bee. The bee shot far, and fell down into the flowers along the bank. "Well, that should do it." He rubbed his aching ass.

They heard a rustling in the flowers on the bank. To his surprise, Medea stood up, rubbing her head.

"Medea?" Rhys hadn't seen her in the flowers. "What are you doing there?"

"You really do want to kill me, don't you?" she spat, her eyes turning pitch black with anger.

"Uh oh," said Zann, realizing what was about to transpire.

"Damn," muttered Darium. "I think you made her angry."

"Y-you were the bee, weren't you?" asked Rhys, realizing now she had shapeshifted into the form of an insect. "How was I supposed to know that? That was a stupid thing to do, Medea. I could have killed you. Why did you do it?"

She stormed over to the men. "Rhys, I heard you speak my name and figured you were telling your brothers about us spending the night together. I wanted to hear what you had to say. However, now that I have heard what came from your mouth, I wish I hadn't."

"Medea, I can explain." Rhys watched as her whole face seemed to change and contort. She became very angry. He didn't like to see this side of her at all. It was not becoming in the least.

"You used me, Rhys Blackseed!"

"No, I didn't." Rhys saw Rapunzel and his mother coming from one of the cottages and hurrying in their direction.

"You want to kill me so you can become king, admit it! And you tried to do so just now by swatting at me in my bee form. I bet you wished you had killed me." Fire seemed to burn in her black eyes now, and it was very unsettling.

"Medea, that's not true, and our time together last night should have proved it to you. I don't want to kill you. And I also don't like the fact you were spying on me." This angered him now.

"If I wasn't, I'd never know how you really felt about me, would I?" she retorted.

"I don't want to kill you. Honest."

"How can I believe that? You almost just smashed me to death with your hand."

"I told you, I didn't know the bee was you," he said through gritted teeth, thinking this was a nonsensical conversation.

"Well, I heard what you said to your brothers," she shouted. "You're considering doing away with me and my sister just so you can be king!"

"Now wait a minute." He held up his hands, trying to calm her. "I said, any man would consider such an offer, but I turned it down. Perhaps you missed that part."

"I heard you say you considered it."

"Just for a brief moment, I suppose, but it was only the temptation getting to me. You know I would never do it."

"Do I?" Her hands were on her hips now.

Rhys glanced up to see both his brothers shaking their heads, making him realize that mayhap he shouldn't have admitted to anything. Not when Medea was so angry. "Medea, the important thing is, I turned down the King's offer. Don't you understand that? Do you hear what I'm saying?"

"Oh, I hear you. I've also heard more than I ever want to know!" She raised her hands and blasted black light at Rhys. It hit him hard in the chest, flipping him high in the air. He landed on his back on the ground with all the air knocked from his lungs. He struggled to try to breathe.

"Rhys, are you all right?" Darium and Zann rushed over to help him.

"Medea! Medea, what are you doing?" yelled Rapunzel, running over the bridge toward her sister.

"Rap, I thought Rhys was different from most people, but now I see he is the same as everyone else in my life who has deceived me or let me down."

"Sister, control your emotions. Please," warned Rapunzel, reaching out to take her sister's arm. "You know what happens if you don't."

"Leave me alone, Rap." Rapunzel went flying through the air next, barreling into Alaina. They both fell to the ground. "I will make him pay for what he did, if it is the last thing I ever do."

It didn't even sound like Medea talking now. Rhys had no doubt that it was the darkness inside her making her act this way. Medea stormed toward Rhys, but Rapunzel intercepted.

"Nay, I won't let you hurt him. You'll leave him alone." Rapunzel used her own powers now to blast Medea, sending her stumbling and falling to the ground.

"No one cares about me. No one ever has," screamed Medea, getting to her feet.

"Medea, calm down and we'll talk about this. Then we'll go find the dragon, and head back home where we belong," said Rapunzel.

"I'm not leaving the land of Mura, and you can't stop me from staying. This is my home now. I plan to be the ruler of Mura, not that conniving, deceitful Rhys Blackseed."

"Medea, this isn't you," said Rhys, getting to his feet, and heading toward her, finally catching his breath and being able to speak. "I know you have darkness inside you. That is what's making you act this way. You don't really mean it." He inched closer to her.

"You know nothing about me, Rhys Blackseed. Nothing at all!" she screamed.

Rhys lunged for Medea, knocking her down. They rolled over and over atop the ground while he used his powerful strength to hold down her arms. He did every-thing he could to try to stop her from using her dark magic.

"Get off of me, Rhys."

"Medea, listen to me. I was wrong to consider the offer from the King, and I'm sorry. It was a weak mo-ment. Everyone has them. But honestly, I could never kill a woman, and you know it. Look into your heart and see that it is true what I say. I could never kill someone I care for as much as I do you."

"You lied to me, Rhys. You don't care about me at all. I was better off alone!" She mumbled some words that Rhys couldn't decipher, but it almost sounded like some kind of spell to him.

"Uh... Rhys?" said Zann from behind him.

"Brother, I think we're going to need that super strength of yours really soon," mumbled Darium.

"Not now," spat Rhys, still struggling with Medea. But when he heard the women scream, he turned his head to see a sea serpent rising up from the creek. The fae were out of their cottages, and running around in confusion, not knowing how to stop it. "Damn it, you didn't, Medea," he said with a deep sigh, realizing she'd just conjured up the monster to get him to release her. He had no other choice then to do just that, or risk someone being hurt or even killed.

As soon as he released Medea, she stood up, glaring at him again with black eyes.

"I'll have everything for myself that you supposedly turned down, and even more," she said, laughing wickedly now. She seemed so evil. It was just like everyone had been warning him about her. Rhys didn't like seeing her this way. This wasn't her. It was a dark magic she inherited at birth from her mother control-ling her. She didn't have a choice. If Medea truly couldn't control it, like he'd been told, then he realized she might be consumed by the darkness. That is the worst thing he could ever think could happen to her.

"Medea, stop this," he pleaded. "You don't mean to be this way."

"Oh, I do mean it, and so much more."

Rhys felt that if he could just get through to her, mayhap he could help her to fight the darkness. He wanted to touch that loving, caring side of her, so he brought up their night together, hoping to spur it.

"We spent a wonderful time together in the lippenbur lilies last night."

"Don't even mention that," she snapped, only seeming to cause more anger from her.

"I meant every word I said, and I hope that you did too. You said you never felt so special or loved."

She stopped talking and seemed to be remembering their time together. "Yes," she admitted.

"I think you deserve more of that, Medea, and I want to be the one to give it to you."

"You do?" she asked, almost calming down for a moment.

"We belong together." He slowly walked toward her, hoping to grab her again. "If we talk about this, I'm sure we can come up with a solution to your little problem."

Her head snapped upward and a scowl washed across her face. "My little problem?"

"Uh oh," he said, realizing he shouldn't have referred to her dark magic as a problem.

"You're the one with a problem, because I am going to get everything you ever wanted in life, and you will be nothing when I am done. Just you wait and see."

"Wait," he said, lunging for her, but with a swish of her arm, she disappeared, and he grabbed on to nothing but air. "Damn!" he spat, angered that he wasn't able to stop her.

"Rhys, are you coming?" yelled Zann, as he and Darium both tried to fight off the beast with their swords, even though it was having little effect.

"I don't have time for this," spat Rhys, running over and jumping on to the back of the sea serpent, gripping it tightly around the neck. The serpent hissed and flipped around, its long tail slashing out at everyone, causing a frenzy. "Get out of the way, everyone," Rhys yelled, using his strength to strangle the sea serpent before it killed someone. A few more flips and struggles, and finally, the monster stilled, dropping dead back into the water.

"You did it!" cried Rapunzel. "Thank you for saving us, Rhys."

"No trouble," he said, sloshing his way out of the creek, shaking water from his hands. The fae folk all gathered around, staring at the dead beast in their creek. Sea serpents seemed to be common on this side of the mountain, but where Rhys lived, they never seemed to see a one.

"What will we do with it?" asked one of the women.

"How can we move it? It's too big and heavy," said another.

"I think I can help." Darium sheathed his sword and stepped forward, holding his hands out. "I'm not sure yet how to actually use my new elemental powers, but I can try." He was able to levitate the sea serpent from the water, but not being used to his newfound powers yet, he couldn't hold it there for long. The beast dropped back down into the creek, causing the fae folk to gasp and cry out as water splashed up on them. "I guess I need a little more practice," said Darium, studying his hands.

"Darium, allow me," said Alaina, stepping forward. "Your elemental power of the air will get stronger in time, but right now, Son, don't overexert yourself. You'll need your strength when you encounter the dragon. You all will, if you're going to be successful in capturing it."

Alaina easily called upon the air to help them, since she was able to control the weather. A whirlwind spun around above the sea serpent, picking it up in a funnel.

"I'll send it into the Masked Sea," she told them, swishing her hands and sending the funnel out to the sea where it deposited the dead sea serpent. Then the cloud of swirling air dissipated.

"Thanks, Mother," said Rhys with a sigh of frustration. "I only wish I had been able to make Medea realize how much she really means to me."

"It's a dragon!" screamed one of the fae, pointing to the sky.

"Run! Hide!" yelled several others, causing chaos again for the fae.

"Oh, damn," said Rhys looking up to see the dragon flying right over the Whispering Dale. "I think someone is riding it," he said, peering into the sky. When it came closer, he could tell there was a man on the dragon's back.

"It's a man," said Zann.

"I wonder who it is," remarked Darium. "I've never seen him before."

When it swooped over their heads, Rapunzel gasped. "Marco?" she said with a hand to her mouth.

"Marco?" asked Rhys. "You mean, your Dragon Lord husband?"

"Nay. It can't be." Rapunzel shook her head. "He

couldn't have come through the portal and also found us this quickly. I don't believe it at all."

"The dragon answers to me now, Sister," called the man from the air.

"Sister? Oh, no. I think I know what is happening," said Rhys, shaking his head, realizing just what was going on. "Rapunzel, I believe Medea has shapeshifted into the form of the Dragon Lord to trick the dragon in order to control it."

"That's Medea?" asked Zann, stretching his neck to see better.

"You're right," said Rapunzel. "That is not my husband, but it is my wretched sister. We are all in trouble now."

"What do you mean?" asked Darium.

"You all heard what Medea said before she left," Rapunzel pointed out. "She threatened that she would be ruler of Mura and that she was not leaving here and going back through the portal."

"That doesn't sound good," said Darium.

"Not at all," agreed Zann.

"Zoroct's eyes, we are all in trouble now," said Rhys. "I think she means to use the dragon to seize Kasculbough Castle and kill the King." Rhys couldn't believe what was happening. Just last night he spent the most wonderful time with a beautiful woman whom he thought he could possibly even love. But now, Medea's evil side emerged and threatened everything and everyone in Rhys' life, and he couldn't accept this. He had to stop her. He couldn't let her kill his king and take Kasculbough as her own. There had to be a way.

"Nay. She wouldn't really do that. Would she?" asked Alaina.

"Yes, she would," said Rapunzel, sounding sad to admit it. "In the past, Medea helped her mother do the exact thing when they seized Tanglewood Castle. Now, she's about to do it all again, but this time on her own."

"It is exactly what she threatened to do," Rhys pointed out. "I can't believe this is really happening."

"Believe it. The darkness inside Medea now controls her," Rapunzel told the others. "You are all about to see a side of Medea that you have never experienced before. And I assure you, it will be terrifying. Medea can't control this dark side of her, and over time it has grown stronger. Sadly, there will most likely be a lot of death and destruction on Mura before she is finished."

Thirteen

"This is all my fault," said Rhys, pacing back and forth along the edge of the creek. "I should have been able to stop Medea, but I failed. I couldn't get her to listen to me."

"Women will do that to you," said Darium, sounding like the voice of experience now that he was married. "They'll lure you in until all you can do is think about nothing else but them. They have minds of their own, and will hardly ever listen to a word you say."

"Right," agreed Zann. "Look what happened to you, Darium."

"Hey, I didn't mean me." Darium scowled at Zann. "Besides, I never said I didn't like it. Being married is the best thing that ever happened to me. I'd do it all again and not be sorry. I love Talia and love being married."

"I was starting to have feelings for Medea as well," said Rhys. "She may have a dark side to her, but I've also seen the light within her and I believe it is stronger." Rhys thought about Medea's smile, her innocence, and how much it meant to her to have his friendship... his love. His heart went out to her. She'd seemed so distraught when she'd told him about her loneliness. But when she was with him, she seemed so happy and full of life. "Damn, I've really made a mess of things. I wish she'd never heard about that deal I almost made with the King. That is what set her off."

"Rhys, you did nothing wrong," said his mother. "You were there for Medea when she needed you. Now you need to look out for yourself."

"Nay," he said, throwing his hands in the air. "I need to look out for Medea. Only now, I have no idea how to do that. I don't even know where she is." The crystal pendant resting against his chest started to glow. He reached down and held it, immediately feeling comfort. "I have to get her home. Back to her home," he said. "That is where she'll be the safest, far away from Mura and sea serpents and kings who want her dead. She needs to go through that portal, even if I don't like the idea of her leaving."

"Hrmph. Easier said than done," grunted Darium. "Nothing involving Medea seems to be easy."

"My sister has been misguided, Rhys." Rapunzel walked up to him. "She is young and inexperienced. Her mother died before being able to teach her much."

"What do you mean?" asked Rhys. "She's had twenty years to learn, if I'm not mistaken. Didn't her mother just die recently?"

"Yes, Hecuba did die recently, but... but..." Rapunzel looked back and forth from one of them to the other.

"What is it?" asked Rhys. "If there is something else I need to know about Medea, please tell me."

"Her birth was a magical one," Rapunzel explained.

"Aye, I know. She has magic. Both light and dark," said Rhys with a nod.

"Nay, it's more than just that."

"How so?"

"What is it you're trying to say, Rapunzel?" asked Alaina in a gentle voice.

"Well, I'm sure you'll all find out anyway, so I suppose it's no secret. Everyone back home already knows. When my sister was conceived, dark magic was involved. Lots of it. Her mother, Hecuba deceived my father in the shapeshifting form of a beautiful woman. Once Medea was conceived, she was born almost immediately."

"I don't understand," said Rhys, his brows creasing.

"You see, her birth was magical, most likely some dark spell her mother put on her somehow. I don't really understand it either. Hecuba had me trapped in a tower at the same time when Medea was born, so I watched over her until she turned eighteen."

"What?" gasped Zann. "So, you were a prisoner for eighteen years? Rapunzel, you really don't look old enough for that to be true."

"I'm not, and that is not what I mean." Rapunzel released a deep breath and continued. "You see, Medea's childhood went very quickly."

"How quickly?" asked Rhys preparing himself to hear something absurd, since he figured it was what Rapunzel was leading up to.

"Well, Medea was under a dark spell from Hecuba. Therefore, she aged one year for each day that passed. It didn't stop until she turned eighteen."

"Good gods, you have got to be jesting!" Rhys held his head since this information made it hurt. "No wonder she has such a childlike innocence about her at times."

"I wish I was jesting, but I'm not." Rapunzel continued. "Medea attained her magical abilities quickly as well. She and I were at odds constantly, ever since she was born. You see, she was a lot like her mother until she changed... in the end, that is."

"In the end? What end?" asked Rhys. "Something isn't adding up here."

"There is a part of the story I left out, but I guess I might as well tell you that, too."

"Please do," said Zann. "This is proving to be very amusing." He grinned and folded his arms over his chest, eager to hear more.

"Let's see, how do I say it?"

"Just tell us the truth," said Alaina. "Unless you'd like me to read your mind, and I can relay the rest of the story."

"Nay. I'll do it. She is my sister and I owe it to her, I suppose."

"Go on," said Zann impatiently.

"My brother, MacKay, had a shard of Hecuba's magical mirror embedded in his heart."

"A magical mirror?" asked Zann, nodding. "Nice. I could use one of those."

"My brother would have died if it wasn't for Medea."

"So, then she does have a good side to her," said Rhys, wanting to hear her say *yes* more than anything right now.

"She does," said Rapunzel, getting a sigh of relief from Rhys. "However, her guilt has isolated her from the rest of the family ever since that day."

"Guilt?" asked Darium. "For helping to save your brother's life? I don't understand."

"Nay, I don't suppose you would unless I explain more." Rapunzel's expression became sad. At first Rhys didn't think she was going to finish her story, but then she continued talking. "Medea had to make a choice. She ended up sacrificing the life of her own mother in order to save MacKay. It was a hard choice to make, but she could only save one of them. In the end, she did the right thing, letting the light outweigh the dark. To make up for all the pain her mother had caused my family, Medea chose to save MacKay's life instead."

"So the light is stronger than the darkness after all," said Rhys. "I knew it."

"Mayhap it was at that time, but I'm not sure it still is," said Rapunzel. "Medea has had nothing to do with the rest of our family. She can't face us after that. She's managed for two years now to keep her distance, hiding away at Tanglewood Castle. Her own father and siblings really know nothing about her. I know her the best since I was there from her birth."

"It all makes sense now why she told me she feels so alone." Rhys felt sorry for Medea. His heart ached for her return. "We've got to help her. Let's go." He hurried over to his horse, ready to do whatever it took to save Medea from the darkness and get her back into his arms again.

"Wait, Brother." Darium hurried after him. "What are you planning to do?"

"There's nothing we can do. She's in control of the dragon now, unless you've forgotten." Zann pointed out a very important piece of information. One that could change everything.

"I didn't forget." Rhys looked down and grabbed the crystal in his palm, giving it a light squeeze. "I am hoping to use that to our advantage. If I have to trick her, I will. But somehow, I will make certain that Medea and Rapunzel are both on that damned dragon when I open the portal and send them through."

* * *

Medea rode the dragon in a circle over the Whispering Dale, so furious with Rhys that part of her wanted to strike him down dead right where he stood. She had thought she'd finally found the man for her, but realized now that she was wrong. Rhys was no different from any other man back in England. She still couldn't believe that he had considered killing her.

She was only thankful she came up with a plan. Now that she could shapeshift, all she had to do was shift into the form of Marco and use a little spell, and the dragon listened to her. It worked like a charm, but she wasn't sure how long it would last. Hopefully long enough to carry out the rest of her plan.

"Fly over the Pyramids of the Gods," she instructed, sounding like Marco as well as looking like him. The dragon was easily fooled. It really must have thought she was its Dragon Lord, because it listened. This was fun and all too easy.

One circle around the pyramids, and she directed the dragon higher, liking the feel of the wind against her face. She looked like her brother-by-marriage, Marco, right now. However, she couldn't stop thinking of how she looked earlier and also how she felt while at the Whispering Dale or spending the night in the field of lippenbur lilies with Rhys.

She pictured her long black braid entwined with the exotic lippenbur lilies and fae flowers that had made her feel pretty and enticing for the very first time in her life. So much so, that she even wanted to become a fae.

"Bah! Who wants to be one of the fae, anyway?" she asked herself, feeling the darkness inside her growing stronger now.

Power was more important than beauty. She felt invincible, and that was all that mattered. She was just as strong as her mother used to be. With each day that passed, her powers matured more and more. Soon she'd be even more powerful than her late mother. That was a great feeling, and made her excited wondering what else she could do. With power came fame, and wealth, and everything that went along with it.

"Fly higher," she commanded. The dragon took off up to the tip of Mount Catskulp, the highest mountain peak on Mura.

Medea flew in a circle, peering down at the mountains and also inspecting the waterfall far below. The crystalline waters fell over the high cliffs, emptying into a clear pond filled with colorful floating water lilies of pink, and yellow. It truly was a land filled with magic and beauty.

As she noticed the land south of the mountains, things started to look different. This was the part that Rhys told her wasn't magical at all. He said it was a horrible place to live because of the greed and fighting from the three kings of Mura.

She could see the three castles of the kings of Mura below, each one of them looking as if they had a fortified keep. They must also have strong armies, and defenses of all kinds. The kings ruled over their area, each wanting the others' land as well. Serfs and villagers, along with knights, nobles, and soldiers, all answered to the kings, each of them living in their king's castle or in a small village right outside the gates.

"I want that," she said aloud, devising a plan in her head of how to capture each castle for herself. It shouldn't be hard with a dragon at her command now, she supposed. All she had to do was to take what she wanted. Never did she need to yearn and wait until something was offered. Soon, she'd be Queen of all of Mura. Everyone, including Rhys, would bow down to her then. That part made her smile.

Deciding the first kingdom she'd conquer was the one where Rhys was a knight, she directed the dragon to the east coast where the kingdom of Kasculbough was situated. This would show him. Rhys almost agreed to kill her, following his king's command. He was considering doing it to claim the throne someday as his own. Well, wouldn't he be surprised when the throne was hers instead of his? If so, he'd have to answer to her. After all, he was supposedly the most loyal knight in the kingdom of Kasculbough, so there was no way he could refuse her orders.

As she rode through the sky, she started to feel sick to her stomach and didn't understand why. Never had magic made her feel ill before. Putting her hand on her belly, she realized she felt severely bloated and uncomfortable. Something almost felt as if it was moving inside her. Actually, this ride in the air was making her dizzy and feeling as if she wanted to retch. She felt lightheaded, and decided she needed to land before she fell off the dragon altogether.

She directed the dragon lower, right above Kasculbough Castle now. Below her she saw the dark stones of the keep and the red roofs of the outbuildings in the courtyard. There were crops growing inside the bailey, as well as a deep pit situated off to one side. The entire castle was surrounded by a moat filled with water.

Take the castle. You deserve it. Rid yourself of those who won't bow down to you. The thoughts in her head were so loud now that she could think of nothing else but this. It was almost as if she were listening to the words of her mother, but this time the thoughts were coming from deep inside her instead.

"Take the castle. Kill everyone if you have to!" she shouted, feeling the power of her mother flowing through her veins right now. Then she thought about Rhys again, and had the overwhelming need to be in his arms. She missed him. Her emotions were unstable and she couldn't control what she felt at all. One minute she was angry, and the next she felt calm. Vengeance struggled with forgiveness inside her. This all made her feel extremely sad.

Greed overtook her next, and now she didn't care. Then she felt ever so lonely once again, thinking about how good it felt when Rhys saved her from the sea serpent at the pyramids. She wanted to taste his sweet, strong lips against hers once more. Nay. She wanted so much more. She wanted to lie with him and spend another magical night in the field of lilies under the stars. That only got her thinking about Rhys deceiving her again. Before she knew it, the anger had returned. All of the emotions swerving back and forth was too much, making her dizzier and dizzier. It was getting harder to hold on to the dragon's leathery mane as well.

"It's the dragon!" she heard one of the guards on the wall walk shout out. She looked down into the courtyard of Kasculbough, realizing it was naught but a frenzy of running people down below. Women and children hurried to hide. Screams as well as crying filled her ears. King Osric's soldiers formed a triangular formation, clutching their weapons and holding their shields high above their heads.

"Blast them with fire!" she shouted, and the dragon obeyed. As she dipped down from the sky, the dragon breathed fire right at the group of soldiers. Unfortunately, the soldiers were prepared. They lifted their shields made of metal, pushing them together and making a roof over their heads. The fire from the dragon bounced off without harming a one of them.

"Damn," she shouted, taking off back up into the sky. Then she saw the King down below, and her lips turned up into a smile. She realized that she didn't need to take out the armed men. All she had to do was to capture or kill the King, and she'd hold all the power over them.

"Swoop down there. By the King. He's next," she commanded the dragon.

The dragon started its descent, but something was wrong. There was a lurching sensation in Medea's stomach that made her feel extremely odd. When she looked down to her waist, she gasped. Her stomach was huge! Then, against her wishes, she started to shift out of the form of Marco and back into herself.

The dragon must have realized then that it had been tricked. It looked back over its shoulder and roared loudly.

"Ooops," said Medea, holding out her hand to see that she was once again herself. "That's a good dragon," she said, patting it on the head. "Now, kill the King. Please?" she added, but it didn't do any good. When they swooped down to the King, instead of blasting the man with fire, the dragon shook her off of its back and took off back up into the sky letting out a loud, angry roar.

"Oooomph." Medea landed hard in the courtyard, on the ground right at the King's feet.

The soldiers shot arrows at the dragon and chased its path with their swords drawn. The dragon retreated, quickly making its way back to the Quamm Caves. This left Medea there by herself. All alone. Again.

On her hands and knees, she retched. Then she looked up slightly to see the shoes of the King. Her belly hurt like the devil. It was so big right now that she felt like she'd swallowed a melon.

"Who are you?" growled the King.

Medea's eyes roamed up higher and higher, stopping at the King's face.

"Hello, King. I'm... Medea. Remember me?" She

tried to sound fierce, but it was becoming too difficult since she felt weighted down and as if she wanted to die.

"You're the witch." The King unsheathed his sword and his men ran over to him.

"I'm Medea," she repeated, barely able to speak. "It's a name you won't want to forget." She had meant to blast him with her powers just then for more effect. Unfortunately, it took all her strength just to lift her hand. She thought she felt lots of movement in her belly now, and didn't understand what was happening to her.

"Seize her," commanded the King, pointy a beefy finger right at her.

His guards grabbed her and yanked her up and to her feet.

"Don't touch me," she snapped. "I'm a powerful witch and I could kill you all with just a... just a... oooooh... ow!" She cried out in pain, looking down to her feet to see a puddle of water mixed with blood dripping down her legs and to the ground. Her belly hurt more than anything now.

"Throw her in the dungeon," screamed the King, but his men hesitated.

"She's pregnant, my King," said one of the guards.

"I am?" Medea looked down to her belly again and groaned. She had only just lain with Rhys, so it was much too soon to be pregnant. Then again, she realized, when her mother had conceived her, she had been told her birth happened very quickly. She realized now exactly what was happening to her. It was if her life was repeating itself, but with her as the mother this time. She moaned in pain, falling to the ground.

"Sire, I think she is birthing the baby," said one of the King's men.

"What? Here?" asked the King. "Nay! Take her to the tower chamber, and call the midwife. Fast!"

"I'm a powerful witch," she said, under her breath, her eyes closing since she felt so drained of energy. Then she cried out in pain, feeling something happening. It was pain like she'd never felt before.

She was pregnant and having Rhys' baby. That is, a very magical baby was being born even sooner than she'd been born, if she wasn't mistaken. She wasn't sure if by using her dark magic she had sped up the birthing process, or if this is how it would be every time she was pregnant, since her own birth and aging happened so fast because of one of Hecuba's spells. This couldn't be happening. It shouldn't be. Should it? Sadly, Medea started to wonder if she was becoming just as evil as her mother.

"Rap? Rhys," she wailed as the guards dragged her into the keep. Medea was frightened for the second time in her life and this time it wasn't because of a sea serpent. She had all her powers, but it didn't matter. If she could use her powers to stop all this from happening, she would, but unfortunately, she didn't know how, or even if it was possible. Medea had no idea what she was supposed to do. All alone once again, she would have to face this herself, and that made her very sad. Medea really needed Rhys at her side right now, because she wasn't sure she was strong enough to birth a baby—his baby—all by herself.

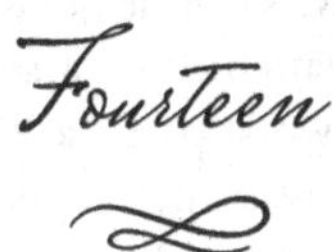

<h1 style="text-align:center">Fourteen</h1>

Before Medea even had time to come to terms with what was happening, she found herself holding her newborn baby daughter in her arms. Lying back on the bed in the King's tower chamber, she stared down at the wailing infant, still in shock and unable to speak.

"What a nice baby," said the midwife who had helped to deliver the child. "What will you name your daughter?" The woman washed her hands in a basin of water. There were two guards standing just outside the door.

"I- I-I'm not sure," Medea muttered, using all her energy just to answer the woman. She felt so tired that she could probably sleep for a week right now.

"Well, the baby sure is beautiful and looks a lot like you," said the midwife. "Except for that oaken hair and those big green eyes. Does she get that from her father, I suppose?" The midwife was most likely just trying to make conversation, but Medea wanted her to shut up so she could think.

"I suppose so." Medea swallowed deeply, looking down at the squalling baby. This was not unlike a dream. It had happened too fast, and she was having a hard time believing it was real. She still felt her head spinning, and was so dizzy that she wasn't sure she wouldn't fall right out of the bed.

What would Rhys say if he knew? Medea wondered. Would he want a daughter or a son? Would he want children at all? The worst part was that she didn't know if Rhys would even want her anymore, now that she'd given in to the dark side and left him. Confusion muddled her brain.

"What is your name, my lady?" asked the midwife, sounding too kind to her. Medea didn't feel as if she deserved it.

"I'm M-Medea."

"Hello, Medea. I am Henriette. Do you have someone to help you care for the child? Or did you want me to summon the nursemaid?"

"Nursemaid?" She looked at the woman and her mind went blank.

"To feed her. Or are you planning on doing that yourself?"

"I don't know. I suppose I am." Now, she really felt frightened. She looked down to her breasts. Her mother never nursed her as far as she knew. Medea wasn't even sure she knew how.

"I'll let you two rest now. The King wants to see you, but I will tell him it's too soon since you just gave birth."

Before Medea could even respond, the door burst open and King Osric strutted in, accompanied by two of his guards.

"Sire, it's not a good time," protested the midwife. "Medea has just given birth and she needs to rest."

"Hush, Henriette," snapped the man. "What was your name again, witch?"

"It's Medea, sire," Henriette responded for her, and Medea was glad.

"I asked the witch, not you!"

"It is Medea, just as she said." Medea only answered so he wouldn't punish the nice midwife. She wanted to blast him with her magic right now in response to his ruthlessness, but unfortunately, she was so tired from birthing the baby and shapeshifting, that she was too weak to even use her powers.

"What's that?" He looked down at her baby.

"This is my daughter," said Medea. Just saying it out loud felt odd.

"I know it's a baby, you bitch!" he spat. "But it is human or magical?"

"I- I'm not sure," she answered softly, really not knowing the answer to the King's question.

"It doesn't matter. It's a girl, is it not?"

"Yes," she said, only because the King was looking right at it.

"Then it is of no use to me. Guards, kill them both." Osric turned on his heel to leave. The guards reached out for Medea and the baby, frightening her enough to give her the strength she needed.

"Nay! Don't touch me or my child." Medea pulled the baby closer, holding it up against her chest, feeling the warmth of their bodies touching. It felt good. Her daughter was a tiny little thing, but with a head of thick, oaken hair, just like her father. The baby cried and looked up to her with innocent, big, green eyes, seeming very scared. Medea had to protect her child. She was the only one now who could save the little girl's life. A feeling of love engulfed her as the baby cuddled up to her, trusting her completely. Medea knew now that she would give her own life to save this child, if need be, and never regret it.

Then she looked up at the guards with their

weapons in hand. Her eyes trailed over to stare into the eyes of the terrible king who ruled Kasculbough next. That immense feeling of love within her disappeared quickly and darkness took its place. How could anyone order a little baby to be killed? He was truly a wretched man. Without even using her hands this time, she was able to shoot the dark energy from her eyes, knocking the King's men to the ground.

King Osric spun around seeing his guards on the floor. Then he turned back to her, drawing his sword.

"I would put that blade away if I were you, or you'll be next," she warned him.

"Are they... are they dead?" he asked, looking down at his men. Smoke rose up off their bodies.

"I don't know and neither do I care," she retorted. "Now, get out of here. I am tired. My baby and I need to rest."

"You're evil," he spat. "You are a witch filled with dark magic."

"So, what if I am?"

"Magic is prohibited on Mura," he told her, as if that meant anything at all to her.

"Really." She rocked the baby in her arms, and to her surprise it actually stopped crying. "Too bad, since none of that will matter once you're dead and I'm the one sitting on your throne."

The King lunged at her with his sword pointing the way. This time, she made an invisible barrier around the bed, protecting both her and the baby. King Osric smashed into it, dropping his sword and falling to his knees.

"You see, it is of no use trying to hurt me. My powers make me invincible. Soon, when I rule Kasculbough, that will be invincible, too."

"I don't understand this. You weren't pregnant when I saw you in my courtyard yesterday."

"There are some things about witches that can't be explained or figured out, so don't bother to try."

Two guards ran up the tower stairs and stopped at the door, as the midwife watched with wide eyes from the shadows in the back of the room. When the soldiers were about to enter the chamber, King Osric raised his hand and stopped them. "Wait there," he commanded his men before looking back at Medea. "I would like to make a deal with you, witch."

"My name is Medea," she snapped. "Don't forget it. If you call me *witch* once more, I'll have your brains exploding out of your head next. Do you understand?"

"Medea," he said with utmost respect, talking softly and gently. "I'm sorry. "Can you tell me; will your children be as powerful with magic someday as you are?"

"More so, I'm sure. However, I will know more about that in the next few days."

"Few days? You will be able to tell that soon?"

"If my child is like me, she'll grow quickly."

"How quickly?" he asked, cocking his head, seeming interested.

"Well, I aged one year for each day that passed, until I reached eighteen."

"Amazing," he said, his eyes becoming even wider. The smile started to return to his face. "Tell me, how fast can you have these babies?"

"Well, I don't know for sure. This one was only conceived last night."

"Really." The King got a big smile now and chuckled lowly. "I can see us raising a whole army of boys, or mayhap even girls together. It won't matter as long as they all have magic. They'll be our warriors. We'll seize Evandorm and Sethor both. Together we will be the sole rulers of all of Mura."

"*We?*" she asked, making a face. "I can do that all by myself, if I so choose. Why would I want anything to do with you?"

"You'll need a man to help you conceive these soldiers," he pointed out. "That will be my job."

The thought made her cringe. "You wanted me killed," she reminded the man.

"Nay, I didn't. I swear, that is not true. Who did you hear that from?"

"I heard it directly from Rhys Blackseed's mouth, and he is your best and most loyal knight."

"Blackseed," he growled. "Those brothers are all liars. They'll say whatever they have to in order to get what they want."

"What do you mean?" She looked down at her baby and smiled. She really was cute, like the midwife said.

"It was Rhys Blackseed's idea to kill you. He told me that you were a threat and he'd take you out if I made him my heir."

"What?" Her head snapped up. "I don't believe you. He said it was your idea and that he turned you down."

"Hah!" The King laughed heartily. "Did he say that before or after you figured it out?"

That made her stop and think. Could Rhys have just said that because he knew she'd discovered the plan and he was trying to save his own ass?

"He probably also told you some lie to get you in his bed," continued the King, making more sense than she wanted to admit. "I'm guessing that whelp is his, isn't it?"

"Yes, Rhys is the father, and my baby is not a whelp!" She slammed him against the wall without even touching him. The guards ran in with weapons drawn, so she used her powers to send them against the wall as well.

"Sire, she is powerful," shouted one of the guards from the floor. "We need backup."

"Don't get her mad," said the other guard in a soft voice.

"Guards, take the other two men out of here. I want Medea to be able to rest," instructed the King.

"You don't want to imprison her, my King?" asked one of them. "She is a threat, my lord."

"Aye, don't you want her dead?" asked the other.

"Nay. Why would I want to hurt my future Queen?" The King followed up his sentence with a forced laugh.

"Future Queen?" Medea repeated in surprise. She wasn't sure where this was coming from. Then again, if the man wanted to have babies with her, she supposed she would be his Queen. Still, she didn't need or want him. She could rule by herself.

You don't want to be alone again, came a voice in her head, clouding her thoughts. *Take the man up on his offer. You can rule all of Mura with a powerful king doing your bidding. You don't need to feel lonely. He wants you. He wants to create a family. This is what you've always wanted.* The dark voice of her mother filled her ears, and she couldn't push it away. She wondered if Hecuba was mentoring her from the grave. Either way, she found it hard to ignore it. *It is your fault I am gone, and I'll never forgive you unless you do what I say.*

"That's right, Medea," said Osric. "With you at my side, the two of us will be the most powerful rulers of Mura. I want you to marry me on the morrow."

"Marry you," she repeated, feeling as if she were in a foggy daze. "Why in the world would I even consider doing that?"

Because then you'd have everything you ever wanted.

This man is rich and powerful and can give you every-thing. You need him. You will rule together the entire land of Mura. You will have power and wealth. Most of all, with all your children you'll have together, you will never be lonely again. You got rid of me, Daughter, and that is why you are so lonely. It is your own fault. Do this, I warn you, or I will never forgive you and you will al-ways feel the stab of guilt and the pain of being alone.

"Because you know I'm the only one you can trust, that's why," said Osric. "Plus, you'll need help raising our army of children. You don't want to do it all alone, do you?"

"Alone," she repeated, looking down to her baby, realizing she wasn't really alone anymore. Still, in a way, without a man at her side, she would have to raise the child all by herself. She'd felt the emptiness of not growing up with a father present. Aye, she needed a man in her children's lives. But the man she really wanted wasn't Osric, it was Rhys.

Rhys doesn't want you, but Osric does, came the voice of her mother in her head once again. *Don't be a fool, Medea. Do what I would do. Use this man for your own needs. You deserve it. Be the powerful witch and queen that I tried to teach you to be. King Osric is the man for you, and no one else.*

The thing Medea feared most in life was being alone, and that was exactly how she felt since the death of her mother. It was painful and sad and she didn't want to live that way anymore. Medea vowed to find a man and raise a family and never be alone again, but it seemed no man wanted her once they saw her darkness. She had thought Rhys was the man she'd spend the rest of her days with, but now she could see it wasn't so. He didn't love her, he didn't need her. He didn't want her anymore, now that he'd seen her dark side, she was sure.

Plus, Rhys deceived her, and wanted her dead. Even when she told him she wanted to stay in Mura, he still seemed to want to send her home.

That's right, Medea. Now you see that fool Rhys for what he really is. You don't want a life with him, even if you have already birthed his baby. Go with Osric—he can help you and will always be there for you. That's what you should do. Take the King up on his offer now, before he changes his mind. Do it, before you are left all alone once again. If you waste this opportunity, you'll be the only one to blame for your miserable life.

The darkness inside Medea grew stronger every time she heard her mother's thoughts from the grave. She started listening to the voice in her head and found it too hard to push it away. Her greed became the only thing important to her right now, and it made her feel filled with power. King Osric could offer her everything she'd ever wanted, just like the voice in her head told her. With him, she'd have a family and also a kingdom. With him, she would never be alone again. She couldn't turn down his deal. It was too good to pass up. She would listen to her mother and finally be forgiven. Medea would not continue to make mistakes again.

Move fast, Medea. Do it now. Do not wait. Take what is yours, what you deserve. You can rule Mura with Osric at your side and have an army of children quickly. Then, get rid of the man, once you've used him for all you need.

"Yes, Mother. You are right," she said softly, feeling the influence of the dark witch who seemed to somehow live on inside her.

"I've reconsidered. I'll marry you," she agreed, watching the King smile even more. A pain went through her heart as she thought about Rhys and how much she'd miss him. Then she pushed the thought away. Rhys had lied to her. He had used her when he knew how lonely she really was. She couldn't trust him again. Rhys Blackseed had never offered to marry her or do anything with her other than to couple with her out of lust. The King offered marriage, a family, lots of children, and a title she would have earned instead of stolen.

That's right, Medea. That's a good girl. You don't want someone like Rhys. You want Osric. Listen to me, because I know what's best for you. I was the one who gave you life. Do this, and I will forgive you for taking mine.

"Yes, Mother. I will," she whispered, rocking her baby and giving the infant a kiss on the head. Tears dripped down her cheeks. She had to do this, because if she didn't, she would go to her grave feeling guilty for her mother's death. "I'll do it, so you'll forgive me," she whispered.

Good, Medea. And when you are done with the King, dispose of him. Keep listening to me, Daughter, and I will always be here to guide you. With me here, you will never feel lonely again.

Fifteen

"Look, there's the dragon," called out Zann, as the traveling party headed over the mountains on horseback, making their way back to Kascul-bough. The three men and Rapunzel made the trip. Alaina had stayed back with the fae since they were so shaken by everything that had happened. She had told them to go ahead and that she would meet up with them soon.

"My sister is not on the dragon," said Rapunzel, looking up at the sky. She rode atop the horse with Rhys.

"What does that mean?" asked Rhys.

"Medea wouldn't have gotten off the dragon and let it fly away on its own. Something must have happened to make her leave it," said Rapunzel. "She might be hurt."

"Medea is a powerful witch, so I don't think you need to worry about that," said Rhys.

"Not necessarily," Rapunzel continued. "We are in a strange land, and there is no telling how it might affect her powers. Plus, she's been exerting a lot of energy lately with all the shapeshifting that she's just learned to do."

"Did her mother teach her to shapeshift?" asked Darium.

"Nay," answered Rapunzel.

"Then how does she know how to do it?" asked Rhys.

"I guess it's just in her blood, since Hecuba was so good at it," stated Rapunzel.

"Kind of like me, Brother," said Zann. "No one taught me to shift, it just kind of happened on its own."

"I suppose," said Rhys in thought. Everything about Medea was mysterious. Mayhap that is why he'd taken a liking to her. He liked things out of the ordinary. "Do you really think she's hurt?" Rhys' heart softened toward Medea now. No matter how dark she became, he knew there was goodness inside her, because he had seen it. There was light magic as well, and he wanted more than anything to help her find it. He also would never want anything to happen to her.

"Rhys, I think I should transport and go ahead of you and try to find her," suggested Rapunzel.

"Did someone teach you to do that, or did it just happen on its own?" asked Zann curiously.

"Well, I have some powers, but I've just discovered them lately," explained Rapunzel. "I wasn't really taught to do it, but have watched my father transport many times. I guess it just came naturally. However, I'm not sure how far away it will work. I might have to just keep transporting up ahead a little at a time until I can make it all the way back to Kasculbough."

"Then go," said Rhys. "Medea might need you."

"What about the dragon?" asked Darium. "We can't just forget about it. What if it goes back to attack the fae folk?"

"I don't think it will," said Rapunzel. "My guess is that it went back to the caves and will return to the castle in the morning. Marco's dragon can be lazy at times."

"Doesn't that dragon have a name?" asked Zann.

"It does, but it is kept secret. Only Marco knows it," Rapunzel explained. "This way, no one can claim power over it by saying its name."

"Oh, kind of like the fae," said Darium. "Talia didn't even want to tell me her name when I first met her, because of that reason."

"What about food?" asked Zann. "Isn't that thing going to be hungry by now?"

"It only eats once every few days, and he was fed right before Medea took him," Rapunzel explained. "If the dragon does want to feed, it'll look for cattle or sheep first."

"First?" asked Zann. "Well, what if the dragon can't find a cow or a sheep to munch on? Then what will he eat? Us?"

"I can't answer that," said Rapunzel. "I'm not sure. I suppose it's possible it will try to eat people, but I hope we'll find it and get it home before that happens."

"Hopefully, it likes the taste of gnomes," mumbled Zann. "There were plenty of those inside the cave. However, they were so small that I hardly think they will fill the dragon's belly."

"Rapunzel, if you can find Medea, tell her... tell her I'm sorry. About everything," said Rhys.

"I can tell her, but when the darkness gets ahold of her, she won't listen to anyone."

"Then I hope you can get to her before the darkness takes total control. I honestly care for Medea. I don't want her to be evil. I want her to be happy and good."

"Don't we all," said Rapunzel with a sigh, waving her arm and disappearing.

"I'll never get used to that," said Darium, jerking and blinking when Rapunzel rapidly disappeared.

"Well, you'd better try," said Rhys.

"What does that mean?" asked Darium.

"I mean that Zann and I got used to giggling fae for you." Rhys looked over at him and grinned.

"Yeah. So?" Darium continued. "I fail to see how this has anything to do with Medea."

"It does, Brother, because I am not going to let her go."

"Rhys, you're talking nonsense," said Zann. "She belongs on the other side of the portal, not in Mura. She needs to go back. You said so yourself."

"I've changed my mind," said Rhys. "Medea seems so happy here and I believe she should stay on Mura if she wants to."

"Brother?" Darium rode up next to him. "I know that look. What are you planning to do?"

"I thought sending Medea back through the portal would protect her," explained Rhys. "But I see now that what she really needs is to be protected from herself. If I can help her do that, I want to at least try. Medea deserves a chance at happiness. She can't help it if she was born with darkness in her. But if I can help her control it, then mayhap she can live a normal life after all."

"That's a lot of *ifs*, Brother," said Darium.

"Well, here is one more for you," said Rhys. "If I can ever get Medea to forgive me, I think I'm going to ask her to marry me and be my wife."

When Rhys looked over at his brothers, both of their mouths were hanging open and neither of them said a word.

"Well then, since that's settled, I say let's pick up the pace." Rhys urged his steed forward down the mountain, anxious to see Medea once again.

* * *

Medea paced the floor of the tower room with the squalling baby in her arms, not knowing what to do to make the infant stop crying. She'd sent everyone away, including the midwife and refused the nursemaid that was offered. It was getting dark now, and the air coming in through the tower window became cool. She put the baby in the crook of her arm and headed over to the window to close the shutter. Right as she reached out for it, Rapunzel appeared in front of her, scaring her and making her jump back.

"Oh! Rap, you scared me," cried Medea.

"Medea? Are you all right?" asked her sister with concern in her voice.

"I'm fine, but you almost made me drop the baby. What is the matter with you?"

"Baby?" Rapunzel walked over and took the baby from her, cradling it in her arms. "She is so precious. Whose baby is it?"

"It's mine, of course."

Rapunzel's mouth dropped open. "Did you... did you have a baby? Is this Rhys' baby, Medea?"

"Yes and yes. Now give her to me." Medea pulled the baby out of Rapunzel's arms.

"Oh, my," said Rapunzel, holding her hand to her mouth. "If your baby was born in less than a day from being conceived, then it seems as if your child is going to be just like you. What is her name?"

"I don't know." Medea continued to rock the baby, but it just kept crying. "I haven't been able to think straight with all this noise. I haven't decided yet what to name her."

"Sister, if the baby is crying, that means it wants something. When is the last time you fed her?"

"I didn't."

"You didn't?" asked Rapunzel, sounding appalled. "Why not?"

"Because, I tried to nurse her, but I don't have milk."

"That's probably because you haven't had time to make any, with the magical pregnancy and birth happening so fast."

"I also tried giving her a bottle of milk, but she wouldn't drink it and I don't know why. Rapunzel, what do I do?"

"Well, the poor thing has got to eat."

"What did my mother feed me?" asked Medea.

"She had me feed you a blue liquid in a bottle, but I'm not sure what it was. It was something magical that you needed to grow and survive, since you aged a year every day."

"Oh, I think I know what it was, now. I remember finding some later when I got older. I tasted it and it was pretty good. I think I can replicate it." With a snap of her fingers, Medea materialized a bottle of blue milk. She put the bottle to the baby's mouth, and the child calmed instantly. "It worked! It seems since she is a magical baby, she needs a magical formula."

"That's good," said Rapunzel. "Medea, let's go back to the Blackseed's cottage and we can talk about everything there."

"Nay! I will not go there. Rhys lied to me and I never want to see him again."

"That's not true."

"King Osric told me the truth, so don't try to deny it. It was all Rhys' idea to kill me, just because he wanted to win favors with the King and become his heir."

"You can't really believe that. Rhys cares for you. A lot, Medea."

"He doesn't, and I don't care for him. At all."

Medea looked up to see her sister shaking her head. "Osric is the one for me. He's the one I need in my life, not Rhys."

"Nay, this is not you talking, Sister. That sounds more like Medea to me. It is the darkness taking control of you. I can see it since your eyes just turned black."

"I don't care what you say or think. It doesn't matter to me." *Get rid of her, Medea. She is only going to ruin your plans. Don't listen to a word she says. She never was anything but trouble.* "Rap, leave," commanded Medea, sticking her chin in the air.

"No. I'm not going to leave unless you come with me," Rapunzel protested.

"Well, I'm not going back to Rhys and that is final."

"Why not?" asked Rapunzel. "Rhys asked me to tell you that he's sorry, you know."

"He did?" Medea felt a stab to her heart. Part of her wanted to believe this was true. Just as she started to soften toward him, she heard her mother's voice in her head once more and now it was getting louder and impossible to ignore. *Rhys deceived you, Medea. He wanted you dead. You don't want anything to do with him.*

"I don't want to hear you mention Rhys again, Rap," she warned her sister.

"But Medea—"

"Ever! You can just tell him that I will never forgive him. I want nothing to do with him from now on."

"Medea, why are you acting so odd?" asked Rapunzel. "You and Rhys have a daughter now. Of course you want to see him. He's the father of your baby. Since you've already got a child, you two might even get married someday. Isn't that what you've always wanted? Then you'll never have to worry about being alone again. You'll have someone to love and someone to love you in return."

Osric will do all that. Don't listen to a word she says. She is trying to trick you. "I don't care about love anymore. That's not important," said Medea. "Nor do I want to ever marry Rhys."

"You don't?" Rapunzel's brows dipped. "Why not? I don't understand. You two seemed so happy together at the Whispering Dale."

"I won't marry Rhys, Rap, because it's too late."

"Nay, Medea. It's never too late. You two can make up, I'm sure of it. Every couple has quarrels. This will pass, I assure you."

"Nay!" she shouted. "You don't understand, Sister. I can't marry Rhys. I've already agreed to marry King Osric. We are going to raise an army of magical babies and make them into soldiers when we seize both Evandorm and Sethor." *Yes, Medea. This is the right thing to do.*

"Medea, what are you saying?" asked Rapunzel, sounding as if she were in shock.

"I am saying that I made the King a promise and I won't go back on it. When I say something, unlike other people I know, I mean every word of it." She also wanted more than anything to be rid of the guilt of her mother's death but didn't want to tell Rapunzel. She had a plan now, and when this was over, her mother will have forgiven her, and she wouldn't need to carry that guilt any longer.

"I certainly hope you don't really mean that," said Rapunzel, her mouth dropping open in surprise. Medea's sister looked sad and shocked, both at the same time. "Medea, if you marry King Osric, the darkness inside of you will rule *you*, as well as all your babies, for the rest of all time."

Sixteen

B y the time they'd made their way over the mountain, it was already nightfall. Rhys' brothers convinced him to wait until the morrow when they were refreshed to make an appearance at Kasculbough. It had been against Rhys' wishes, but when Rapunzel returned and told him the news that he had a child, he couldn't think straight. It was so unbelievable, that he didn't know what to do.

Back at the cottage, Rhys paced the floor while Darium's wife, Talia served them all something to eat.

"Rhys, please eat something," said Talia from the table. Rhys' mother had yet to return from the Whispering Dale.

"I can't," he said, pacing some more and running a hand over his hair in thought. "I'm too upset. I still can't believe I have a baby. A daughter," he said, thinking the more he said it, the faster it would lodge in his brain as being real.

"What's the matter, Rhys? Don't you want a baby?" asked Talia.

He looked up at her and made a face. "Aye, Talia, of course I do. Someday. Doesn't every man want children?

But instantly? This can't be real!" He was back to disbelieving again.

"It's not unlike the way Medea was born," explained Rapunzel. "Medea's magic is strong. Plus, you have different magic than her, altogether. There is no telling what can happen when you mix the two together. Not to mention, the baby was conceived in the very magical land of the fae in a field of lippenbur lilies, no less. It all makes perfect sense to me."

"Well, I think it's wonderful, and I am happy for you two. I can't wait until I have children," said Talia. "Plus, you have a girl, Rhys, which is rare for your family."

"Aye," agree Rapunzel. "She's a cute little girl who looks just like her father."

"Really? She looks like me?" Rhys' head snapped toward her and his eyes lit up with excitement.

"Aye. She has a full head of oaken hair, just the color of yours," reported Rapunzel.

"If the baby looks like Rhys, then it's ugly," said Zann, shoveling food into his mouth, no longer caring that he was eating fae food that was naught but seeds and roots.

"This is the first girl born to a Blackseed in a long time," commented Darium, taking another helping of food for himself. "Rhys, I think you might just have broken the Blackseed curse."

"Broken the curse?" asked Rhys. "Nay, not at all. I think I just created a new one." He started feeling upset again. "How could this have happened?"

"It's called lust," came a wiry little voice from the door. Elric walked in, leaving the door wide open. "You big oaf, what's the matter with you?" The elf walked over and slapped Rhys on the leg, not being able to reach much higher since he was so short. "You just sired a child of darkness. That baby will be evil, just like its mother and her mother before her. It'll be darker than The Dark Abyss, I tell you."

"Nay! Don't say that." Rhys kicked at the elf, but the little man sped away in a blur, appearing at the table now. "Why are you here? No one invited you, elf."

"No one had to invite me." Elric giggled. "I am a sage. I go where I want and do what I please."

Darium was about to take a bite out of a hunk of bread, but Elric ripped it out of his hand, chowed it down in the blink of an eye, and sped around the other side of the table to stand next to Zann.

"Stop that," growled Darium. "I don't like you taking my food."

"You don't need it."

"Yes, I do."

Elric made a face. "Oh, that's right. Now that you don't do much sin-eating anymore, you're probably hungry all the time."

"Elric, what is it you want?" asked Rhys. "Because, if there is no real reason for you being here, then please leave."

"Leave? Nope, can't do that." Elric shook his head furiously. He was still wearing the stupid jester hat he'd worn when he was the court fool at Macada Castle, even though his clothes were now all green. The little bells on the hat jangled. "I'm here on a mission, to give you a message from the gods." He snatched the wine goblet away from Zann, sucked down the liquid with a big slurp, and put the goblet back in his hand before anyone even realized what happened.

"Can someone please make him leave?" complained Zann, staring into the empty goblet. "I'm starting to see why Darium doesn't like him."

"Oh, shut up, you fool." Elric picked up a cloth

napkin and snapped it at Zann in a whipping motion, as if he were riding a horse and trying to make it go faster. Zann jerked backward to avoid being stung.

"Do that again, and I swear you'll be sorry," warned Zann. "I'll shift into a wolf, hunt you down, and eat you as an appetizer, since I never seem to get much meat in a meal anymore."

"Oh, Zann, watch that temper." The elf made a tsking sound with his mouth. "If not, you're going to turn evil, just like the witch girl."

"Her name is Medea," said Rhys through gritted teeth. "And she is not evil."

"Hmph. If only that were true." The elf eyed up a piece of cheese in Rapunzel's hand next.

"Tell us your message, and then leave," Rhys commanded.

"Okay, okay, calm down, man." Elric's eyes remained on the cheese. Rapunzel handed it to him. He nibbled it quickly like a rabbit, and then licked the crumbs from each of his fingers when he finished.

"Elric, if you'd like, I can set you a place at the table," offered Talia, in a kind gesture that the elf didn't deserve.

"No thanks," said Elric, licking his lips and burping. "I'm not really hungry. But now that you mention it, what's for dessert?" He stretched his neck looking over to the kitchen.

"Pie," Talia answered.

"The message, Elric," Rhys ground out, before the elf could even respond to the pie comment.

"Oh, yes. The message. It seems the gods wanted me to remind you, Rhys, that Medea was a very bad girl when she visited their temples."

"If you mean because she didn't leave an offering at

the pyramids, and that she stole the crystal key, then I already know about it."

"And the ring. Don't forget she also tried to take back your ring," the elf reminded him.

"Yes, I know," said Rhys. "Zoroct told me she'd have to pay for all of it, and she already has. She was unable to move or use her powers when leaving the pyramid. A sea serpent almost got her, but I took care of it."

"Nay, nay, nay. That's not what they mean." The elf chuckled as if he were amused.

"That was only a sample of what's to come."

It sounded as if what Rhys feared would happen was going to transpire. "What are you saying? Are the gods going to punish Medea *again*?" asked Rhys, hoping it wasn't so, but guessing it was probably true.

"Wouldn't you like to know," said Elric. "The gods told me everything."

"The gods don't even like you, so why would they tell you a single thing?" asked Rhys. "Plus, they warned me not to trust you."

"Naw, don't believe that. They say that about everyone," said Elric, swiping his hand through the air, making light of the situation. "Besides, I'm the official messenger of the gods."

Darium was drinking and spit wine across the table when he heard that. The elf zipped away in time, and the liquid hit Zann in the face.

"Sorry, Brother," said Darium, burying his nose in the goblet.

Zann groaned and wiped his face with his sleeve.

"The gods have to say things like that to sound important, but it's just a lie," said Elric as he kept changing his position in the room. He circled the table, his eyes staying focused on the food. "Don't pay any mind to it, I tell you."

"Nay?" asked Rhys. "Then why should I listen to this message you're telling me now? I trust you about as much as I trust that a skunet won't spray its stench. And I'd welcome a skunet into my home right now, over you."

The elf scrunched up his nose and tapped his foot on the floor impatiently. "If the gods didn't insist I tell you, I'd walk out right now without saying another word after that rude remark."

"Believe me, you'll get used to it," mumbled Darium, having been called a skunet many times in his life because of his two-toned hair.

"Go ahead," Zann challenged the little man. "Leave if you don't like it. It won't bother us a bit."

"Nay, wait," said Rhys, not wanting the elf to leave before he heard the message. If it was about Medea, he wanted to know. "What is the message? Tell me."

"Fine, I'll tell you. When the gods give a punishment, it is bigger than what already happened to Medea, I promise you. They do nothing in a small way. That was nothing, what already happened to her, I tell you. Nothing at all."

"All right, we get it," snarled Rhys. "Now out with the rest of it or I'll choke it out of you if I have to."

"Nasty, nasty," said the elf in a sing-song voice. "You are almost starting to sound like you have a dark side now too, Rhys."

"Keep stalling and you'll find out for sure," Rhys warned him.

"All right," said the elf. "No need for demonstrations. The witch is about to have something horrible happen to her. Something so shocking, that even she will never believe it. All because she didn't respect the gods."

"Horrible? How horrible?" asked Zann, picking up

a piece of bread. When he saw the elf eyeing it, he held it closer to his chest.

"If you want to know that, you're going to have to give me something in exchange for the rest of the information." Elric stretched out his arm with his palm up in the air.

Zann sighed and held out the bread.

"Not that, you fool. If I wanted that, I'd just take it." The elf hit Zann's hand, making him drop the bread.

"I'm tired of your games. I'll give you something you won't forget," said Rhys, drawing his dagger from his waist belt and heading over to the table.

"All right," said Elric, holding his hands out. "They are going to take something away from her that is important, and they're going to give her a test."

"A test? What kind of test?" asked Rhys.

"I don't know. They didn't tell me. Gotta go," said the elf, still eyeing the blade in Rhys' hand. He zipped over to the door in a blur, but stopped before leaving. "Talia-Glenn, what kind of pie was it you were offering?" he asked.

"Pazzleberry," she told him.

"Hmmmm."

Rhys headed for the door, still holding the dagger, just trying to frighten the irritating pest.

"Not my favorite, but thanks anyway." Elric was gone in a flash. Rhys closed the door after him, putting his dagger away.

"Well, now that we've gotten rid of him, what do you all think he meant by that?" asked Rhys.

"It's my guess that he really likes pazzleberries, but didn't want you skewering him, so he pretended not to," replied Zann.

"Not that," said Rhys. "I'm talking about the message from the gods. It sounds like something really bad is going to happen to Medea. I don't like this."

"I don't think we will have any influence over the decision of the gods," said Rapunzel. "We will have to wait to see what happens before we can try to help Medea. In the meantime, what is our plan for capturing the dragon?"

"I bet you miss your husband and baby," said Rhys.

"I do," Rapunzel admitted. "Every minute away from them feels like eternity."

"What is like to have a baby?" asked Rhys, curious to know now that he was a new father. "Do you like it?"

"Yes, I love it. So does Marco. My little boy Zane likes to ride the dragon with his father, even though I'm against it."

"Zane is a good name. It sounds a lot like Zann." Zann smiled proudly.

"Speaking of dragons, I'd like to know the answer as to how we'll capture it, as well," said Darium. "After all, that beast is going to start getting really hungry soon."

"Well, mayhap I can try to wrangle it. Then we can throw some ropes around it to keep it from flying," suggested Rhys.

"Nay, ropes will never hold a dragon," said Rapunzel. "It would have to be something like enchanted chains instead."

"Is that something you can do, Rapunzel?" asked Darium.

"I could try, I suppose," she answered. "Although I've never attempted it before."

"We're desperate," said Rhys. "We'll take all the help we can get."

"Then to catch it, we'll have to fool it somehow," suggested Zann. "Something like what Medea did by shapeshifting into the Dragon Lord."

"Nope. Shapeshifting into Marco won't work any-more," said Rapunzel. "Dragons remember. If they're fooled once, they are sure not to be fooled again by the same means. I cannot believe the dragon didn't realize Medea wasn't its Dragon Lord to begin with, since there is a definite connection between the dragon and Marco. Medea's powers must be getting stronger to pull off something like that. If I didn't know better, I'd say she had help."

"Help? From who?" asked Darium. "I don't believe anyone of Mura would help her do something like that."

"Nay, they wouldn't," agreed Rhys.

"I wish I knew the answer to that, but I don't," said Rapunzel. "I know Medea's mother, Hecuba is dead, but I swear some of the things Medea does are what I would expect from that evil witch instead."

"Mayhap we can lure the dragon to us using some kind of bait," suggested Darium.

"Like what?" asked Rhys.

"Food?" said Zann. "Or mayhap a female dragon?"

"Those are both good ideas, but I think I know something that dragons are attracted to even more than food," said Rapunzel. "Marco just told me this recently."

"What's that?" asked Talia.

"Marco said most dragons are vain and attracted to reflections of themselves."

"Like their reflection on the water?" asked Zann. "Little good that will do us."

"I suppose you're right," answered Rapunzel. "That might be why the dragon is staying so close to the sea in the caves. We'll need to lure it into some kind of enclo-sure. Mayhap we can do that with a polished shield. Or lots of them. The shinier the better."

Rhys put his hand to his chin in thought. "I think I

know where we can get everything we need to pull this off. I can get the shields from the armory at Kascul-bough Castle."

"Well, a lot of good that will do us, if we don't have a place to hold the beast," remarked Darium.

"I think I can solve that problem too," added Rhys. "We can use the oubliette—the large pit in the courtyard where the King throws his prisoners. If we capture the dragon in it, mayhap we can hold it there until we figure out how to fly it back to the portal. What do you think, Rapunzel?"

"That could work," she told him with a thoughtful nod. "Once the dragon goes into the pit attracted by its image on the shiny shields, I can use my magic to do the rest. I'll construct enchanted bars over the top of the pit that will hold it. Or at least for a while. Dragons are very strong. If angered, they can become vicious and de-structive."

"Rhys, do you think you can get King Osric to trust you enough to believe that you are doing this for him since he ordered you to capture the dragon?" asked Darium.

"I don't know," said Rhys in thought. "Since Medea is there now, he might not want my help. I really need to know the situation of what is going on before I can an-swer that. However, either way, I think I can sneak in and convince some of the soldiers to work with me. There are a lot of them who pay fealty to Osric, but would rather not."

"That sounds risky," said Talia.

"Medea is worth the risk," answered Rhys. "Mayhap I can sneak up to the tower and try to convince Medea to help as well."

"Nay, Rhys, that won't work and I'd advise you not to try to talk to Medea right now." Rapunzel seemed sad and upset. "My sister's emotions are going crazy, probably since she just had a baby. Right now she pretty much hates you."

"Hates me?" This disturbed Rhys more than anything. "Nay, that can't be. Medea and I are attracted to each other. I'm sure by now she's figured out the truth as to how I feel about her. We have a child together."

Rapunzel let out a sigh. "Rhys, I'm sorry, but since King Osric convinced her that you were the one who suggested killing her, she wants nothing to do with you."

"The bastard," growled Rhys, feeling his own anger growing now. "He most likely said that to save his own neck. I still can't believe Medea took him at his word. Why would she believe him over me?"

"It is odd," agreed Darium. "Especially since it seemed the two of you were hitting it off together."

"I'll just have to change her mind about me, and help her see the light," said Rhys.

"I'm afraid that might not be so easy." Rapunzel seemed as if she knew something else but was purposely not telling Rhys.

"What is it, Rapunzel?" Rhys asked. "Please, I need to know everything."

"I suppose you have the right to know," she answered. "Rhys, I hate to tell you this, but my sister has made an agreement with King Osric that I don't think you're going to like."

"An agreement?" asked Rhys, surprised and curious at the same time that Medea would do this. "What kind of agreement? Has she vowed to kill me now?"

"I don't know about that, but I do know that she has agreed to marry the King. They are going to seize the other two castles and rule all of Mura together with their army of magical soldiers that they're going to make."

"She's going to marry Osric? And have his babies?" This wasn't at all what Rhys wanted to hear. He slowly sank down atop Darium's bed. "Nay." He shook his head slowly, staring off into nothingness. "It can't be. She can't marry him. I won't let it happen."

"What about the part of seizing the other two castles and ruling all of Mura?" asked Zann. "Rhys, did you even hear that part at all?"

"It's not true. It can't be," mumbled Rhys.

"I assure you, it's true," Rapunzel confirmed the fact.

"She can't do it," Rhys muttered, not wanting to believe any of this. "She doesn't really want this."

"Brother, she's a powerful witch filled with evil right now," Darium reminded him. "She can do whatever she wants. And since I've seen the results of evil entities lately, I can confirm that there will be nothing you can do to change her mind."

"Nay. I won't stand for this," Rhys said stubbornly, jumping to his feet and starting to pace again. "Medea is not like that. I've seen a different side to her. She would never do those things on her own. Someone is influencing her."

"You've only seen the good side of my sister, while the darkness in her lay dormant," explained Rapunzel. "I have to agree with Zann and Darium. I don't think there is anything you or anyone can do to stop her, now that she's made her decision. As a matter of fact, Rhys, I don't think she'll ever agree to even talk to you, let alone give you the opportunity to get close enough to her to try."

"She's right," said Darium. "If the King is against

you now, you won't be able to step foot into the court-yard again either."

"Then I'll find another way to contact her, but I refuse to give up." Rhys would not let it go.

"Rhys, what other way is there?" asked Talia, cleaning up dishes from the table.

"I think I know a way to do it." Rhys stopped pacing and folded his arms over his chest as he stared at the ground. "I won't even try to approach her at the castle. I agree, that would be a mistake. Instead, I need to lure her to me, similar to the way we're going to lure the dragon into the pit."

"I don't understand. With a reflection of herself?" asked Zann with a chuckle.

"Nay, nothing like that," said Rhys. "I know a better way, even though I hate to use it. You see, I discovered that Medea is scared out of her mind of being alone, and having no one love her."

"She's not alone. She'll have the King," remarked Darium.

"And her baby," added Talia.

"Exactly," said Rhys, looking up at the others with a smile on his face. "If I know Medea, and I think I know her at least a little, since we've spent intimate time together, she will treasure that baby more than anything right now."

"She already does," said Rapunzel. "She didn't even want me to hold it, when I was just trying to help her to get the baby to stop crying."

"Mmmm hmmm," said Rhys, feeling more and more confident about this plan. "All we need to do is to distract her long enough for one of us to sneak in and steal the baby away from her."

"What?" asked Darium. "You're going to steal her baby?"

"You have gone daft, Rhys," said Zann. "You can't steal a woman's baby."

"Nay, Brothers, I haven't gone daft," Rhys told them. "It seems you are all forgetting it is also my child. I am the father, and have just as many rights to raise my daughter as she does."

"But she's the mother," protested Talia. "You can't take a newborn away from its mother."

"As Rapunzel pointed out to us, Medea is also filled with darkness right now that she cannot control," Rhys reminded them. "I personally think being around that darkness is harmful to my child."

"Perhaps you are right, but this is a magical baby," said Rapunzel. "It's not going to be easy to deal with the child either, believe me. I know, since I was the one who basically raised Medea. And I tell you, it was not pleasant."

"Oh, come on, Rapunzel," said Rhys with a chuckle. "It's just a little innocent baby. How much trouble can it really be?"

T hankfully, the next day, Darium was summoned to Kasculbough to sin-eat, therefore giving them a perfect opportunity to proceed with their plan.

"Remember," said Rhys from atop his horse as he and his brothers prepared to leave. "You've got to keep the King distracted so I can sneak to the tower to get the baby. After all, I don't think I'm welcome there right now, or else I'd just walk right in."

"I'll do the best I can and take my time sin-eating," replied Darium.

"Right. And I'll go in my wolf form, and distract the guards by making a few circles around the courtyard," said Zann, repeating his part in the plan. "When they start to chase me, Rhys will make his way to the tower to get the baby. Damn, why did I agree to this? What if they start shooting arrows at me?"

"That's what I'll be there for," said Rapunzel, exiting the house with Talia at her side. She and Talia had baskets filled with food over their arms. "I can use my magic to deter any arrows from hitting you."

"Talia, you're not coming with us," said Darium.

"Yes, I am, Husband. I want to be a part of this plan as well."

"Nay. You'll get hurt. You stay here and wait for us," said Darium once again.

"We are bringing offerings of freshly baked hand pies to tempt them," stated Talia proudly. "Actually, what they won't know is that I added enough semi-poisonous herbs into the food that it'll make them instantly sleepy and they'll fall fast asleep. It's enough to slow them down, but won't kill them."

"What makes you think you can get the soldiers to eat the goods right away?" asked Darium.

"I'm a fae, sweetheart. I have powers too, if you've forgotten."

"Nay, I still don't like the idea of the women being there," protested Darium.

"If there is any danger to her, I swear I'll get Talia out of there quickly," promised Rapunzel.

"You can do that?" Darium seemed to be considering the idea now.

"You already know that I can transport. I can also bring one person with me," Rapunzel explained.

"If so, then you can grab Medea and drag her back through the portal once Rhys opens it," said Zann, coming up with a plan of his own.

"Mayhap," said Rapunzel. "But if I go back through the portal without Marco's dragon, he'll have my head."

"Can't you just bring Marco back here to control the dragon?" asked Zann.

"I don't know. Perhaps. However, I don't want to take the chance that we wouldn't be able to get the portal open again once we're through it. If so, the dragon would be trapped in Mura, and that isn't going to make anyone happy."

"I agree," said Rhys, fingering the crystal pendant hanging on the chain around his neck. "I may have the key to the portal, but I've yet to try to make it work. We don't know what is going to happen. We'd better not risk it. The two women should go back through the portal at the same time as the dragon."

"Then mayhap we should be focusing on capturing the dragon instead of plotting to steal a damned baby." Zann grew frustrated, as always.

"We'll need Medea's cooperation if we're going to keep the dragon in the pit," explained Rhys. "I know that Osric is going to want to use that dragon for his own purposes once it's there. Medea is our only hope to pull this off, but I need to get her back on our side first."

"Then let's go, and stop wasting time talking," said Darium. "The sooner this is over with, the faster I can get back to my honeymoon. Murk," he called out to his raven. It flew over and landed on his outstretched arm. "We'll need your help too," he told the bird. "I want you as a scout to warn us if there is any danger." He turned and looked at his wife. "Keep a close eye on Talia," he told the bird. The raven squawked and flew off into the sky.

"Darium, stop worrying about me," said Talia. "If I am in trouble, I'll call the animals and all of nature to help me. You're forgetting that I can do that."

"I suppose I am," muttered Darium.

"Darium, remember that you can also use your new-found elemental powers if we need them," Talia told him.

"Thanks, Talia, but I don't feel confident about that yet," answered Darium.

"I'm not even sure what to do with them."

"I'm sure your mother could teach you," said his wife.

"Our mother has once again abandoned us, in case

no one has noticed," stated Zann, with malice in his voice as he mounted his horse.

"Well, I'm not going to abandon Medea or my daughter." Rhys turned his horse and led the way to Kasculbough.

* * *

Medea woke up to find that during the night, her baby had aged one year. She held her daughter in her arms, feeding her the magical blue milk from the bottle. Somehow, Medea felt gypped that she'd missed the entire first year of the little girl's life. This made her sad. It also made her unhappy that her baby was growing so quickly, just as she had. Did this mean her baby was magical too?

This thought didn't bother her, but the thought of the child having darkness inside her, did. After having finally had a few hours of sleep, things were looking better this morning. The sun shone in through the open window, and the sound of chirping birds outside reminded her of the beautiful Whispering Dale. It made her think of the intimate time she had spent with Rhys. Her heart ached for him this morning, making her want to be with him. The more she looked into their beautiful baby's eyes, the more she realized that her little girl really did look a lot like Rhys.

There came a small knock at her chamber door. Before she could answer, the door swung open.

"Prepare yourself for our wedding," said Osric, strutting in as if he had the right to intrude. "We'll be wed right after the Sin Eater is finished."

"Get out!" she shouted, holding up her hand and blasting the King with a bolt of magic. He flew back into the two guards standing watch at the door. They caught him before he could fall.

"What do you think you're doing?" he growled, not used to being treated this way.

"You have no right to barge into a lady's chamber without being invited in." She put the baby on the bed and stood up, still in her nightdress.

"Oh, is that all?" he asked. "I'm sorry, Mudera. I'll be sure not to anger you like this once we're wed."

"My name is Medea not Mudera! I'd think you'd at least know my name since you want to make me your wife." Medea's darkness might have been dormant throughout the night, but now it had been awakened by the disrespectful king with no manners.

"What happened to your baby?" gasped the King, straightening his clothes. "It cannot be the same one I saw yesterday. This one is three times the size."

"This is indeed the same baby," she retorted. "It is a magical baby. I told you that it would age quickly. My daughter is now a one-year-old."

"You told me, but I guess I didn't comprehend it." Fascinated, he walked back into the room. "It's amazing." He approached the bed.

The baby crawled around the bed, exploring the pillows.

"This is fantastic," he continued. "We'll make an army quicker than I even imagined. So, how fast can you crank these things out?"

"Pardon me?" she said, not liking the way he spoke about her child. "It is not a *thing*. It is a child. A baby. My daughter."

"Sure, sure it is," he said, waving away the suggestion, staring at the baby. "So how long after conception can I expect my first soldier to appear?"

"I-I don't know," she answered. "This baby was

born in one day after conception, but you need to remember the baby's father was magical too. You are only human."

"What?" he asked, his head snapping upward. "I thought this was the child of my knight, Rhys Blackseed. I recently discovered that his mother is a fae, but are you saying that he has special powers too?"

Medea could have kicked herself for pointing out this fact, even though the King probably would have figured out the details by himself in time. Still, she knew magic was prohibited on Mura and part of her didn't want Rhys to get in trouble.

"I don't think you need to concern yourself with my business," she snapped, feeling her anger and the darkness inside her growing just looking at the man.

"Of course, my lady, you're right."

His use of the title of lady simmered her emotions a little. She liked being referred to that way for some reason, even if back in Tanglewood she hated to be called *my lady* or *Queen*.

"When you are Queen, I will make certain never to pry into your business again."

"When I'm Queen? How about you start right now by addressing me with respect?"

"Don't sound so upset. After all, you'll be Queen soon, since we're to be married this morning. Let me see this magical daughter of mine." He reached out for the baby, and suddenly Medea became panicked. She didn't like the man calling the child his daughter. This was Rhys' baby, not his. She certainly didn't want him touching the baby either.

"Nay! Get away." Once again, she used her powers, sending the King sliding out the door.

"Medea, you really should learn to control your temper," grumbled the King, letting his guards assist him to a standing position once again. "Now, I've called for your handmaid to help you dress for the wedding. I've also taken the liberty of securing a gown for the wedding that I'd like you to wear."

"I don't need anyone's help. Now leave!" She scooped the baby off the bed and cuddled the little girl to her chest, as she turned her back on the King and walked over to stare out the open window.

"Of course, my love," said the King from behind her.

Medea shivered when the King called her his love. It didn't feel right. The only person she wanted to hear that from was Rhys. Osric didn't love her, and she certainly didn't love him. The only man she truly had feelings like this for right now was Rhys Blackseed.

"My lady?" came a small voice from the door. Medea looked back over her shoulder to realize that the King had left and Henriette stood in his place. She held what looked like a white wedding gown in her arms.

"Henriette?" she asked. "I thought you were the midwife, not my handmaid."

"I am both," said the woman, who looked old enough to have a child Medea's age. "May I come in to assist you in dressing?"

"I suppose," Medea answered with a sigh.

The handmaid entered and closed the door, stopping in her tracks when Medea turned around and she saw the baby in her arms.

"W-what happened to the baby?" she gasped.

"My child is magical," explained Medea. "If it's like me, it'll age one year each day until she turns eighteen."

"H-how can this be?" The woman truly looked scared. Now that Medea's anger was subsiding, she felt as if she wanted to calm her handmaid. After all, Henriette had been kind to her, and Medea liked her.

"Don't be frightened," she said with a smile. "It's the way my magic works."

"I see." The woman's eyes fastened to the baby. She stared at it, blinking, and looking astonished.

"Did you want to hold her?" asked Medea. This seemed to help the woman relax.

"Oh, could I? I do love babies."

"Of course. Put the gown on the bed." Medea was reluctant to hand her child over, but knew if she wanted the handmaid to trust her, she was going to have to let the woman hold the baby. "Here you are," she said, giving the handmaid the little girl. The handmaid's expression changed drastically and she smiled, hugging the baby to her chest, rocking it slowly.

"She is so cute. What is the baby's name?"

"I-I don't know," said Medea. "I haven't decided yet."

"Mayhap you should name her after your mother. What was her name?" The handmaid sat down on a rocking chair, rocking the child on her lap now. The little girl cooed with contentment.

"My mother?" Medea thought of the evil woman and didn't want her daughter to be that way. "Nay, I don't think so. Her name was Hecuba, and I don't like that name."

"Then how about if you name her after her father? But a girl's version of the name of course. What is her father's name?"

Medea felt protective over that information and didn't want to tell her. "I don't think that would be a good idea either."

"Oh, look, the baby is sleeping. I'll just put her down on the bed."

"She is sleeping? Already?" Medea glanced over to

her daughter in shock. The baby had kept her up most of the night, and it hadn't been easy at all to stop her from crying. This was amazing in an odd sort of way. "Oh, well then, why don't you help me dress and fix my hair?"

"Of course, my lady." As Henriette helped Medea don the wedding gown, Medea got to thinking about something the King said.

"Did I hear the King mention that the Sin Eater was coming to the castle this morning?"

"Yes, my lady," answered Henriette. "The King's falconer died suddenly in the night so the King called for the Sin Eater."

"I see." She held up her arms as the woman pulled the gown over her head. If Darium was going to be here, did that mean Rhys would be with him? If so, she wondered if Rapunzel had told him about the baby. Part of her wanted to see Rhys again. Part of her wanted to show him the child they'd conceived together in the field of lilies. But then, another part of her kept thinking of how he had deceived her. Nay, she decided. She never wanted to see Rhys again.

After dressing her, Henriette combed out Medea's hair. "There you go, my lady. You look beautiful." The woman smiled, perusing her from head to toe. "I am sure you are going to be the talk of all Mura."

"I'm sure I am," she said, thinking of the plan she and the King had to seize the Kingdoms of Evandorm and Sethor, claiming the title as King and Queen of all Mura. This plan had felt strong and right yesterday. However, now she was starting to waver a little in her decision. It didn't feel so good anymore.

Medea heard voices from outside and headed over to the window to look out. She gazed down into the courtyard, seeing Darium approaching the King. At the

King's feet was the dead body of the falconer. Bread and ale had been placed atop the corpse's body.

"My King," said Darium with a bow. His raven was on his shoulder, but flew up to the tower window, perching on the sill right by her. It stared at her as if it was trying to say something. "Today, we've brought food for everyone so I won't have to eat alone," Darium continued.

"Rap?" Medea mumbled to herself, seeing Rapunzel and Talia accompanying Darium. They held baskets of food. The women started to pass out hand pies to all the guards. When a little child asked for some, Darium brushed the boy away.

"This is a special treat only for the King and the soldiers," said Darium, making Medea suspicious. She wondered what was going on.

"I don't want any." The King refused the food, but Darium remained persistent. The raven scared her as it flapped its wings and left the sill, heading up to the roof of the castle.

"At least drink with me then, as I sin-eat," Darium told him. "For the sake of your poor falconer." He took a bottle of wine that Talia handed him from the basket, first drinking the ale from the chest of the corpse. Then he filled the empty goblet with wine from the bottle and handed it to the King.

"I don't need to drink to a dead man," complained the King. "Besides, I'm getting married in a few minutes. I'll celebrate afterwards."

"Then let us drink to your wedding, Sire," said Darium, making Medea very suspicious now. She didn't think any of Rhys' family would approve of her marrying King Osric.

"Nay, I don't want any," said the King, sounding irritated with Darium.

The next thing she knew, Zann appeared in the courtyard in his wolf form, howling and running around in crazy circles. All the men tried to catch him. When one guard on the battlements raised an arrow, Rapunzel turned around and used her powers to redirect the path of the arrow. It just missed the wolf's back end, scraping up against it.

"What's going on here, Blackseed?" growled the King.

"That's what I'd like to know," mumbled Medea. "Henriette, I need to get down to the courtyard. I think there is trouble. Can you watch my baby for me until I return?"

"Of course, my lady." Henriette walked over to the bed, sitting down by the little sleeping girl.

"I'll be right back," Medea promised.

Not wanting to waste time in actually walking down the stairs, Medea used her powers and disappeared, reappearing in the courtyard.

* * *

To Rhys' surprise, the plan was going smoothly. He was able to sneak through the courtyard and over to the keep without being spotted. He didn't think he'd even need to use the grappling hook and rope hanging at his side to scale the tower. He would probably be able to climb the stairs instead.

"What is going on here?" he heard, turning his head to see Medea materialize in the courtyard. His heart jumped. She was wearing a wedding gown, and looked more beautiful than ever. Her hair had been combed out, and her ebony locks spilled over her shoulders in a soft cascading flow like that of a waterfall. The neckline on the gown was low, and showed cleavage. Too much cleavage, in his opinion. Suddenly, he felt jealous, He didn't want Osric looking at her when she was dressed like that.

"Medea, my bride, the wedding will start in just a minute," said the King. "There seems to be a loose wolf in the courtyard that we need to rid ourselves of first."

Rhys didn't like King Osric calling Medea his bride. Rhys was about to storm over there when he heard a low growl from his side. He looked down to see Zann in his wolf form.

"Zann, good job," he said, as his brother shifted back into himself. Of course, Zann was naked. Rhys reached into the bag slung over his shoulder, throwing Zann his clothes. "I'm going up to the tower now to get the baby."

"Rhys, shouldn't we be preparing to capture the dragon? It's bound to show up soon." Zann took a few deep breaths since it was always exhausting to shift.

"Yes, you're right," Rhys agreed. "But we need Medea's participation, and taking the baby is going to bring her to me. This needs to be done first. Make your way to the armory and start collecting only the shiniest shields. Get as many as you can find and bring them to the pit."

"Me? You're the knight here. I think you should help me."

"I will. But first, I need to get my child. That's more important."

"Have it your way," said Zann, hurriedly dressing. "You know, I almost got shot out there. I felt the arrow graze my butt." He rubbed his backend, trying to see it.

"Rapunzel redirected the arrow, so you can stop complaining, Brother. Now, tell the women to get out of here," he said, noticing a few guards yawning and dropping to their knees. "I think the poisoned food is working."

Rhys quickly entered the keep without being seen. He made his way over to the tower and ran up the spiral staircase, approaching the bedchamber. There were no guards there, and he figured they heard the commotion and left to go out to the courtyard.

Rhys still wore his tunic with the King's crest on it. So, even if someone did see him, they hopefully would believe he was still one of King Osric's knights. He reached out for the door latch, but hesitated when he heard a baby crying from within the room. That was his baby, he reminded himself. It was the child that he and Medea conceived together. This whole thing still made his head spin. Realizing he needed to get out of here before Medea returned, he opened the door and stepped into the room.

The handmaid, Henriette, whom he knew well, sat on the bed trying to calm the squalling child.

"Sir Rhys?" The woman looked up in surprise. "It is nice to see you again. I didn't think you were still in the King's service."

"Well, I'm here, aren't I?" he answered, instead of outright lying.

"Lady Medea asked me to watch her baby until she returned. That is why I'm in here."

"Of course," he said, walking over and looking down to the little girl in the woman's arms who looked to be about a year old. She was a beautiful child with a full head of brown hair, matching the color of his own. Her eyes were also clear and emerald green instead of dark like her mother's. Rapunzel was correct in saying that his daughter took after him. He liked that a lot. It made his heart swell with pride. "May I hold her?" he asked, wanting more than anything to cuddle his daughter to his chest.

"If you can get her to stop crying, it would be appreciated." Henriette handed Rhys the baby and got up off the bed, straightening her wimple. She also handed him a bottle filled with blue milk.

"What in Zoroct's name is that?" he asked.

"I am not sure, but I think it is magical milk," answered the handmaid, giving him the bottle.

"What is her name?" Rhys held his daughter in his arms, feeling his heart open wide with love.

"Lady Medea has yet to name the child."

"I see." Rhys couldn't help but think of where the baby had been conceived. It was in a field of lippenbur lilies and it had truly been a magical night. The child was just as beautiful and as precious as those flowers of the fae folk. The little girl looked up to him with teary eyes. He reached out with his free hand and wiped away her tears, much the same way as he had done to the baby's mother.

"Don't cry, my precious little lily," he told her. "You daddy is here now."

"Daddy?" gasped the woman. "I didn't know you were the father of the child. However, now that you mention it, I can see the resemblance."

The baby was already a one-year-old little girl, and Rhys wished he had been able to see her when she'd first been born. Everything was moving so quickly in his life right now that it seemed like naught but a dream. He rocked the child in the crook of his arm and then bent over and kissed his daughter on the center of her forehead. The child cooed and giggled, reaching out and touching the crystal hanging around his neck. When she did, Rhys swore he smelled the scent of lippenbur lilies. He also saw a quick flash of light, and felt a connection with the child. It made him feel strong and alive. He was proud to be the little girl's father. Rhys' heart opened wide.

"Did you see that? There was a flash of light," said the handmaid. "It happened right after you kissed the baby and she touched that crystal at the same time."

"A flash of light? Did you really see something?" he asked, not sure he wanted to admit that he had not only seen it but felt it, too. Something magical transpired between him and his daughter, but he wasn't exactly sure what it was. Since he was so used to hiding magic, he didn't feel comfortable discussing it with the handmaid.

"I-I guess I am mistaken," said Henriette, not willing to talk about it either. "Well, I suppose you have things to do, Sir Rhys. There seems to be a ruckus down in the courtyard. I am sure you'll want to look into it." The woman reached out for the baby.

"Nay. I'll keep my daughter with me for now." Rhys was not about to hand the baby back to her. He pushed the bottle of blue milk into a bag hanging at his side. "I'm not needed down in the courtyard. You can go back to your duties now, Henriette. You are dismissed."

"But Lady Medea told me to watch her child. I'm not sure I should leave without her permission. Plus, I am not sure I should leave the baby with you."

"You are naught but a servant, Henriette. It's not proper for you to speak to a knight in this manner."

"I'm sorry, my lord. Please forgive my ignorance," she said, bowing her head.

"Go down to the courtyard and give Medea a message for me, please."

"Of course. What shall I tell her?" asked the woman.

"Tell her I need to talk with her. It is very important."

"I will tell her you are awaiting her in the tower," said Henriette.

"Nay, not here."

"Then where?"

"Just give her the message. She'll know where to find me."

"Of course, my lord." The woman left, quickly heading down the stairs. Rhys was about to leave after her, but heard voices at the foot of the spiral staircase and stopped. He realized it was the King's guards coming back up to the tower room. "Damn," he whispered. He needed to leave here with the baby before he was discovered. He couldn't be stopped from taking the child if his plan was to work.

He headed back into the room, closing the door. Then he placed the baby on the bed and hurriedly tied the rope around himself. Darium's raven landed on the windowsill, shrieking.

"I know, I know, Murk, but thank you," he said, realizing the bird was giving him a warning. He picked up the child and headed over to the window, sending the raven back into the sky. Once the grappling hook was securely latched onto the sill, Rhys held the baby protectively in one arm, and used his other to lower himself to the ground. He was halfway down when the baby started wailing.

"Shhh," he said, hoping to silence the little girl. If he couldn't, the child would give away his presence here. He couldn't grab the bottle now since he needed to hold on to the rope. "Quiet, my little Lily," he said, deciding to name the child since Medea hadn't bothered to do it. "You are going to get us into a lot of trouble."

As soon as his feet hit the ground, he felt Medea's presence. He whirled around to see her standing there with her hands on her hips and a frown on her face.

"What do you think you are doing, Rhys Blackseed?" she spat.

"Medea. Nice to see you again, too," he said, flashing her one of his best smiles.

"You are stealing my baby?"

"Our baby," he corrected her. "And I wasn't really stealing her. I just wanted to see my daughter, and I knew you wouldn't let me."

"Hand her over!" she all but screamed. Her eyes started getting really dark now. He knew that meant that the evil inside her was starting to take over.

"Now wait a minute, Medea. I only came for little Lily, because I knew you'd come looking for her. Then, I'd have a chance to talk with you. If I just showed up here, you'd want nothing to do with me, since the King told you that awful lie about me."

"Lily?" she questioned. "Is that what you called her? That's not my baby's name."

"Nay, I know it isn't. The handmaid said you didn't name the child. I took the liberty of naming our daughter Lily, since she was conceived in a field of lippenbur lilies."

"That handmaid let you have her?"

"Now, don't be mad at Henriette," said Rhys, holding up a hand. "None of this is her fault."

"I'll be mad at whomever I want to, and you are number one on the list, Rhys Blackseed. How could you ever even consider kidnapping an innocent child?"

"I told you, I was only taking Lily with me for now, because I knew you'd come for her and I would then have the chance to talk to you. I would never hurt her. She's my baby, too."

"Stop calling her Lily." The child continued to wail.

"Medea, you can't believe those lies that King Osric told you about me. I swear, it was his idea to kill you, not mine. Besides, you know how I feel about you. I could never hurt you. I saved you from the sea serpent and the wrath of the gods—that should prove it." The raven cried out from the sky, flying in circles above Rhys' head now. The baby cried even louder.

"I suppose you're right. I wouldn't put it past King Osric to make up that lie. But even so, you are not proving a thing by what you're doing now. Give me my baby." When Medea tried to take the child from him, something happened. A buzzing noise filled the air, and some sort of shock wave hit Medea, knocking her to the ground.

"Medea? Are you all right?" asked Rhys in surprise, not sure what just happened.

"Why did you do that?" Her eyes bore fire. "You are purposely trying to keep my baby from me and I don't like it."

"Nay, I didn't do that, Medea," he said. "Honest. I don't know what happened." The raven continued to shriek, and the baby cried even harder. But above all the noise, he heard something else that took his interest. It sounded like the sound of large flapping wings. He looked up to the sky and swore. "Damn it, not now!"

"It's the dragon," screamed Medea, hurriedly getting to her feet.

The dragon flew over to the courtyard, while Rhys took off at a run, protecting the child against his chest. Medea was right behind him.

When he got to the courtyard, things only became worse. The plan to put the soldiers to sleep by eating Talia's food worked too well. The only ones not prone on the ground sleeping were Darium, Talia, Rapunzel, King Osric, and a few stray guards. It seemed their plan had backfired. They would never be able to capture the dragon now. They needed more help.

"Everyone, get to safety!" Rhys shouted, as the dragon swooped downward. With outstretched talons, it picked up a stray pig from the courtyard, and took it back up into the sky. It tossed it into the air and devoured it whole.

Women shrieked and children cried in fear.

"Capture it!" called out the King, but he had no men there to help him do much.

"I've got the shields," called out Zann, running from the keep with his arms full of shiny shields.

"Let me help," called out Darium, taking half of them and heading at a run for the pit.

"Medea, get me atop that dragon," screamed the King. "We need to use it now to conquer Sethor and Evandorm."

"I'm not going anywhere or doing anything until I have my baby." Medea reached out once more for the baby, and once again ended up on the ground.

"It wasn't me!" shouted Rhys, watching Medea's features change. "I don't have the power to do that." Her face almost seemed to twist and distort when the darkness filled her.

"You will die for this, Rhys. No one takes my baby." Her eyes became black and so did her disposition. It didn't seem like Medea's words at all, and even her voice sounded different. Rhys was starting to feel as if she were somehow possessed.

"I told you, I didn't do it," he spat. "I don't know what is going on."

"I do," said Rapunzel, running over to them with Talia on her heels. "I think it was the baby. She doesn't want to go to you, Medea, because you are acting evil."

"That's not true. My baby loves me," screamed Medea, turning into someone else now entirely. Rhys had never seen her look so mean. Her eyes narrowed to slits and were darker than ever. Her face contorted, making her look older than her real age. She almost seemed to have a dark aura around her. It was almost as if she were standing in a black cloud. It only made the baby cry even more.

"I will make you pay for this, Rhys. You turned my own child against me."

"Sister, stop it," shouted Rapunzel. "This isn't you. You sound more like Hecuba right now. Please, stop it. Rhys is the baby's father. He would never hurt your daughter."

There was no reasoning with Medea when she was like this. There was too much darkness controlling her to even get through to the light hidden inside.

The dragon swooped downward again, coming right for them. Rhys realized he needed to do something about the beast now, and would worry about talking to Medea later.

"Rapunzel, take the child to safety, please," he said, pushing the baby into her hands, giving her the bottle as well. "Bring her to my mother. She'll be safe amongst the fae."

"Nay! Sister, you will not leave here with my child." Medea's anger was out of control now. She raised her hands in the air, and a cart filled with hay shot over their heads. The roof blew off the mews and kennels, and the swords of the sleeping soldiers flew through the air on their own.

"Get Lily out of here. Now!" ordered Rhys, ripping his sword from his scabbard, ducking just as a sword sailed over his head.

Rapunzel disappeared, transporting out of there with the baby.

"I'll call the animals to help us," said Talia, shouting to be heard over the loud roar of the dragon.

"Nay," said Rhys. "The dragon is hungry, and that will only entice it. We won't sacrifice any more animals."

"Then I hope you have another idea," said Zann, running back from the pit with Darium. "We put the shields inside, but the sky is dark. There isn't enough sun to reflect and capture the dragon's attention."

"They're trying to capture our dragon," King Osric shouted, ripping his sword from his belt and holding it toward the men. Zann and Darium instantly drew their weapons as well. "Medea, stop them. And get that dragon down here so we can conquer the other two kingdoms."

Rhys looked over at Medea, catching her eye. The darkness inside her was getting scary. She honestly looked as if she wanted to kill someone, probably him.

"Medea, fight the darkness. You can do it. Don't give in to it," Rhys told her.

Medea's face was stone-like. She raised her hands in the air and chanted something that Rhys couldn't understand. The dragon swooped downward. Rhys and his brothers swiped at it, but of course it did no good. Then, before Rhys knew what was happening, Medea was atop the dragon, and she'd taken King Osric along with her.

"Yes! We're going to do it, my dark Queen," shouted Osric from atop the dragon, holding on tightly to Medea as they rode through the sky.

"Medea, come back," yelled Rhys, feeling so helpless as the dragon made a circle above Kasculbough and then headed toward Evandorm. "Don't do this," he shouted, but it was too late.

Medea's darkness had consumed her. Now, somehow, she controlled the dragon. She would use it to her advantage to do the bidding of the evil king.

"Zoroct's eyes, we're in trouble," Rhys told his brothers.

"We've got to warn Evandorm and Sethor," shouted Zann. "They'll all be killed."

"There's nothing we can do. We'll never make it there in time, before them. It's too late," said Darium. "It seems as if Medea has no intention of returning until she has killed off the other kings and helped Osric claim both kingdoms."

"I can make it to Evandorm in my wolf form," said Zann. "It's not far, and if I run, I'm sure I can make it." He shifted into a wolf and took off at a run.

"This can't be happening," said Rhys, lowering his sword. "I refuse to believe the woman I care for, and the mother of my child could kill others. I don't believe that she could be so filled with greed, anger, and hate that she would want to claim that much power."

"Believe it," said Darium. "Your girlfriend is about to become the darkest spirit in all of Mura."

"This is bad. Really bad," said Rhys.

"With a fire-breathing dragon to do their bidding, and also Medea's black magic, we are all doomed," agreed Darium. "This will even be worse than the evil that escaped through the portal of the Land of the Dead."

"I hope you're wrong," said Rhys, shaking his head, feeling somehow this was all his fault. As much as he wanted to believe his brothers were mistaken, he was afraid that what they said was true. Medea's darkness had totally consumed her. Rhys wasn't sure there was anything that he or anyone could do to bring her back to the light.

Eighteen

Medea rode through the sky atop the dragon, with King Osric hanging on for dear life. She hated everyone and everything at this very minute. Rhys took away her baby, and that was the only thing that had helped her keep her sanity. She could feel the struggle of the light and dark within her, and the darkness was starting to win.

Kill the Kings and claim their thrones, came the voice of her mother in her head. *You will hold all the power of Mura. You want it. You deserve it. It belongs to you.*

"Here's Evandorm," yelled Osric from behind her. "Bring the dragon down and burn them out. Kill them all and it will be mine. I will rule all of Mura. It will be all mine. I will be the only king."

She noticed that King Osric was no longer using the word *we*, and had reverted to *I*. He was a greedy, horrible man. She supposed it should bother her, but at this moment, it really didn't.

"Down, dragon," she commanded, and surprisingly it listened. She wasn't sure but the dragon almost seemed frightened of her. "Burn their village." She managed to get the dragon to swoop down, noticing all the armed soldiers and people running in the courtyard.

"That's right. Blast that group of soldiers," yelled the King, shaking his fist and cheering. Just as the dragon was about to kill them all, she heard the shriek of a bird. She turned her head see it was Darium's raven. It flew right in front of them and was about to be scorched. The raven reminded her of Rhys, and then she thought of the baby—their baby. Right as the dragon was about to singe the people, she managed to pull it up. The fire hit the roof of the castle instead, sending up a large plume of black, billowing smoke. The flags atop the spires flying the crest of the King of Evandorm blazed with flames like lit torches.

"What did you do?" screamed the King. "Go back and kill them. Do it!"

Medea looked down to the courtyard to see Zann. She somehow couldn't kill Rhys' brother. That bothered her, although she didn't know why.

Kill the wolf, she heard in her mind, but she tried her hardest to shake the thought away. She liked Zann and didn't want to hurt him.

"I'm going to Macada Castle," she said instead, managing to use her magic to direct the dragon to the next castle.

"Nay. Wait!" shouted the King, almost falling off when she pulled up and turned the dragon quickly. "I haven't seized Evandorm as mine yet. Go back," he cried.

"Shut up!" she shouted, starting to get irritated with the man. She chanted a spell to keep the dragon under her command. Then she directed it to the west coast of Mura. Macada Castle and the kingdom of King Sethor came into sight.

On the way there, she passed over the Goeften Forest, seeing Darium Blackseed's little cottage down below. Talia was out front, looking up into the sky directly at them. Medea started thinking of the meals they'd shared there, as well as the hospitality. This was the first place she and Rapunzel went after they came through the portal. Part of her started to long for the friendship of Talia and the others. They were like friends to her, and that was something she never had back in England.

Remember, Rhys was going to kill you, came the dark thought in her head.

"Nay, that's a lie," she mumbled, but the dark voice of Hecuba within her was strong and convincing.

He only said that to steal the baby. Rhys needed a way out and you gave it to him, you fool. Of course he wants you dead. Then the baby will be all his.

Hearing this only managed to make her furious once again.

"Faster. Faster!" she commanded the dragon, kicking her heels into its sides. The dragon didn't like it and turned its head and roared at her. The wind hit her hard in the face, blowing her hair around her.

"Get your damned hair out of my face, witch," spat King Osric. "I can't see a thing."

She didn't like the way he spoke to her, and did nothing to tie back her hair. When they got above Macada Castle, she saw everyone running around in chaos once again.

"There's the King. He's up on the battlements with his guards. Scorch him!" cried Osric in vengeance.

Medea had the dragon swoop in closer, controlling it by using her dark magic to make it go where she wanted it to. "Scorch them," she commanded the dragon, feeling the darkness growing and taking control of her again. But just as the dragon was about to do her bidding, she noticed a little girl holding the hand of one of soldiers on the battlements. The child would be killed as well. This made her think of her daughter and how she would never want anything to happen to her. She turned the dragon just in time. Instead of the men being killed by the dragon's fiery breath, it hit the back of a hay cart that went up in flames.

"Damn it, can't you aim this beast?" shouted Osric. "Let me do it. I'll control the stupid thing. You need to show it who is in charge." The King stabbed the tip of his sword into the dragon's wing. The dragon screeched and shrieked, rising up almost in a vertical position. The King dropped his sword and it fell down into the court- yard of Macada Castle. Then, he started to slip, grab- bing on to Medea, and pulling her along with him.

"Nay!" Medea shouted, trying to shake him off, but he clung tightly and she couldn't loosen his hold. "Take us back, dragon," she commanded, holding tightly to the dragon's leathery mane. She didn't want to trans- port, because if she did, she would lose the dragon.

The dragon was in a frenzy now. Instead of flying back to Kasculbough, it took off over the Picajord Mountains.

"Help me," cried the King, gripping on to Medea's skirt. He bounced up and down against the dragon's sharp scales every time the dragon turned. King Osric was poked and pierced by the spikes of the dragon's tail as well. Blood oozed from his wounds. Then the drag- on's wings hit him in the face. His hand was slipping and he was about to fall off. If he fell, it would mean his death.

"Damn you, die then. I don't care," Medea ground out, meaning to let him fall. Then, she looked down and saw something that melted her heart of ice. They were directly above the Whispering Dale on the other side of the mountains. She could see the field of lippenbur lilies where she'd made love with Rhys and where her daughter had been conceived. The alluring scent of the flowers of the fae drifted up high into the sky filling her senses. She breathed it in, and almost cried. Part of her longed to be happy again, the way she was when she visited the Whispering Dale with Rhys.

"Pull me up," shouted the King. "You can't let me die."

Her heart softened. Did she really want to see anyone die? She reached down and pulled the King back up onto the back of the dragon. And when she did, she looked down to see the colorful fae cottages and the enchanting arched bridges that went across the creek. There, on the bridge was Rapunzel, holding Medea's baby. Alaina, Rhys' mother, was with her. They looked up in the air, seeing her, making Medea feel so ashamed of her actions that she wanted to die.

"Medea, please don't let the darkness claim you," screamed Rapunzel. "Your baby needs you. Rhys needs you. So do I, Sister."

Medea felt something wet on her cheek. When she reached over to touch it, she realized it was a tear. The dragon beneath her was wounded now, and would no longer listen to her commands. The King was wounded as well. The dragon flew rapidly back to the Quamm Caves where it had been making its lair. Right over the top of the caves, it bucked like mad, trying to get Medea off its back. With her heart opened now, her dark magic was losing its power.

She could no longer control the dragon, and neither could she continue to hold on to it for much longer. Reaching back, she grabbed on to the King's arm just as they fell from the dragon and plummeted to the earth far below.

"Naaaaay!" screamed the King, as they headed for

their death atop the sharp rocks of the caves. But just before they hit, Medea was able to tap into her powers of transporting. When they fell, they landed in the black waters of the moat of Kasculbough Castle instead.

Medea surfaced and so did the King, coughing and spitting out water.

"You wretched witch," shouted King Osric. "How could you do this to me?"

By now, whatever sleeping potion Rhys' family had used on King Osric's men had worn off. The soldiers came running to their king's rescue.

"I'm injured. Be careful you fools," yelled the King. When his men pulled him out of the water, Medea could see his shredded clothes and the lacerations made by the scales of the dragon. His face was mangled and his body bruised. He was bleeding profusely and couldn't even stand on his own.

Medea climbed out of the moat. Her white wedding dress had turned a shade of gray mixed with brown from all the dirt and smelly water. Her hair was matted down, and green scum from the water clung to her body.

"Take me to my solar," said the King, barely able to speak since he was so weak. He had to be carried there because of his condition.

"My lady, are you all right?" Henriette was the only one to come to help Medea.

"I'm fine," she answered, pulling a slimy strand of long hair away from her mouth.

"Let me help you get back to the tower. I have a hot bath prepared for you in your chamber since I thought you might like one when you returned."

"Thank you," said Medea, looking around as they walked over the drawbridge and back into the court-yard of Kasculbough. Somehow, she had hoped to see Rhys, but he was not here. Right now, she'd even feel better if she just saw one of his brothers, or mayhap his mother or Talia. Sadly, she knew she wasn't going to see any of them since she knew where they were. Medea had seen the location of all of these people from the air, except for Rhys, the person she wanted to see the most.

All the friends she'd made here, as well as Rhys' family, were all with the ones they loved. They were at their homes where they should be. Home. The word hit her like a boulder to the gut. Where was her home now, she wondered? It used to be at Tanglewood Castle in England. However, that seemed like naught but a dream. How could she ever return there after what she'd been through on Mura?

Medea had felt at home in the Whispering Dale and amongst the fae folk. She liked it there so much that she had never wanted to leave. She had even felt comfortable and accepted when she'd visited the Blackseed cottage. Now, she felt like she didn't belong at any of these places, and neither would she be accepted anywhere after what she had just done.

"I'm sorry your wedding didn't take place as planned," said Henriette, being kind as usual, helping Medea up the spiral staircase to the tower bedchamber. Medea was so soaked from the rancid moat water that with every step she took her shoes squeaked. Her body reeked like sewerage or perhaps decomposing bodies of enemies that were at the bottom of the moat. She couldn't stand the smell of herself. "I'm sure the King will reschedule the wedding as soon as you are both healed," Henriette assured her.

"Yes," Medea answered, thinking about how the King acted when he was on the dragon. People said she had a dark side, but this man was power-hungry and mean and so much worse. He didn't care whom he killed to get what he wanted. She didn't like that in the least.

Entering the tower room, the first thing Medea found herself doing was looking for her baby. Of course, her daughter wasn't there.

"I'm sorry about what happened with your baby, my lady," said Henriette. "I understand you're upset with me and I will accept any punishment you feel is fit."

"Punishment?" Medea looked up, deep in thought.

"I deserve to be punished for not protecting your baby." The woman lowered her head.

Medea knew that her baby was in good hands. Rhys, his family, and Rapunzel would make sure the child was safe. She realized now that the one the child wasn't safe with, was herself.

"There will be no punishment nor any reprimanding, Henriette. It wasn't your fault."

"Thank you, my lady. That is very kind of you. Let me help you change out of your wet clothes. You must be chilled and want to warm your body in the hot bath."

"There's no need to help me. Take the rest of the night off," Medea told her. "I can tend to things myself."

"Thank you, my lady," said Henriette, bowing and backing out the door. "Do not hesitate to call for me if you need anything at all. If not, I will see you in the morning."

"Henriette?" Medea stopped the woman just as she was about to close the door.

"Yes, my lady?"

"Tell me something. Why are you so kind to me, when I have been nothing but mean?"

"I am your maidservant," she answered. "It is my job."

"Oh. I see." Medea's heart sank to hear that the woman only did it out of duty. "That will be all," she said, dismissing the woman. Henriette closed the door and once again Medea was all alone.

She opened the shutter on the window, wanting to watch the moon and stars while sitting in the bath. It was getting dark already, and it looked like a storm was approaching. With a flick of her hand, she was naked and sitting in the hot tub. The water felt comforting to her aching body. It wasn't easy riding on the back of a dragon and it had taken a toll on her. Especially since she had just birthed a baby. She needed to rest. There was soft soap and a clean cloth that the handmaid had left for her, along with rose petals that were sprinkled atop the water.

Medea picked up a rose petal, holding it between two fingers, feeling the softness of it. Then she brought it to her nose for a sniff. It smelled nice, but could not compare to the scent of lippenbur lilies. She washed and relaxed in the hot water, becoming very sleepy. Henriette was right about the bath. It felt wonderful. What didn't feel good was the fact that she was once again all by herself. Now she didn't even have her baby for comfort.

Medea thought about transporting herself to the Whispering Dale to steal her child back, even though it was exactly what Rhys wanted. The main reason she didn't do it, was because when she tried to take her little girl from Rhys earlier, the baby had used her magic to keep Medea away. Even her baby didn't want her near, because of the darkness inside her. It made Medea cry.

Staring out the window at the stars and moon starting to appear, Medea thought about the magical night with Rhys in the field of lippenbur lilies as she continued her bath. She longed to be there right now. Why couldn't she be with him again?

"I would give anything to be Rhys' wife and raise our child together," she said aloud, being totally honest with herself. "I wish it could be so," she whispered, staring straight up at the brightest star in the sky.

She'd had an exhausting day, and her eyes started to close. Too tired to even get out of the bath, Medea leaned her head back and fell asleep, hoping to dream about Rhys and baby Lily, since this is the only way she would ever see them again.

Nineteen

Rhys managed to sneak back into Kasculbough Castle later that night, having helped his brothers at both Macada Castle and Evandorm to put out the fires and tend to the injured. Thankfully, there had been no actual deaths from Medea's little escapade with the dragon. Unfortunately, both King Grinwald and King Sethor were so furious that they were already planning an attack on Kasculbough. What a mess Medea had made of things.

Even so, Rhys didn't want anything happening to her. He missed her and longed to talk to her and hold her in his arms once again. Standing below her tower window, he tugged on the rope that was still attached to the grappling hook fastened to her window. He looked around once more, and when he was sure no one was watching, he scaled the tower, making his way to Medea's room.

Rhys pulled himself into the room and landed with a soft thump inside the chamber. It was dark in there. In the moonlight coming through the window, he could see Medea relaxing in a tub of water with her head back and her eyes closed.

"Medea?" he whispered, making his way over to her.

When he got closer, he heard her whimper in her sleep. He glanced down to see that she'd been crying. "Medea, sweetheart," he said, putting his hand out to gently touch her. Her body felt freezing cold. Dipping his fingers down into the water, he realized it was frigid. "Medea," he said again, but couldn't seem to wake her. Removing his weapon belt so he wouldn't hurt her, he then scooped her out of the water and carried her over to the bed. As he put her down between the covers, he noticed she was shivering and her teeth chattered.

Rhys looked around, but the only clothing he could see in the dark room was the foul-smelling, dirty wedding gown laying on the floor in a puddle of water next to the tub. Not wanting to leave her like this, he decided there was only one thing he could do to help her warm up.

After bolting the door, he quickly undressed. He took off all his clothes, and lay down in the bed next to her. Then he pulled the covers up around them both. He laid his arm over her for warmth. Medea whimpered again and turned on her side, snuggling her face up to his chest, never waking.

"My sweet, sweet, Medea," he said, kissing her wet hair, not even caring that he was getting wet now too. With his arms around her, he stroked her head and kissed her cheek. Then, watching the moon and stars out the window, his eyes drifted closed and he fell asleep with Medea in his embrace.

* * *

Medea woke in the night, thinking she was dreaming. She found herself out of the tub and snuggled up in the warm protective arms of Rhys atop the bed. It felt so good that it made her want to cry. She had been dreaming of Rhys and also of her baby all night long. Her heart ached with sadness. Never had she felt as lonely as now.

"You're up," she heard the deep, sexy voice of Rhys, thinking this dream was ever so real. "Medea, are you all right?"

When she heard that, she looked up to see Rhys' beautiful green eyes looking down at her in concern. It was at that moment that she realized this was no dream. This was real.

"Rhys?" She bolted up to a sitting position in bed, looking down at his face bathed in the moonlight streaming in through the open window. His long oaken hair fell around his shoulders, making him look ever so handsome. She could even see the crisp, curly hair on his wide, strong chest. "Is this a dream? Are you really here, Rhys?"

"Aye, it's real. I am here, Medea."

Then she thought of everything that happened, and how he took her baby from her. It only managed to make her start feeling sad and mad again.

"Go away, Rhys. I don't ever want to see you again," she said, hitting him with both fists against his chest. Filled with emotion, she started crying.

"Hush," he told her, grabbing both of her wrists in one of his big hands. "Medea, please don't do this. I came here to tell you I'm sorry. I wanted to tell you that I... that I love you."

Her heart jumped into her throat and she stopped struggling with him. "What did you say?"

"You heard me."

"Aye, but what did you mean?"

He smiled and chuckled lowly. "What does it usually mean when someone says they love you?"

"I wouldn't know," she answered. "No one has ever

told me that they love me before. I'm not sure how to react."

"Well, then, I'll tell you what it means. It means that I want to spend the rest of my life with you, raising little Lily together. I want us to be a family."

Medea gasped and held her hand to her mouth. This is everything she wanted. That made her think once again that it was only a dream, since good things didn't happen to her.

He had no right naming your child, came that all too familiar dark voice in her head.

"I told you, Rhys, Lily is not the baby's name." The voice in her head made her push aside Rhys' previous words. Medea sniffled and wiped a tear from her eye with the back of her hand.

"Then what do you want to call her, Medea?" he asked. "I'll call our daughter any name you choose, but she needs a name, sweetheart."

"I-I'm not sure."

"I named her Lily because she was conceived in a field of lippenbur lilies. I think it's fitting. It was a magical, special place, and a night I will never forget."

"Oh," she said, starting to decide that she rather liked the idea now. She sank back down and laid her head against his chest. "I suppose we could call her Lily." She took a deep breath and released it, hoping the voice of her mother wouldn't start up again in her head. "Although I was almost thinking of calling her Rae, since she is such a ray of sunshine in my life."

"Then why don't we call her both names?" Rhys suggested. "Lily-Rae sounds pretty. And since our daughter is part fae, it's perfect. You know, those faeries always seem to have two names."

"All right," she said with a smile and a nod. "Lily-Rae it is. I like that." Then she bolted upright in a sheer panic. "Rhys, where is our baby? Is she safe? Why don't you have her with you?" Still being half asleep, this thought just occurred to her and caused alarm.

"Calm down, sweetheart," he told her, pulling her closer to him. "You know that she is in the Whispering Dale with my mother right now. When Rapunzel returned to the cottage in the forest earlier, she told me that you saw them there when you flew overhead on the dragon. She also told me you almost fell to your death."

He wanted you to die. He was hoping you feel to your death. The voice in her head broke through once more.

"So is that why you're here, Rhys?" she asked. "Are you here just to see if I am alive or really dead?"

"Nay. Of course not. Rapunzel also told me that she saw you and the King disappear when you used your magic. I figured you'd come back here."

"Oh, I see." She took another deep breath and released it. It all made sense to her. "We ended up in the moat," she told him. "I don't know how I missed my mark."

"What were you aiming for? The tub of water?" he asked with a chuckle.

"Actually, the wagon of hay." She giggled now too.

"Medea, I don't want you to marry King Osric. And I want you to believe me when I tell you I didn't come up with the idea to kill you. That was all him."

"I know that, Rhys. After I saw how evil the man is, I realized that he had come up with the plan to have me killed and just told me a lie about you. You are not that way at all."

"True, but I was tempted by darkness within me at first, Medea, and I am not proud of it. I told you all about that already. I did consider taking the King's offer briefly, and I only hope you can forgive me. It was wrong, and I am ashamed that I almost gave in to the dark side within me."

"Rhys, you don't have darkness in you. Believe me, I know what darkness is."

"Yes, I do have it, Medea. Everyone has light as well as darkness in them. We just need to find control so the good wins over the bad."

"Mayhap you're right. I'm not really sure. But I suppose I just have a lot more darkness in me than anyone, because of my mother and her evil ways. I keep hearing her voice in my head and it is getting harder and harder to ignore it. I'm afraid I'm going to end up just like her, and that scares me to death."

"Medea, don't say that." He rubbed his hand up and down her back. "I didn't know your mother, but I've heard how awful she was. I am sure that will never happen to you."

"It's already happening, Rhys and I cannot control it. It's the truth and you know it. Darkness is strong within me and it is starting to take me over. Even my own baby doesn't want me near her." She started to cry again.

"You are a good person, Medea, I've seen it in you. You are young yet, and inexperienced, that is all. In time, you'll learn to control the darkness and let the light rise to the surface instead."

"Nay, it's too late for me, Rhys. It is too late and now, I'll never see my daughter again. I don't deserve to. Not after the way I acted."

"You will see her, I promise. Just give it some time, that's all."

"Time?" asked Medea looking up at him. "My daughter seems to be aging a year for every day she lives, just like what happened to me. It's going too fast."

"I know all about that. Rapunzel told me."

"Rhys, this is terrifying. My daughter might be the same age as me or mayhap even older before I see her again. Everything is spinning out of control. I just want to enjoy Lily-Rae as a child and watch her grow up together with you. I want to experience things in her life with her. I don't want her to turn into me."

"We will do all that, and we'll do it together, I promise," Rhys assured her. "Marry me, Medea. Be my wife."

"What? Really?"

"I said it before and will say it again. I want to spend my life with you and raise a family together."

Now Medea was back to thinking that she was dreaming again. Could this possibly be true? Good things didn't happen to her. Not in her life. This couldn't be real. Could it? "For real?" she asked him once more, just having to hear him say it was.

"For real," he answered, being the best thing she ever heard. "Unless you're still planning on marrying King Osric, that is."

"Nay!" she cried. "I don't want anything to do with that man. It was only the darkness inside taking me over when I agreed to be his bride and queen in the first place."

"So... what does that mean? Will you marry me or not?"

"Before I answer, tell me something. Why do you even want me, Rhys? I'm not a good person, and don't know the first thing about raising children. You could have your choice of noble ladies right here in Mura. You could have anyone you want."

"I've already chosen. I want you, Medea."

Medea shook her head, biting her lip, trying not to cry. "I don't know, Rhys. I can't condemn you to a life with an evil wife. You deserve so much better. Mayhap it would be best if you took Lily-Rae and raised her by yourself. Don't even tell her a thing about me. I'll go back through the portal and she'll never have to know her mother was evil. Then I'll—"

Her words were cut off as Rhys' mouth covered hers in a deep, sensuous kiss. All the tension inside her left, and her body relaxed in Rhys' arms. The kiss lingered, and when their lips parted, she spoke once again.

"Why did you do that?" she whispered.

"It was the only way to shut you up and to keep you from drowning in your self-pity."

"Self-pity, is it?" She hit him playfully on the chest.

"That's exactly what it is." He ran his finger down her chest, circling one of her nipples, causing a tingle to flit over her skin.

"Rhys. That is making me excited."

"Well, then I suggest we do something about it."

"I think that's a good idea." She rolled atop him, straddling him with her legs. His hands went to her hips, closing around them.

"Oooo, I like this new, experienced Medea who just claims what she wants," he told her in a deep, sultry voice.

"I learned from the best," she replied, reaching down to kiss him. She felt his manhood hardening beneath her. "Is making love always the same?" she asked. "I mean, will I feel the same way I did when we did it in the field of lilies?"

"My answer is *nay*."

"Nay?" Her heart dropped. She looked down at him and saw him smile.

"It's better with each time," he told her, waggling his eyebrows. "Let me show you." He pulled her to him, sitting up partially, taking her breast into his mouth. Caressing her bottom with his hands, he suckled her at the same time, making the motions of a baby trying to nurse.

"Rhys, I wasn't able to nurse," she told him.

"Well, we can still pretend, can't we?" He pleasured her with his mouth, causing her head to fall back. His hands touched her in just the right places to make her moan aloud. She rubbed up against his hardness, feeling herself coming to life. He was big and oh, so pleasing. Now that she knew how it felt to have him inside her, she couldn't wait any longer to feel it again.

Positioning herself, she took him inside her, slowly sliding down his slick shaft until they'd joined as one. Now she felt complete. She was joined with Rhys, and they felt like one. She also didn't feel lonely anymore. Together they did the dance of love, not stopping the thrusts in and out until they had both reached their peaks and cried out with elation.

Both of them breathing hard, she lay down next to him, feeling safe and protected and loved in his embrace.

"Do you think we made another baby?" she asked with a giggle.

His body stilled. "Don't take this the wrong way, Medea, but I sure hope not. Because, if all of our children are going to be born and grow up as fast as Lily, I don't think I can handle it."

"Neither can I." She smiled at him, and they both laughed together. "I know what you mean," she said. "I haven't gotten the knack of the first baby yet."

"I need time to figure out how to be a father," he told her. "What am I saying? I need time to figure out how to be a husband, too."

They lay in each other's arms until they both were able to steady their breathing.

"Yes," she said aloud, in a strong and steady manner.

"Hmmm?" His eyes were closed as he was already falling asleep. He opened one eye. "What did you say?"

"Yes," she answered with even more conviction now, knowing this was exactly what she wanted. "You asked me to marry you, Rhys Blackseed, and my answer is *yes*, I will. I want you as my husband, and also as the father of all my children."

"Which we hope will only be one at a time," he mumbled, kissing her on the nose.

"I am happy about this, Rhys." Medea fell on her back and stared up at the ceiling. "I love you. I'm sure I do. And this is what I want more than anything in life. I wished for it on a star a little while ago and now it is already coming true. I did it while I bathed."

"That all happened in the bath?" he asked, looking amused.

"Yes. I made a wish upon a bright star I saw out the window. I said I would give anything to be your wife and to raise our child together, and now it is happening. How odd is that?"

"That isn't odd at all," he told her, pulling her closer in his embrace. "When we focus on the good things we want in life, they tend to manifest faster."

"Are you happy, Rhys? I know you are half asleep, but you sound as if something is bothering you."

"The only thing bothering me, sweetheart, is that I'm not sure how we're going to tell King Osric that you will now be my bride instead of his. That, and also how to not have him try to kill one or mayhap both of us when he finds out. I assure you, he's not going to be happy that a powerful witch like you is no longer going to be doing his bidding."

"Don't worry about that," said Medea with a smile. "I'll always have my powers to protect us both from someone like King Osric. Just leave him to me."

Twenty

By the time Medea awoke the next morning, Rhys was already up and dressed.

"Rhys?" she said sleepily, having had a wonderful night's rest in her lover's arms. "Why are you already awake? It looks like the sun has just started to rise."

"Something's wrong," he told her, strapping on his weapon belt. I think Darium's raven is trying to tell me something." He nodded at the raven sitting on the window ledge. It squawked and flipped its head around. "All right. I'm coming," he told the bird. "You are just as impatient as my brother."

"What do you think is wrong?" She sat up, pulling the sheet up around her naked body.

"I can't be sure, but my guess is that Evandorm and Sethor are preparing their revenge because of the attack by the dragon yesterday."

"War," she said, getting up, wrapping the sheet around her and walking over to the window to look out. The raven flapped its large wings and headed off into the morning sky. "Rhys, this is all my fault. Many are going to die now, because I couldn't control my anger and the darkness welling up inside me. I have to do something to stop this. I don't want anyone to die because of me. I'm coming with you."

"Nay. Stay here for now, Medea. Leave it to me and my brothers, sweetheart." He put his hand on her shoulder and gave her a quick kiss.

"But why? I am powerful and I can help you."

"I know that, Medea, but to be honest with you, I'm afraid your dark side will take over again and possibly make things worse. Until you learn to control it, I think it would be better not to get involved."

"Mayhap you're right," she said, letting out a deep sigh. She had already made a mess of things, and she didn't want to be the cause of more damage or deaths. "Be careful, Rhys."

"You know I can take care of myself. There is no need to worry."

"Lily-Rae," she said, her head snapping around to gaze out the window again. "She might be in danger."

"She is with my mother. The baby is fine."

"Will they be staying in the Whispering Dale?"

"My mother is bringing the baby to Darium's cottage this morning so I can spend time with her later."

"I want to see our daughter too, Rhys." Medea put her hand on his chest. "She's going to grow up so fast, and I don't want to miss it."

"Medea, it's nice to hear you talk that way." Rhys looked deeply into her eyes. When he did, she saw the concern within them.

"You're worried about something. What is it?" she asked him.

"I'm a father now, and soon to be a husband as well," he told her. "I am just worried about my family, that's all."

"Rhys, you know I can protect myself as well as the baby. I want to go to the cottage. I need to see my child."

"We will. But later. Together," he replied.

"My lady?" came a voice from the corridor as well as a small knock on the door. "I am here to help you dress."

"It's my handmaid," Medea whispered. "I'm not sure it's good if she sees you in here."

"You're right. I'll leave by the window," he whispered back.

"My lady? Are you awake?" The knocking continued. "The door seems to be locked and I cannot enter. Is everything all right?"

"Yes, I'm fine. Just a minute, Henriette," she called back to the woman. "Rhys," she whispered. "I'll stay here right now, just so the King doesn't become suspicious and send his men to the cottage to find you. I don't want him to find the baby. But please, hurry back with word on what is happening. And protect our child. Our little Lily-Rae."

"You know I will." He kissed her once again, and used the rope with the grappling hook to lower himself out the tower window.

"My lady?" The latch on the door jiggled as Henriette tried to enter. "Is something wrong?"

Medea blew a worried breath from her mouth and ran over to open the door for her handmaid.

"The door was locked, my lady." Henriette looked confused.

"I just didn't want any of the guards entering when I was in the bath last night. I must have fallen asleep forgetting to unlock it," she told the woman.

"Oh, I see." Henriette held a blue gown in her arms, entering the room and laying it on the bed. "I brought you another gown to wear since your wedding dress was ruined in the moat." Medea glanced at the soggy, dirty dress laying on the floor next to the tub. Then the

woman spread out the blue gown, touching it rever-
ently, as if it meant something to her.

"Thank you, but I don't need the gown, Henriette."

"You can't wear that soiled one to your wedding,"
said Henriette, her eyes becoming wide.

"Nay, I don't suppose I can," said Medea with a giggle. "However, I'm sure you know by now that I can just
materialize a gown for myself whenever I want to. Why
did you bring this one to me?"

"I'm sorry. I guess you don't need it," she answered,
sounding very disappointed. "I just hoped you would
wear this one. It is a special gown to me." Henriette ran
her fingers over the soft velvet, seeming to get lost in her
thoughts.

"Special? How so?" asked Medea, wanting to know
what the woman was thinking.

"I made this gown myself. It was years ago. I constructed it for my daughter, Rose to wear at her
wedding."

"You have a daughter? I didn't know that. And she's
married? How nice."

"Nay, I don't have a daughter anymore. And Rose
never had the chance to marry. She died the morning of
her wedding."

"Oh. I'm sorry," said Medea, her heart going out to
the woman. "That must have been so awful. How did
she die?"

"King Osric killed her."

"What?" gasped Medea. "Why would he do such a
thing?"

"He didn't want Rose marrying one of his knights.
That is who she fell in love with. He wanted my
daughter all for himself."

"Your daughter was a noble?"

"Nay. Far from it. At the time, King Osric's wife was

still alive. He wanted Rose as one of his strumpets. When he realized she was going to run away with the knight... he killed them both, right here in the courtyard."

"That's terrible," said Medea, putting her hand on the woman's arm to try to comfort her. "I can't even imagine how it feels to lose a child. If I lost my daughter, I think I'd go crazy."

"I felt that way for a long time. I also felt a lot of anger for the King."

"Why did you stay here still working for the King afterwards, Henriette? Why didn't you just leave?"

"This is the only job I knew. I was a widow, and Kasculbough was my home." Tears dripped down the woman's cheeks. "I was all alone, my lady. I had no one, and nowhere else to go afterwards. I had to stay. Please, Medea. You remind me a lot of my daughter. Won't you at least wear her gown today when you marry the King?"

"I-I can't," she said, feeling awkward about this entire situation.

"I understand." The woman's face turned solemn and she started to scoop up the gown.

"Nay." Medea's hand shot out and she stopped her. "You don't understand. I will wear the gown for my wedding, but I won't be marrying the King."

"What?" she looked up in horror. "You have to marry King Osric. He is in the courtyard now making the preparations."

"I don't love him, Henriette. He is an evil man. You, out of everyone, knows that is true. No one should ever be required to marry such a bad man as King Osric."

Henriette's gaze dropped to the bed. "Excuse me for speaking so freely, my lady, but I've heard tongues wagging that you are evil as well."

That hit Medea hard. She realized that what the woman said was absolutely true. "I am sorry that I wasn't able to control the darkness in me," she apologized. "But Henriette, I have someone who loves me for who I am. He accepts me even with the darkness that covers my soul. No one has ever done that before."

"Is it the father of your baby of whom you speak?"

"Yes. Rhys and I are going to marry and raise our daughter, Lily-Rae, together." The thought made her so happy that Medea couldn't help but smile.

"Lily-Rae?" asked Henriette.

"Aye. That is what we decided to name her."

"Your daughter is named after a flower just like mine was. Well, I hope you two will be happy together."

Medea's felt so sorry for Henriette and only wanted to wear the dress so the woman could see it on someone. Rose meant the world to her, and now she was gone. Henriette said Medea reminded her of Rose, but Medea knew this couldn't be true. She was sure the woman's daughter was good and filled with light. Medea could never live up to that. Still, she wanted to do what she could to help ease Henriette's pain and loss.

"Will you allow me to wear the gown anyway?" she asked.

"If you'd like to, I'd still be honored," said Henriette. "Medea, I don't know why, but I have started to think of you as my daughter, even though we have just met."

Medea was truly touched by the woman's words and knew that right now, Henriette needed someone to fill the void of Rose. If Medea could do that for her, mayhap it would help one person not feel as lonely as she had through the years. She let Henriette help her don the gown, noticing the smile return to the woman's face. It was truly one of the prettiest dresses she'd ever seen.

"This gown is gorgeous," she told Henriette, admiring the woman's handiwork. I've never seen such fine stitching. You did an excellent job."

"My work has been said to be fine enough for the goddesses of The Haven," the woman said with a proud smile. "However, I know that it isn't true, and I would never claim it to be. After all, I would never want to anger a god or goddess."

"I have to agree with that," said Medea, knowing firsthand that it isn't a good idea to anger them. "Well, I am not all that familiar with your gods and goddesses, but I'm sure your handiwork is at least fit for a queen."

"Excuse me, my lady." A guard stuck his head into the room. "The King summons you to the courtyard anon."

"Thank you, I'll be there momentarily," Medea answered, looking back up at Henriette. "You have been so kind to me. I'm not used to that."

"I think of you as the daughter I lost, and can only hope you will consider us friends, Medea." Henriette picked up the wet gown and walked behind the dressing screen to hang it up to dry.

"Of course, I do," Medea answered, fixing her hair.

"I value my friends," the woman told her. "I would do anything at all for the people I care about if it helps them," she said, still behind the screen. There was a moment of silence, and the Henriette stepped back out into the room. "Would you, too?"

"Would I what?" asked Medea, putting her hair into a braid.

"Would you do anything at all for your family or friends to help them, even if you had to make great sacrifices to do it?"

"Well, I never really thought about it before, because no one ever meant much to me until now."

"It is really important to me to know. Would you?" The woman seemed to be acting odd all of a sudden, but Medea figured it was because she was still thinking about the death of her daughter.

"Yes, I suppose I would," Medea told her.

"I hope you mean that, and that you're not just saying what you think I want to hear."

Medea suddenly felt incredibly responsible for her words, and the value put upon them. In the past, she might have said things just to suffice people, because she didn't care. However, now that she had a baby, and was going to marry Rhys, things inside her were changing. She saw things and people in a different light.

Medea knew what love felt like now. It was something that had been creating quite a void inside her for a long time. Now, she felt the light pushing through that darkness that she'd been born with, and it felt good. It felt right. Knowing someone like Henriette and hearing her story, helped to bring those feelings to the surface. Medea truly wanted to change, and to start over. A new life in a new land was exactly what she needed and wanted. There was no doubt in her mind.

It felt good having people care about her. She wanted to do the same in return for them. Friends were important, and she realized that now. And just like Henriette valued them, so would she.

"I do mean it, Henriette," she said, being sincere. "If there is ever anything at all I can do to help you, just ask. I promise, I won't let you down."

"I am so glad to hear you say that."

You don't owe her anything. She can't be trusted. Don't give her promises. Don't do it. Do not trust her, Medea. The dark voice was back in her head again, making Medea feel odd. She didn't want to listen to the voice of her mother anymore. It was time Medea started making her own decisions.

Medea took a deep breath and released it, pushing the voice away. It almost made her panic, but she didn't know why.

"My lady, I think you should get down to the courtyard now," Henriette continued. "The King is waiting for you."

"Yes," said Medea feeling confusion in her brain as she headed to the door. "I'm sure the King is going to be furious when he finds out I will not marry him after all."

"What will you do if you have no choice and end up having to marry him?" asked Henriette. "Doesn't that frighten you?"

Medea stopped in the doorway and turned to face her new friend, thinking this was an odd question. Still, she supposed Henriette was right. Medea wouldn't put it past the greedy king to do whatever he had to in order to get what he wanted.

"That will never happen, Henriette. I am going to marry Rhys. Besides, I'm not afraid of the King. I have my magic to protect me. King Osric is the one who should be fearing me instead."

"I hope you're right," mumbled the woman as they descended the stairs.

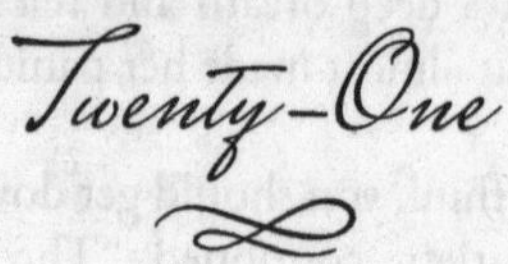

Twenty-One

"I'm here," Rhys called out, hurrying into the cottage in the forest, eager to spend time with his new daughter. He stopped in the doorway when he saw the elf sitting at the table and Talia placing a large pazzleberry pie in front of him. Darium and Zann were standing there with their arms crossed over their chests, staring down at the little man.

Rhys' mother and Rapunzel were sitting on the bed with Lily, who looked to be two years old now. The baby's hair was much longer than yesterday, and she was even standing up, jumping on the bed. It surprised Rhys to see this. Now he understood why Medea was so adamant about coming to see the baby. Lily-Rae was growing up too fast and they were missing it all.

"Your raven seemed like it was trying to give me a message, Darium. What's up?" asked Rhys.

"Dada," said little Lily-Rae from the bed, looking up and smiling at him. She giggled and held out her arms. His heart jumped into his throat. She knew who he was. Somehow, she recognized him as her father and this choked him up with emotion.

"My little Lily-Rae, I am so happy to see you." Forgetting all about the elf, Rhys rushed over to the bed, picking up the little girl. "She said Dada. Did you all hear that?" he asked excitedly, holding Lily-Rae up in the air.

"We heard it," grumbled Zann. "Rhys, where were you all night?"

"I was with Medea," he told them, not wanting to hide the truth. "She cannot wait to see Lily-Rae again. I couldn't wait to see her either. Just look at her smile. She's smiling!" he said, not able to hold back his excitement.

"Lily-Rae? Is that what you named her?" asked Rapunzel. "I like it."

"I like it too," said Alaina. "It sounds like a fae name to me."

"Well, I liked the name Lily, and Medea wanted Rae, so we gave her two names," explained Rhys. "After all, our little sweet pea is part fae." He tickled the baby's stomach and the little girl giggled, sounding just like a faerie.

"Rhys, I sent the raven because there are some things we need to discuss," Darium interrupted.

"I am guessing Evandorm and Sethor are getting ready to attack Kasculbough?" asked Rhys, still smiling at his child.

"Yes, they are," said Darium. "And there's more."

"What do you mean more?" Rhys put his mouth on the little girl's arm and playfully blew air causing a vibration, making the child laugh even more. "Damn, she's cute."

"Rhys, pay attention," said Zann, sounding as if he was losing his patience. "This is important."

"Sorry," said Rhys, handing the baby to Rapunzel, and walking back to the table. Elric picked up a spoon and slowly started to eat the pie. Rhys had never seen the elf move so slowly before. "What's up with the elf and the pie?" he asked.

"Elric has information from the gods and we're waiting to hear it," said Darium, turning a chair backwards and straddling it, resting his arms on the back of the chair.

"He told us that in exchange for the message, he wanted an entire pazzleberry pie all to himself," added Zann, pacing the room as usual.

"So, what's the message, Elric?" asked Rhys.

The elf ignored him and kept eating the pie... one bite... then another... very slowly.

"Elric? Speak up," said Rhys.

"Elric said he'd tell us, but not until after he was finished with the pie," explained Talia.

"Zoroct's eyes, why are you moving like a turtle?" Rhys asked the elf. "We've all seen you eat and drink so fast that it makes our heads spin. You do everything fast. Except for now. Why?"

"Be patient, you big oaf. I'll get to the message soon. When I'm done eating," said the elf with a smile, taking another bite, chewing so slowly that Rhys figured the man was falling asleep.

"Well, while we're waiting, I'll tell all of you my good news then," said Rhys.

"Really? What is it?" asked his mother. "We could all use some good news about now."

"Medea and I are getting married."

The elf started coughing at hearing this. Rhys didn't care if he choked on the pie. He deserved it.

"You're marrying the witch?" asked the elf as soon as he could talk.

"Aye, that's what I said. And her name is Medea," Rhys corrected him, not liking anyone calling Medea a witch, even if that is what she was.

"She's got dark magic in her, Brother, or have you forgotten?" asked Zann.

"I know. It's fine. I still love her."

"Love? We're talking love now?" asked Zann, stopping to look up from his continuous pacing.

"Rhys, mayhap you should first think about this more," said Darium. "Slow down a little."

"I agree with Darium," said his mother, getting up and walking over from the bed. "Medea might not be the best choice for a wife. How about if I introduce you to a nice fae instead?"

"Nay. Stop it," snapped Rhys. "I don't want to hear another word about it. Medea and I already have a child, and we love each other. We want to marry and raise Lily-Rae together."

"Rhys, even though Medea's my sister, I'm not sure she would make anyone a good wife." Rapunzel picked up the baby and walked over to join them. "She has a darkness inside her that she just can't control." She looked down at the baby in her arms. "I just hope Lily-Rae didn't inherit it from Medea, the way Medea got her darkness from Hecuba."

"If so, we'll have two evil witches on Mura," groaned Zann, continuing to pace.

"Stop it! All of you." Rhys grabbed his daughter from Rapunzel. "My baby is not evil, and neither is Medea." He realized how silly it sounded as soon as he said it. After all, everyone had seen Medea on the dragon, trying to seize two kingdoms. She had caused a lot of destruction and could have caused a lot of deaths with her recklessness as well. They lucked out this time, but would they be so lucky if it ever happened again? "Well, she's got that side of her under control now," he said. "I've seen the light in her and she is really a good person."

There was silence, and then, of all people, his mother was the one to say something nice. "I'm sure you're right, Rhys. We don't know the girl the way you've gotten to know her. If you believe in her, then so do I."

"Really?" asked Rhys, not expecting to hear this, since his mother had been against Medea since she'd met her.

"Really," said Alaina.

"I guess I agree, too," said Rapunzel. "After all, I know Medea can be good when she wants to be."

"Yes, we're all happy for you. Aren't we, Darium?" asked Talia.

"Sure," said Darium half-heartedly. "Right, Zann?"

"Mmmph," mumble Zann, not sounding at all convincing. Rhys wasn't sure what that meant, but figured he didn't really want to know.

"Congratulations are in order," said Alaina. "When is the wedding, Son?"

"We plan to get married as soon as we can. Or, should I say as soon as Medea breaks the news to King Osric that she's not marrying him after all."

"Won't that make the King angry?" asked Rapunzel.

"I'm sure it will," Darium answered for Rhys. "I'm also sure he is not going to just sit back and accept it, either."

"Medea could be in danger," said Talia. "She's at Kasculbough all alone."

"Oh, don't worry about Medea." Rhys chuckled. "She's got her magic to protect her. She can take care of herself. There is nothing King Osric can do to harm her."

All of a sudden, the elf downed the rest of the pie so fast that he moved in a blur. Then he threw the spoon down with a clank, and leaned back in his chair with his feet resting atop the table. He let out a loud belch and smacked his lips. "Great pie, Talia." He tapped his full belly with his hands. "A man could get fat with all your talented baking."

"Why, thank you," said Talia with a smile, enjoying the compliment.

"All right, Elric. Now that we've established my wife's talent with food, tell us the message from the gods," grumbled Darium.

"Well, let's see." The elf tapped his chin, pretending to be thinking. "What was it again?"

"Mayhap I'll help you remember." Zann knocked the elf's feet off the table with a swipe of his arm. The elf zipped around the room, and ended up standing atop the chair, wagging his finger in Zann's face. He was still so short, even atop the chair, that he couldn't reach Zann.

"Don't do that. It's not nice," snapped Elric. "Just for that, I might decide to keep the information to myself after all. If I do, Rhys might never see Medea again."

"What?" asked Rhys, not liking the sound of this. He had thought the elf was just jesting about this message from the gods, but now he got a bad feeling that something was severely wrong. He handed the baby to his mother, and reached out and grabbed the elf by the scruff of the neck of his tunic, holding him high above his head. "If there is information you've been keeping from us that might put Medea in danger, I swear, I'll kill you myself."

"Now, now, such talk like that is never going to get me to give you the message," said the elf, barely able to speak.

"Put him down, Rhys," said Darium. "And Elric don't even think of stalling any longer or you'll never get a pazzleberry pie from my wife again."

"All right, all right. Put me down, you big oaf, and I'll tell you everything."

Rhys reluctantly put the elf down. He was already dreading what he was about to hear. Somehow, he knew it was going to be bad news, and that it somehow involved Medea.

* * *

Medea walked out into the courtyard to find the King with his advisor, Raudfer, and his men all standing in a circle. There was no doubt in her mind that this was all for the wedding. The man was going to be very upset when she told him she was marrying Rhys instead, but she didn't care.

"My bride," the King said holding out his hand. His leg was wrapped with boards, and she figured it must be broken from their fall into the moat. He leaned on a wooden crutch and had scratches and bruises all over his body. Still, he was here, standing and talking, and that surprised her. After seeing the deep, bloody wounds made from hitting against the dragon, she didn't expect him to be able to even get out of bed at all. "My advisor, Raudfer, is going to conduct the wedding ceremony. Come," he told her, still holding out his hand.

"King Osric," said Medea, walking over to him and shaking her head. "I won't marry you, and there is nothing you can do or say to make me change my mind." Her handmaid, Henriette followed right behind her, not saying a word.

"What did you say?" screamed the King.

"I won't marry you," she repeated. "It wouldn't have worked out anyway."

"Nay, you cannot back out of our deal. You will

marry me, witch. We have plans to rule Mura together, in case you've forgotten."

"Nay, I haven't forgotten. I made that deal when I was under the influence of dark magic and not thinking clearly. However, I'm not under the influence right now, and as far as I'm concerned, I want nothing to do with you, ever again."

"Well, I don't agree with this at all. A deal is a deal," snapped the King. "You must hold up your end of the bargain."

"I assure you, King Osric, that I have no such plans to marry you now, or ever. Neither will I ever change my mind. That is all I have to say," she answered. She probably would have been better off if she'd stopped right there, but instead, she kept on talking. "Besides, I heard the way you spoke yesterday. You kept using the word *I*, not *we* when we were atop the dragon. That tells me that you want to rule Mura by yourself, but just want me by your side because you know I have powerful magic. You want me to scare off your enemies, and also to do your dirty work for you. Well, I won't do it. I won't help you to hurt or kill others, and I certainly will not be a part of you seizing all of Mura as your own. I'm not marrying you, and that is all there is to it."

"Yes, you are marrying me." The King grabbed her hard by the arm and pulled her toward him. This made Medea angry. She felt the darkness inside of her growing again, and she felt helpless to stop it from taking control. Out of habit, she waved her free arm, meaning to send the rude man flying across the courtyard. However, to her utter surprise and to her dismay, nothing happened.

"What's the matter, witch? Doesn't your dark magic work on me anymore?" asked Osric with a low chuckle.

"I don't understand," she answered. "Of course it

works. Why wouldn't it?" She looked at her hand and flicked it again, but still nothing happened.

"You're not so brash anymore without your powers, are you?" continued the King.

"That's nonsense. I have powers," she spat, becoming even angrier.

Kill the fool. Do it now. Don't let him talk to you this way. Her mother's voice was back in her head, urging her to do something dark again. This time Medea didn't fight it.

"I'm one of the most powerful witches ever," said Medea. She tried again to use her magic, but nothing happened. Then she tried to transport, but she couldn't get out of King Osric's grip.

"She's really lost her powers," gasped one of the guards.

"I can't believe it," mumbled someone else. "She's just like the rest of us now."

"Nay!" cried Medea, trying over and over again, waving her arm up, and then down and up again. It was no use. She couldn't even do the simplest thing using any magic at all. Dark magic or light magic, it didn't seem to work. It was all gone, and she was human like everyone else now. All of a sudden, she started to panic. Without her magic, she was defenseless. She didn't carry a weapon and had never needed to learn to fight, so she didn't even know how.

"I don't care if you have no powers," growled the King. "You are still going to marry me, because I say so."

"What?" she spat, terrified to hear this and not understanding it in the least.

"My lord, why would you even want to marry her? She should mean nothing to you now," said Henriette.

Medea's head snapped around toward her servant.

"Yes, my handmaid is right. You don't want me. Without my magic, I'm no good to you. Let me go."

"Why do you even care, servant?" snapped the King. "And how dare you speak to your sovereign in this manner."

Trouble was brewing, Medea could feel it in the air. She appreciated Henriette's help in this situation, but she really wished the woman would stay silent. It was only going to make matters worse.

"I am Medea's friend, and friends do anything at all to help each other," said Henriette, making Medea flinch. This couldn't be good. What was the woman doing?

"I see," said King Osric, nodding at one of his guards who walked up and stood directly behind Henriette now.

"Henriette, thank you," said Medea. "I truly appreciate your input, but please stay silent and let me handle this. I really don't want you to get into trouble because of me." Medea started to fear for the woman. Why was she being so bold?

"I'll answer your question, servant," said the King. "I will tell you only because I want Medea to hear my reason. I will marry you, Medea, even without your powers. I'll do it, because my adversaries already fear you. You see, if you are at my side as my Queen, they will always fear me, and I like that. Their fear is what will be their downfall. Before long, I'll have their kingdoms, even without your help and the use of your dark magic." He laughed heartily. "Your presence alone is going to be enough to get what I want. And with the dragon at my command, I'll have more power than you could have ever given me, anyway."

"Nay, you won't. The dragon will never help you or listen to your commands. Especially not since you hurt it," said Medea. "Besides, you don't even know how to capture it."

"Don't I?" he asked with a chuckle. "Walk this way with me," he said, hobbling, dragging her toward the pit. "Look at that, my Queen-to-be. Now tell me that I don't know what I'm doing."

He pointed down at the pit, and Medea's eyes followed. To her horror, she saw Marco's dragon inside the pit. There were iron bars over the top of the opening, holding the beast inside.

"Y-you caught the dragon? How? When?" She was so surprised that she couldn't believe what she was seeing.

"It was late last night. You might have known it, if you hadn't been in bed with Sir Rhys," Osric ground out.

"Y-you know?" she gasped, thinking her intimate night with Rhys had remained a secret.

"Aye. I knew Blackseed sneaked into the tower. He made it there only because I wanted him to."

"I don't understand," said Medea. "You wanted Rhys to spend the night with me, even though you thought I was to be your bride?"

"Aye," he answered. "I needed you both distracted, so I let it be. The dragon was wounded, so it was easy to catch when it returned to Kasculbough during the night. Plus, a little elf told me about those iron bars to keep the dragon contained."

"Elric," Medea mumbled. "No wonder no one seemed to trust him."

"The gods must have taken away your powers, Medea," said Henriette. "They must be punishing you somehow."

"Aye," said Medea in thought, remembering how the gods threatened her when she so boldly broke into their temples and stole the crystal key. She had also re-fused to give an offering, and tried to steal back Rhys' offering of his ring. Now she regretted her actions with all her heart.

"I don't care if I have no powers, I still refuse to marry you," she cried. "I love Rhys Blackseed and I am marrying him. You mean nothing to me, but he means the world to me."

"You will marry me," threatened the King, grabbing her arm tightly.

"Nay, I won't." She struggled against him, but one of his guards held her back.

"You say Rhys means something to you?" asked Osric.

"Of course he does. He's the father of my baby."

"What about your friends?" asked the King. "Do they mean anything to you at all?"

"My friends? What do you mean?" she asked, fol-lowing his finger as he pointed to something. She turned to see Henriette being held by a guard. The man had a sharp dagger pressed up against her throat. "What? Nay. What are you doing?" she screamed. "Don't hurt her. She has nothing to do with this. Henriette is innocent. Let her go."

"My man will slit the handmaid's throat at my com-mand," snarled Osric. "You will watch her bleed to death at your feet if you don't say the wedding vows and become my wife."

"Nay, please," she shouted, crying now. This was like a nightmare and all she wanted was to wake up again, safe in Rhys' arms. Even with the anger inside her growing, she was not able to do a thing to use her magic to help her one and only friend. She tried over and over again, but she no longer had a bit of magic, light or dark. It was a terrifying feeling. She had never felt so frightened or as alone as she did right now. Medea had always wondered what it would feel like to just be human, and now she realized that she didn't like it after all.

"Don't worry about me, Medea," said Henriette. "Don't give up everything you ever wanted just for my sake."

"Henriette! I don't want you to die," cried Medea. "This can't be happening."

King Osric leaned on his crutch and chuckled.

"There is nothing you can do to help me," said Henriette, weeping. "King Osric killed my daughter and the man she was to marry, and now he'll take my life as well." Henriette seemed to give up hope. Medea didn't like this. The woman had been so kind to her, and also had lived through some horrible things brought on at the hands of the King. She didn't deserve to die. She didn't deserve this at all.

"Oh, but there is something Medea can do," said Osric. "She can marry me right now, and I'll spare your life," he told the handmaid.

"B-but if I do that, I can't marry Rhys," said Medea, tears streaming down her face.

"That's right," said Osric. "So what will it be? Will you choose Sir Rhys or Henriette?"

"What about my daughter?" cried Medea. "What will happen to her if I marry you?"

"You can bring her to live with us, it's fine with me," said the King. "If she has magic, that will help me and be even better. Plus, I'm counting on your magic returning as well. I'm guessing in time it will. Then, we can have that army of magical babies I wanted after all."

"Nay. I can't marry you. I won't!" she said through gritted teeth.

"Your choice," said the King with a shrug. "Kill the handmaid," Osric ordered his guard, terrifying Medea even more. She looked down to the gown she wore, thinking about how Henriette lost everything when the King killed the daughter she loved. The poor woman didn't deserve this. Medea didn't want her to die.

"Henriette, I want to help you, but I don't want to give up the man I love," Medea told the handmaid. "Plus, I don't want to lose everything I ever wanted. This is my one chance at happiness."

"I understand," said the woman calmly. "You are under no obligation to save the life of your friend, even though you promised me you would do anything at all for me, if I ever needed your help."

"I did say that," said Medea, thinking back on their conversation.

"I would do the same for you," added Henriette.

"She won't keep her word," said Osric. "She's an evil witch who cares about naught but herself. I'll bet she won't even flinch when she watches my man slit your throat and you bleed to death," he said to Henriette.

"Nay, don't say that." Medea felt her heart about beating out of her chest. Her knees knocked together. So much confusion clouded her mind that she could no longer even hear the voice of her mother. She was all alone and had to make a decision that she would have to live with for the rest of her life.

"Medea?" asked the handmaid, looking up with longing in her eyes. "I don't want to die. I know I told you I understand, but I really need your help right now. Won't you help me?"

Visions of Medea's mother dying because of a decision she made, swarmed through her head. The guilt from that still ate away at her. If she let Henriette die, it would only add to the weight on her shoulders. But if she broke her promise to Rhys and married Osric instead, she would be letting him down as well as giving up her chance to finally be happy. She didn't know what to do, but she did know that she couldn't have both.

"I want to help you, Henriette, you know I do," said Medea, her entire body trembling now. "But it would mean giving up Rhys and having a family with him, and I already promised to marry him. I have to think about Lily-Rae as well. Still, I don't want you to lose your life." Medea couldn't keep her tears from flowing. She was scared and confused and so alone. Without her magic, she was vulnerable and couldn't stop the King. She never felt so helpless as she did right now.

"Then your answer is no?" asked the woman, making Medea dig deep into her soul, trying to figure out what to do. She'd never had a true friend before, and now that she had one, was she really willing to let the woman die? There was no reason for Henriette to die. She had done nothing wrong. Medea struggled hard with her decision. She wanted a new life with Rhys and her baby. She didn't want to be married to an evil man whom she despised. She loved Rhys. She loved Lily-Rae. The last thing she ever wanted was to lose them, when all she ever wanted was the love of a man and to have a family of her own.

"I- I'm not sure what to do," said Medea, wishing someone was there to tell her the answer. She had always listened to her mother and never had to make a decision on her own. But now, even the voice of her evil mother in her head was silent. No one was going to help her. She needed to know how to save the handmaid's life and still be able to be with the man she loved, but there didn't seem to be a way to do it.

"Kill the wench," snapped the King. "I'll wait no longer for her answer."

"Yes, my lord," said the guard, turning his knife inward. Henriette looked up with sad longing in her eyes.

Medea realized that she just couldn't let the woman die, even if she had to sacrifice her own happiness to stop it. She was once again put in a horrible position, and had to make a choice that would determine if someone lived or died. She'd been responsible for her mother's death and she couldn't go through this again. Even though it was done to save another's life, Medea never forgave herself for it. She decided she did not want to have to watch someone die because of her. Nay, she couldn't do it. This woman was innocent, and Medea would not stand there watching as Henriette was killed.

"Nay! Stop!" she shouted, closing her eyes and biting her bottom lip that was still trembling. "I will marry you, King Osric. I will do it if you promise to never hurt Henriette or threaten her life again. You have already taken everything from this woman, including her daughter. No mother should ever have to endure that kind of pain. Please do not kill Henriette, because she has done nothing wrong. I am the one who has been bad, not her. She does not deserve it."

"So, let me be clear on what you are saying," said the King. "You would give up your happiness for a friend? You would sacrifice everything that you've ever wanted and give up the man you love, just to save a simple handmaid?"

"Yes," said Medea, feeling her heart break. "I don't want to lose Rhys, since with all my heart I love him and want to be his wife and raise a family with him. But I also don't want to see an innocent woman go to her death because of my selfishness." She nodded slowly. "I made a promise to Henriette that I would help her if she ever needed me. I told her I would do it, no matter what I had to sacrifice, and I will not go back on my word."

"Why?" asked Osric. "I need to understand."

"Henriette deserves happiness in her life. I, on the

other hand, have let the darkness within rule me. I have done some horrible things in my life. I have been very bad at times."

"But you couldn't help it, Medea," said Henriette. "It was the darkness inside you making you act that way."

"I know it was," she answered. "But to be honest, Henriette, at times I admit that a part of me liked the way it felt. However, I have changed. I don't want to be that same person anymore. I don't want to hurt people. I don't want to see them suffer. And I don't want to have to live in fear of the darkness controlling me, and possibly hurting those I love."

"But what about Sir Rhys? And the baby?" asked Henriette. "Don't you love them?"

"I do this because I love them, Henriette. I could not live with myself if I sent you to your death because of my own wants and greed. I also don't want my family to have to live with someone who has such darkness in her heart, that she let another die when she could have stopped it from happening. I want happiness with Rhys and Lily-Rae more than anything in the world, I swear I do. But I also want to make the right choices from now on. I want you to live, Henriette."

"If you want Sir Rhys so badly, then let the handmaid die," said the guard.

"Nay. I just can't do that," she answered softly.

"What about Blackseed?" asked the King. "What will he think about your decision?"

"He will understand my decision and support it," said Medea, knowing this was true. "Rhys is a good man. He would not want me to let innocent people die if I had the power to stop it. I will never let that happen again."

"Power," mumbled the King. "My, how your idea of power has changed."

"Let me in!" Shouting was heard from the gate.

Medea looked up to see Rhys fighting off three men at once, trying to get into the courtyard atop his horse. Darium and Zann were with him. And in a cart being pulled by a horse was her sister, Rapunzel, Rhys' mother, and her darling baby. Driving the cart were Talia and Elric.

"Lily-Rae," cried Medea, clasping a hand over her mouth when she saw how big the little girl had become overnight. Tears filled her eyes once again. The thought hit her hard that she would never be there to see Lily-Rae turn into a young lady. The King said her daughter could live with them, but she didn't want the girl to grow up around such an evil man. Nay. She would tell Rhys to raise their daughter, because Rhys and his family were good people. That is where Lily-Rae belonged.

"Stop, Medea! Don't marry him," yelled Rhys, still fighting off guards at the gate.

"Let them pass," called out Osric, surprising Medea that he should say this. King Osric stood up straighter and actually handed his crutch to his guard.

When the newcomers all approached, Rhys held out his sword, making his way forward. "Let her go," commanded Rhys.

"Nay, Rhys, don't," she told him, still crying. "King Osric is going to kill Henriette. I had to promise to marry him to spare her life."

"What? Nay." Rhys looked over to the handmaid, who was still being held by a guard. "Medea, I love you and want to spend my life with you. I thought you loved me too."

"I do!" she cried, her entire body shaking. "I love you and little Lily-Rae more than life itself."

"Medea, please. Don't marry him," Rhys begged her once again.

"I cannot let Henriette die because of me, Rhys. Please try to understand. I don't make this decision lightly. Take care of our baby for me. Tell Lily-Rae every day that I love her."

"We're going to get married and raise her together." Rhys had a tear in his eye now, too.

"It's better this way, Rhys," she told him. "The darkness inside me is dangerous and I don't want it to ever affect my child. I don't want to continuously worry that someday I might hurt her or even you."

"You won't, Medea. You are a good person. I've seen the light within you."

"Protect her, always, Rhys. And always remember that I love you," Medea said in a soft voice.

"Nay, Medea. I won't let you go." Rhys was not making this easy for her. She wished now that he and the others had stayed at the cottage.

"Mama," shouted Lily-Rae from the cart, making Medea so sad that she felt a sharp stabbing pain in her heart. She held much love for Rhys and Lily-Rae. She also felt love for Rapunzel and her family back in England. The light inside her was growing and her heart was not so closed off anymore. She was sure of it now. She could feel it.

Medea felt love for Rhys' family too, and even Henriette, whom she would do anything to save. Love wasn't something she was used to. She wasn't sure she had ever really felt it until she met Rhys. But now that she experienced the feeling, she realized that it was stronger than any darkness and always would be. The immense feelings bubbling up inside her became so strong now that it was overwhelming. Her head spun and her knees buckled beneath her, as her body trembled so badly that she felt as if she were about to faint.

She heard shouting from outside the gates, and realized it was the other kingdoms coming to attack. Medea also thought she heard a noise in the sky. When she looked up, she felt confused. It was the dragon. Marco's dragon. But how could this be? The dragon was in the pit. She saw it with her own eyes. It couldn't be up in the sky too.

"Medea, are you all right?" Rapunzel materialized at her side just as she was about to fall, holding out her arms to steady her.

"W-what's going on?" asked Medea.

What she saw next shocked her more than anything. The dragon flew over the castle, breathing fire down at the soldiers from the other kingdoms that had started to attack. They turned and rode away from Kasculbough, not looking back. Then the dragon dipped down, and flew right toward them.

"The dragon is going to kill us!" shouted someone from the crowd.

"Run! Hide," yelled a guard, sending everyone else scattering, as terror broke out in the courtyard.

Rhys dropped his sword, jumping up as the dragon swooped lower. He threw his arms around the dragon's neck, wrestling with it, trying to keep it from moving or attacking. He struggled, using his powers of intense strength to pull it to the ground and pin it down. He threw one leg over its body to hold it there so it wouldn't hurt or kill anyone.

"Darium, Zann, get the pit ready. Hurry!" he shouted, holding the dragon all by himself.

"They can't. There is already a dragon in the pit," said Medea, running over to the pit to show them. She stopped when she approached it, realizing it was empty.

There were no iron bars above it either. Somehow, it had all just disappeared. All she saw was a bunch of shiny shields down at the bottom of the deep pit.

"The pit is ready," shouted Zann.

"We can help you," yelled Darium.

"Nay. I've got it. Get out of the way." Rhys dragged the dragon over to the pit, its wings flapping wildly as it tried to get out of his hold. However, since Rhys held it with his great power, it wasn't able to fly away. Rhys picked it up over his head and dropped the dragon into the hole. "We've got to hold it here somehow," he called out to his brothers.

"I can help," said Rapunzel, waving her hand and creating a magical iron grate above the pit to keep the dragon from flying away.

With the other armies gone now and the dragon contained, Medea looked back over to the King.

"Shall we capture them and put them in the dungeon, my King?" asked one of the soldiers.

"Nay," said Osric. "They are not to be harmed."

"I don't understand," said his advisor.

"Then let me explain. Everyone, please gather around." Osric, motioned for everyone to join him.

Slowly, people came out of hiding, and everyone gathered around the King. When everyone was there, Osric removed his leg brace and threw it down. Then he waved his hands over his head and a bright light encompassed him. Medea watched in awe as Osric's body shifted, and he turned into Zoroct, the god of power.

Everyone gasped and clutched each other. Some of the peasants even dropped to their knees. The guards stood there with open mouths, not knowing what to do.

Zoroct looked exactly like the statue by the pyramid that Medea had seen. This frightened the soldiers, and they all lowered their weapons and backed away. Then Henriette shifted into one of Mura's goddesses, although Medea didn't know which one.

"I-I don't understand," said Medea. "What happened to King Osric and Henriette?"

"I'd like to know what in the name of Belcoum is going on?" growled Rhys.

"Don't mention Belcoum's name around me," said Zoroct in a deep, powerful voice that shook the ground.

"This was all a test for the witch," said the elf, climbing down from the seat of the wagon. "The gods set it up."

"Rhys, I don't have my powers anymore," cried Medea, running to him and falling into his arms.

"I know, Medea. "The elf told us," said Rhys. "That is why I hurried here to help you."

"Then, you all knew about this?" she asked, as Rhys' brothers gathered around.

"Nay, we only knew that you lost your powers, but that's it," said Darium, holding out his arm, and letting his raven land upon it.

"I'm confused," said Medea.

"So am I," added Rhys.

There was a blur and the elf ended up next to Medea. "They only knew what I told them about your powers. I wasn't allowed to reveal more."

"I knew," Alaina spoke up. "The gods swore me to secrecy and wouldn't let me use my elemental powers to help you, Rhys."

"So... this was some kind of test from the gods?" Rhys shook his head, not wanting to believe it.

"Yes," answered the goddess. "I am Cnoir, the goddess of love. I had to test Medea to see if the light within her would outweigh the darkness, since I heard her wish that she'd give anything to marry Rhys and raise Lily-Rae with him."

"You heard that?" asked Medea in shock.

"Of course, my dear. We know, hear, and see all," continued Cnoir. "I am happy to tell you that you passed your test."

"That's right," agreed Zoroct. "The love inside you outweighed the evil. You were willing to give up your own happiness so Henriette wouldn't be killed. You proved that you can love after all."

"The greatest love is sacrifice," said Cnoir. "You were willing to do that, not only for Henriette but also for your baby, since you didn't want her to end up being evil."

"B-but I am evil," said Medea. "Just like my mother."

"Not anymore," said Alaina with a smile. "Now that you've experienced love, the light seems to have taken over."

"Mayhap you're right," said Medea, listening for her mother's voice in her head, but she no longer heard it. She honestly hoped she would never hear it again. "Thank you, all," said Medea. "I'm actually this happened because now, I have confidence in myself. I have faith that no matter what happens or even if I become angry again, I will be able to control that darkness that lives within me, even if it lies dormant wanting to get out. I know I will make the right choices in the future, and let light and goodness show me the way."

"There is darkness in everyone, but you just had more than your share," said the goddess.

Zoroct nodded in agreement. "You are welcome to stay in Mura, Medea. Just don't ever think of stealing from the gods again."

"I promise, I won't," said Medea, hugging Rhys. "Oh! And I'll always leave an offering from now on."

"That reminds me. Elric, give Rhys back his ring." Zoroct stared at the elf.

"He has it?" Rhys looked surprised. "It was my offering. The sea serpent swallowed it."

"Here it is," grumbled the elf, slapping Rhys' ring into his hand. "The sea serpent spit it out and I just picked it up, that's all."

"I told you not to trust the elf," said Zoroct with a chuckle. "He has a habit of taking things that don't belong to him. If he wasn't my messenger, he'd be in big trouble." Zoroct disappeared in a flash of light.

"What about Henriette?" Medea asked the goddess.

"And King Osric?" Rhys wondered.

"I am here," came a voice from behind them. Henriette walked up from the keep. Medea ran over and hugged her.

"So, that wasn't you all along?" asked Medea.

"Yes, it was me," said Henriette. "Our friendship is real."

"I just took her place when she walked behind the changing screen," the goddess explained. "Your friendship seemed true, Medea, but I had to make sure you'd really had a change of heart."

"I did. I swear I did, and that from now on I'll be changed. Forever!"

"You will still need to deal with your anger, and control that darkness on occasion," warned Cnoir.

"I will try, but without magic, I'm not sure I can do it," Medea answered.

"You have your magic back, my dear. Just not the dark magic," said the goddess. "Once you made your decision to save Henriette, your dark magic was stripped from you so you can start over again, and not carry on the mistakes of your evil mother."

"Thank you," said Medea. "Does that mean I will no longer hear my mother's words in my head urging me to do bad things?"

"I cannot answer that," said the goddess. "We stripped your dark magic only, but can do nothing about voices you might hear in your head."

"Could I have been hearing her because I felt such guilt for making a decision that caused her death?" asked Medea.

"Possibly," answered Cnoir. "And it is also possible that you have remedied that guilt by saving a life this time."

"Henriette," said Medea with a nod. "I hope it is so. I have a new life now, and I am looking forward to it."

"What about the King?" asked Rhys once again. "Where is Osric?"

"I can answer that." The King's advisor, Raudfer, walked forward to join them. "King Osric died last night from his wounds, I am sorry to say."

"He did?" asked one of the guards.

"Why weren't we told?" asked another.

"I was keeping quiet, since the gods asked me to work with them," Raudfer explained.

"Good luck," said Cnoir, disappearing before their eyes.

"How can this kingdom survive without a king?" shouted one of the people of Kasculbough.

"We'll be slaughtered by Evandorm or Sethor now for sure," yelled another.

"You have a king." Raudfer held up a parchment. "In this scroll, King Osric names Sir Rhys Blackseed as his successor, since he did not have a son."

"Rhys is king?" asked Darium in surprise.

"Of Kasculbough? Are you serious?" gasped Zann.

"I am serious," said the advisor. "The document was

written up by me. The King signed it in the presence of both me and his second advisor. It is legitimate, I assure you."

"I thought he wasn't going to name me heir unless I killed Medea," said Rhys in confusion.

"He counted on you following his orders, and wrote up the agreement right away," said Raudfer. "Mayhap he would have changed the contract in time, but now he is dead and so the contract stands."

"Well? What do you say, Son?" asked Alaina.

"I—I'm not sure what to say." Rhys looked over at Medea. "Except that I am glad Medea will be *my* wife and not Osric's."

"Now she'll be your Queen as well," said Talia, walking over with their daughter and handing her to Medea.

"Mama," said the child.

"I'll never get tired of hearing that." Medea kissed the little girl on the head. "I only wish I had more time to hear it. She'll be grown so quickly that it will be over before it really begins."

"Not necessarily," said Alaina. "After talking with your sister Rapunzel, we discovered something important."

"What's that?" asked Medea.

"It seems the blue milk you replicated that your mother gave you, had an herb in it that I haven't run across in a long time."

"What herb?" asked Rhys.

"It is something no one can pronounce," said Rapunzel. "But Alaina, being an elemental asked her friend, Rae-Nyst, who is an elemental of the earth, about it. It seems the herb is activated by dark magic, and accelerates growth by three hundred-fold or even more."

"Really So what does that mean?" asked Medea, sniffling.

"It means, if you no longer have dark magic in you, the herb won't be activated," said Alaina.

"And hopefully, Lily-Rae will stop growing at such a fast rate," added Rapunzel.

"But what if Lily-Rae has inherited my dark magic?" asked Medea.

Rapunzel and Alaina looked at each other before Rapunzel answered. "Medea, your mother's darkness, and feeding you that potion for eighteen days, is what kept you growing so quickly. You were stripped of your dark magic, and Lily-Rae only drank the potion for a few days."

"So, if we stop giving it to her, will her growth rate slow down to normal?" asked Medea.

"That's what we're thinking," said Alaina. "But only time will tell."

"Let's hope my mother and your sister are right about this," said Rhys. "If so, it'll allow us more time to enjoy Lily-Rae's childhood."

"I have faith it will. I'm so happy, Rhys," Medea said, hugging the baby and Rhys at the same time.

"Will you be my Queen and also my wife, Medea?" asked Rhys.

"I will. If you... and all of you, will have me," she said, looking out at the people of Kasculbough.

Someone in the crowd started clapping slowly. Everyone joined in and clapped and chanted together.

"Long live the King and Queen. Long live the King and Queen," rang out through the courtyard.

Rhys looked over to the cart to see that the damned elf was the one to start the clapping. When Elric noticed Rhys looking at him, he darted off in a blur.

"Medea, are you sure won't come back to England

with me?" asked Rapunzel. "Speaking of that, how will I get back through the portal with the dragon? I certainly can't control it."

Just as she said it, there was a loud thumping heard. Rhys looked over to see Elric using his magic and lifting the iron bars off the pit.

"Nay! What are you doing?" yelled Rhys, taking off at a run for the pit. Everyone screamed and scattered as the dragon rose up out of the pit and into the sky.

"We're all going to die!" yelled a woman from the crowd.

"My King, shall we try to kill it?" shouted one of the soldiers.

"Nay! Leave it," said Rhys, holding up his hand. He looked up at the dragon, straight into its eyes. "Get down here now and stop terrorizing people," he commanded.

"Rhys, you fool, that's not going to work," shouted Zann.

To everyone's surprise, the dragon settled in the courtyard, bowing its head to Rhys.

"Then again, mayhap it will," muttered Zann from behind him.

"I think the dragon sees you as a Dragon Lord, now that you wrestled it to the ground to capture it," Rapunzel told him.

"I guess so," said Rhys with a satisfied nod. The crystal key pendant glowed on his chest, and Rhys knew it was time to open the portal.

"Rapunzel, it's time to go home," said Rhys. "I will take you through the portal atop the dragon myself. When I return, Medea and I will get married."

"Goodbye, Sister." Rapunzel gave Medea a hug. "And goodbye, Niece," she said, kissing the baby as well. "I am going to miss you. Father and all your siblings will miss you too, Medea. I wish the whole family could meet little Lily-Rae."

"I have an idea," said Medea. "Rhys, can my whole family come through the portal and to Mura for our wedding?"

"I suppose so," he answered with a shrug. "As long as we have the key, I don't see why you can't visit with your family whenever you want, Medea." He picked up the crystal pendant in his hand to look at it. When he did, a piece of it broke off. Both ends glowed.

"Oh no!" cried Talia. "It might not work to open the portal now that it is broken."

"On the contrary, I think it was supposed to happen." Rhys handed the broken piece to Rapunzel. "This is for you," he told her. "Since it is still glowing, I am sure it will work. Now, you and your family can come visit us in Mura whenever you want. Medea and I can come to visit you in England as well."

"Thank you," said Rapunzel, clutching the crystal in her hand. "Well, I suppose I should go now. Good-bye, everyone. I'll miss you, although I am anxious to get back to my husband and my son."

"Can I help you up?" Rhys held out his hand to help Rapunzel onto the back of the dragon.

"Thanks, but I can manage." Rapunzel used her magic and sat waiting for Rhys atop the dragon.

"I'll be back soon," Rhys said, giving Medea and the baby a quick kiss. "Up!" he told the dragon, and it obeyed. It was a wonderful feeling, flying over the tops of the trees, listening to the huge wings of the beast flap air around him. "To the portal," he said, looking down to hopefully catch a glimpse of Medea and the baby once more, but he couldn't find them. "Rapunzel, I don't see Medea and Lily-Rae," he said in concern.

"We're right here," he heard from behind him, so

startled that he almost fell off the dragon. He turned to see Medea sitting behind him holding on to Lily-Rae. The baby waved her arms around in the air and giggled like a little fae. "It's good to have my powers back, Rhys," said Medea. "I hope you don't mind if we come along with you. Lily-Rae wanted to ride on the dragon. I also decided I wanted my family to see the baby right away and not have to wait."

Rhys felt happier than he ever had in his life. "Nay, I don't mind at all," he told her. "I like to keep my friends close and my family even closer."

They flew through the sky, and when they got to the Lake of Souls, Rhys saw the swirling colorful portal opening below them. The crystal key glowed and felt warm against his chest. Life was good. Life was damned good, and he never wanted that to change.

Twenty-Two

A month later

Medea walked down the aisle in the courtyard of Kasculbough Castle holding on to her father's arm. Lucio de Bar had eight children, and cared for every one of them. Medea realized he was just as proud of her as he was of all the others.

She and Rhys had accepted the positions of King and Queen at Kasculbough. The coronation had taken place as soon as they'd returned from taking Rapunzel home through the portal. However, they decided to wait on the wedding until all of Rapunzel's family could attend.

It was a big wedding with all her siblings, their spouses, and children present, and Rhys' family, too. It had taken a while to plan the details and the menu. They made sure to include meat dishes, as well as some without, so everyone had what they liked.

Rhys and Medea had considered getting married in the forest like Darium had, but realized with all these people, they needed more room and proper accommodations to house their guests. A castle was the only place big enough to hold them all.

"Medea," said her father, as the music played and he walked her toward the dais. It was set up outside in the courtyard and was where they would be married. "I am so happy you finally decided to accept your family. We all love you, you know."

"I didn't know that before, but I do now," she responded, meaning every word of it.

"I am so happy for you and Rhys. I also love my new grandbaby, Lily-Rae."

"I'm just happy that Lily-Rae is still two years old instead of eighteen right now." They both laughed at that. Thankfully, it seemed that Alaina and Rapunzel's theory was right, dealing with the blue-milk aging potion. They stopped feeding it to Lily-Rae immediately, and since Medea was stripped of her dark powers, it seemed little Lily was growing up at a normal rate for now. Medea also hadn't heard her mother's voice in her head since the gods stripped her dark magic. However, she still felt her mother's presence, so she knew that Hecuba was not truly gone from her life yet. Still, she would be careful to keep good thoughts and only use good magic from now on, and hopefully she would be able to keep those haunting voices at bay.

Talia, as well as Rapunzel, acted as Medea's bridesmaids. Medea wore the blue gown that had been crafted by Henrietta. The handmaid accepted the position to be Medea's lady-in-waiting from now on, instead of just a simple handmaid. She also acquired the title of being the castle's seamstress and Medea's personal clothier, and midwife, too. Henriette became Medea's closest friend and surrogate mother.

As they approached the altar, Medea felt butterflies

in her stomach. She never had this much attention before, and neither did she think her entire family would support her as much as they did. Medea's father kissed her cheek, handing her over to Rhys. Medea felt so nervous that the bouquet of lippenbur lilies in her hand was shaking.

"You look beautiful," Rhys whispered, taking her arm, standing in front of the King's advisor, who normally conducted the ceremonies of marriage at the castle.

"Thank you," said Medea. "I feel so nervous. My whole family is here, as well as yours, and everyone from Kasculbough. They're all here just for us."

"Of course they are," said Rhys with a chuckle. "Don't be nervous, sweetheart. They are here to support us, and to show they care about us. They are all excited that you are starting a new life. Even little Lily-Rae is happy. Just look at her smiling."

Medea turned her head to see Rhys' mother in the front row holding the baby. Lily-Rae laughed and clapped her hands together. When she did, Medea gasped. The baby manifested a lippenbur lily. Alaina quickly took it away from the baby, looking up at them and smiling.

"All right, let's get this over with," came a grumpy voice, causing Medea and Rhys to turn around. Elric stood on the dais along with the King's main advisor.

"What's this?" asked Rhys. "Why are you here, elf? To ruin my wedding?"

"Nay, you fool. I'm here to officiate the wedding ceremony, since I was the King's second advisor."

"You?" asked Rhys. "You're Cirle, that the King spoke of?

"Yes, me. That's Elric spelled backwards," he answered with a chuckle. "I'm also the one you have to thank for talking that evil king into giving you his throne, Rhys."

"Why would you do that?" asked Rhys.

"I have to admit, it started out as a means just to cause trouble. If I had ever believed for a moment that the King would die and you'd actually take his throne, I swear I never would have done it."

"So you were the spy the King sent to Macada Castle as well?" Darium called out.

"Of course," answered the elf. "Did you think I was really there as the court fool?"

"Let's get on with the wedding," said Rhys. "The King's main advisor will be the one to officiate the ceremony, Elric, not you."

"Actually, Elric is a sage, so he is higher ranked than me, sire," said Raudfer with a bow. "I'm afraid when he asked to perform the ceremony, I had to agree to it."

"Fine. Whatever," said Rhys with a sigh, hearing Darium and Zann chuckling from behind him.

"Do you, Rhys Blackseed take the witch—I mean, Medea de Bar—to be your wife?" asked the elf.

"I do," said Rhys.

"And do you, Medea de Bar take the big oaf—I mean Rhys Blackseed—to be your husband?"

"I do," she answered.

"Why does he have to call you a witch and me an oaf on our wedding day?" Rhys whispered to Medea.

"Rhys, it's fine," Medea whispered back, not wanting any trouble. "I am just glad to be marrying you instead of King Osric, no matter what he calls us."

"The rings, please," said the elf, clapping his hands together. "Hurry up, I hear there is pazzleberry pie to eat afterwards, and I'm hungry."

"All right, we're ready," called out Rhys looking up in the air, making Medea wonder what in the world he was doing. Then she realized what was going on. Her brother-by-marriage, Marco, flew over the roof of the castle atop his red dragon. The crowd stirred restlessly, but Rhys stopped them from running.

"It's all right. The dragon is trained and won't hurt anyone," Rhys called out.

"Congratulations, Medea and Rhys." Marco flew over their heads, dropping a small box that Rhys caught with one hand. Then Marco directed the dragon back up to the roof, landing the beast atop one of the spires to watch the rest of the wedding from there. Darium's raven was up there, but squawked and left quickly, most likely not wanting to be eaten by the dragon.

When Rhys slipped the ring onto Medea's finger, she realized it was shaped like a dragon. The body of a dragon was curved around, and made of gold. The dragon's eye was a ruby. Rhys had a ring to match.

"I love it, Rhys," she said, reaching up and kissing him passionately.

The elf cleared his throat. "Did I say it was time to do that yet?" he complained.

"Sorry," said Medea. "I thought the ceremony was over."

"Not yet. There is one more thing to take care of first." He held out his open palm.

"What?" asked Rhys.

"My payment," he said.

"Not again. What is it you want this time? My ring that you stole from the gods to begin with?" asked Rhys. "Or most likely our wedding rings, right?"

"Bah, nay! I don't want any of that. I have no need for it. I want something much more valuable."

"He wants a snip of your hair," Darium shouted.

"Oh, not that again," groaned Rhys. "This is embarrassing, elf, with everyone watching."

The elf pulled a pair of scissors from thin air, snapping the ends together loudly as he waited.

"You already have some of my hair, and well as my sister Rapunzel's," Medea pointed out to the elf.

"He required the same thing from Darium and Talia at their wedding, but for the life of me, I still don't know why," said Rhys. "None of us knows."

"Well, let's give it to him," she said. "We need to pay our debts." Medea held up a lock of her hair but the elf refused to take it.

"Nay, I have yours, like you said," Elric told them. "However, I don't have his." The elf reached up and took a big chunk of Rhys' hair in his hand and snipped it off.

"Hey, that's enough." Rhys ran a hand over his head. "My hair isn't as long as my brothers', so I don't have as much to spare."

"Stop your whining," Zann called out. "It's only hair, Brother."

"I'm glad you see it that way," Elric said, looking up. "Hmmm, your hair is nice and long, Zann. Since I already have some from Medea, I'll take a snip of yours instead." He pointed at Zann with the tip of the scissors.

"Mine? No way," Zann protested, backing up a step.

"Brother, it's only hair, just like you said," Rhys reminded him.

"Go on, Zann. We all did it," Darium coaxed him.

"I need locks from two people," the elf told him. "I only have one." He held up Rhys' hair to show him.

"Please, Zann," Medea asked nicely. "Will you do it? For us?"

"Brother, the faster you cooperate, the faster you'll

get that big, fat, juicy steak we have that is for you alone," Rhys promised.

"All right. Just do it." Zann walked up to the dais and closed his eyes. He held his breath as the elf snipped off a lock of his hair.

"Not too much," Zann said, his eyes popping back open.

"Stop whining, you big oaf. It's over." The elf braided the two locks together and quickly shoved it into his pocket. "All right, the wedding is over, too," he announced. "I'm going to stop in the great hall to collect my pazzleberry pie, and then I'm off for a nice long nap."

"You do that," said Rhys. "Sorry to say we won't miss you."

"Rhys, be nice," said Medea, taking his hand and turning to wave to the courtyard filled with people. With crowns on their heads and dressed likes nobles, Medea felt for the very first time that she enjoyed being a queen. This time, the title hadn't been stolen, it had been earned through marriage. This time, it was real.

She waved to her family, whom Rhys had already met. Her father stood with Alaina. They were both fussing over little Lily-Rae. Medea looked out to see her siblings with their spouses and children. Hugh, known as Wolf by most, and his twin, Arnon, were there. Stefan, Kin, Ellea, and MacKay proudly stood by as well. Rap was up at the dais with her. All their spouses and children were here as well. It felt so good to have them all present.

And of course, Zann, Darium, and Talia were her new family now. Everyone was so accepting of her that she didn't ever want to go back to the darkness or being evil ever again.

Marco flew down on the dragon once more, and the

crowd parted. He hopped off and held out his hand. "Your carriage has arrived, Your Majesties."

"What?" asked Rhys. "You're going to take us for a ride?"

"No," said Marco. "You are a Dragon Lord now, Rhys, so you can take your bride for a spin by yourself before the feast begins. Go ahead."

"Well, all right," said Rhys. "Why not?" He helped Medea atop the dragon, and took off up into the sky. With the wind in their hair and Rhys' arms wrapped around Medea, they flew over the castle and then up above the waterfall and the Picajord Mountains. It was a beautiful day and the sky was clear. The land of Mura as well as the lands of the nearby islands of Lornoon, Tamaris, and Dolphin Island were visible.

"It is such a wonderful view from up here," said Rhys, wrapping his arms tighter around Medea from behind as they flew on the dragon, turning back now over the Goeften Forest and Lake of Souls.

"Rhys, I think I see a portal opening down there near the lake," said Medea, looking down over the side of the dragon. "It doesn't look like the one that leads back to my home. It's different colors."

"Don't look," said Rhys, keeping his eyes forward. "The last thing we need is another portal. I don't want to see it or even know anything about it. Especially not on our wedding day."

"You're right," Medea answered with a giggle.

"Dada. Mama."

"Rhys? What was that?" Medea turned to see little Lily-Rae settled on Rhys' lap, tucked in between them.

"I guess our daughter wanted to go for a ride on the dragon," he said with a hearty laugh. "Medea, our baby has some powerful magic to transport up here all by herself."

"I am thinking that they both might have powerful magic, Rhys," she answered, watching his eyes as she said it.

"Both?" His attention turned to her now. "Why did you say that, Medea?"

She leaned back against him, hugging both Rhys and Lily-Rae as they flew over the Whispering Dale, and she thought of how she felt when she'd first conceived. "I'm pregnant again," she announced.

"Y-you are?" he asked, sounding a little uncertain about it. "Already?"

"I've known for a few weeks now, but wanted to wait to tell you."

"Are you sure? You don't look pregnant at all, Medea."

"Precisely," she answered with a huge smile, turning back around to face forward. "That means this baby isn't going to be born in a day or two, or even in a few weeks' time. It's going to hopefully take nine months, like it's supposed to, Rhys."

When he didn't answer, she glanced back at him and Lily. "Are you all right?"

"Aye, I'm fine. Just a little overwhelmed is all." Lily reached up and pulled at Rhys' hair and he let her do it. "Lily-Rae, don't pull any of my hair out. The stupid elf already took a big chunk and I need all I've got."

Medea giggled. "How do you feel about everything, Husband? Are you happy to have a kingdom, a wife, and now a new family as well?"

"Oh, I'm more than happy," he told her with a smile, as he directed the dragon back to the castle, flying through the sky that was quickly turning shades of orange and magenta since the sun had started to set.

"More than happy?" she asked. "What exactly does that mean?"

He wrapped his arm around her tightly, directing the dragon with just his legs now. He held on to her and to Lily-Rae, kissing them both, and letting out a deep sigh.

"Well, Medea, I don't know exactly how to explain it. I'm am happier than I have ever been in my life. But at the same time, it is still mystifying to me in a way, with all the magic involved. It seems I never know what to expect, from day to day."

"Don't worry. You'll get used to it, Rhys. I promise."

"Oh, I know. My life will never be the same with all these witches in it, but I would have it no other way."

"Then you're not sorry that you're not still single?"

"Not at all. I feel lucky, extremely pleased, and most of all... ***Bewitched***!"

I hope you enjoyed Rhys and Medea's story and will take the time to leave a review for me.

Even though Medea was born from dark magic, she was also balanced with light magic at birth as well. Medea is a secondary character from my **Tangled Tales Series** which is based on fairy tales. I had a high request from readers to give Medea her happily-ever-after and a story of her own. My readers asked, and I listened and delivered.

I must say, while writing about Medea in **Bewitched**, I wanted to make her a much darker person. Her mother, Hecuba, was a very evil witch in the *Tangled Tales Series*. Medea, who shows up in the last three books of that series, is following right along in her footsteps. However, Medea did start to change by the end of **Heart of Ice: Snow Queen**. I guess that is why in **Bewitched**, she fought me, and wouldn't let me make her appear so evil. I always let my characters do what they want and write their own stories. So, Medea developed much differently than I had expected she would.

That said, I am happy that she did. All that matters is that the light won over the darkness in the end. Love is always stronger than hate. It touched my heart when

Medea finally found love and learned not only how to receive it, but how to give it as well. There were some surprises for me with Rhys in this story, too. Such as, I had no idea he'd end up being a Dragon Lord or that he would be a King of Mura. I honestly hadn't planned for that to happen! However, in the end, I couldn't take it away from him because I felt he deserved it and earned it after everything he'd been through.

If you'd like to read about Medea's siblings, father, her evil mother, or find out what Medea was like as a child growing up one year each day for the first eighteen days of her life, you can do so in reading: ***Lady in the Tower: Rapunzel***, as well as ***A Perfect Fit: Cinderella***, and also ***Heart of Ice: Snow Queen***. Be sure to read the rest of the ***Tangled Tales Series*** as well, since each of the cursed De Bar siblings has an intriguing tale to tell.

If you're wondering about the pesky little elf, Elric, and what's up with him, keep reading. You'll find out more about him and why he wants locks of hair in the next book, ***Beguiled***—Book 3 of the ***Portals of Destiny Series***.

Until then—
  Elizabeth Rose

Elizabeth Rose is an Amazon All-Star, and bestselling, award-winning author of nearly 100 books and counting! Her first book was published back in 2000, but she has been writing stories ever since high school. She is the author of fantasy/paranormal, medieval, small town contemporary, and western romance. You'll find sexy, alpha heroes and strong, independent heroines in her books. Sometimes her heroines can even swing a sword.

Her earlier fantasy romance novels started out with her **Greek Myth Series**, inspired by the TV shows *Legendary Journeys of Hercules* and *Xena: Warrior Princess*. One of the books, **The Oracle of Delphi** was featured on the History Channel during a documentary of the Oracle. Elizabeth joins Oliver Heber Books with her **Portals of Destiny Series** which brings back characters from some of her other fantasy series, making guest appearances.

She loves adding humor to her work, because everyone needs to laugh more in life. Her **Bad Boys of Sweetwater: Tarnished Saints Series**, focuses on 12 brothers, a bunch of kids, and lots of humor. This small-town romance series was inspired by people, places, and things in her own life. The location is the lake and small town of Michigan where she grew up visiting her grandparents.

Living in the suburbs of Chicago with her husband, Elizabeth has two grown sons and one granddog – so far. A lover of nature, she can be found in the summer swinging in her 'writing hammock' in her secret garden, creating her next novel. Her secret garden is what inspired her medieval series, **Secrets of the Heart**, which of course centers around a secret garden too!

Visit elizabethrosenovels.com where you will find book trailers, sneak peeks at upcoming covers, excerpts from her books, as well as original recipes of food that her characters eat in her stories. If you'd like to sign up for her newsletter, join her private readers' group, or follow her on social media, just copy and paste the following links.

Join Elizabeth's Newsletter
Join Elizabeth's Facebook Group

Dark Encounters
Familiar
The Caretaker of Showman's Hill
The Curse of the Condor